Ella Gets to Fly

Ella Gets to Fly

Glen Roberts

This novel was originally published electronically in 2018 as a series of five episodes. The episodes have been combined and edited for re-release in 2020. This is the first paperback edition of the full novel.

Cover concept, design, artwork, and implementation by Glen Roberts using GIMP open source graphics software. Interior layout and implementation by Glen Roberts.

Back-Cover Author Image by Zachary Roberts.

ISBN 978-1-7343605-0-9
Library of Congress Control Number:2020900042

St. Augustine, FL, USA

Dedication:

Hi, Ella! Hi, Claire!

No man is an Iland, intire of itselfe …
John Donne (circa 1624)

Acknowledgments

I'd like to thank everyone who had a hand in the making of this book.

But I can't.

I can't because that would involve thanking everyone who ever contributed in any way to the cosmic context that gave rise to this epic … which is *everyone*, past and present. We all form the milieu in which each the rest of us exist. No man, woman, child, or duck on a pond "is an island, entire of itself," although, I suppose, the moist and lonely duck comes closest. That said … and with apologies to the billions I now knowingly overlook … I'd like to offer my gratitude to a few specific individuals and entities:

First, to my brother, Dale, and his wife, Ann, who took the time and trouble to create and to raise the real Ella as well as her amazingly red-headed sister, Claire.

And to my mom, Marilyn, who, over a substantially longer period of time involving a great deal more trouble, is still raising me.

And to my son, Zak, who … [see the paragraph above but swap the bits around some].

And to the active community of writers in St. Augustine, Florida, USA who have individually and collectively encouraged and supported this attempt, notably The St. Johns County Library, Southeast Branch, First-Thursday-of-the-Month Writers Group.

And to my first, and forever best, critique group of writer-friends, Frank Linn, Carolyn Greely, and Jodi Sykes.

And to Aileen Wietstruk who read an early version of *Ella Gets to Fly* to her granddaughter and gave me hope.

And to eagle-eyed editor, Beth Mansbridge, who somehow spotted and corrected more errors in my manuscripts than there were words.

Oh, yeah. And, especially, to my wife, Brenda, who will ever be the ocean upon which this island floats.

Table of Contents

1
Mean Halloween

A coven of witches, a dozen plus one, flew in low over the farmers' fields so late one Saturday night you'd probably call it Sunday morning.

Charlotte sat straight up on the couch. "Shhh! Do you hear that?"

A low vibrating whoosh filtered through a window we had nudged open to let in the cool air. The eerie hum came from the west, maybe out where the farms started at the edge of town, blocks and blocks away. A flap, flap, flap, like flags on a windy day, accompanied the low drone. An instant later, a harsh staccato cackle confirmed the worst.

Ariel looked at me, her freckles standing out like dots you could connect to make a picture.

"Witches," she said. "And they're coming this way."

"But how can they be?" Charlotte asked. "Halloween is pretty much over."

"They're upset," I said, "because they lost the scary costume competition this year. First time in a century."

No one found my joke especially funny.

"Whatever they're after," Charlotte said, "it's never, ever good."

From all the stories I'd heard in my eleven years of sleepovers at Grandma's, I knew that to be true.

"Where can we hide?" Ariel asked, blurting the words out like a chittering squirrel. "We should really hide."

We all looked around for places to take cover and cringe in fear—except for our friend Holly, who lay sound asleep on the couch at the other end of the room.

Charlotte asked, "When is the last time anyone you know actually saw a witch?"

It hadn't happened in my life.

I whispered, "Grandma told me that witches show up at the worst possible time, like thunderstorms or annoying relatives. She said it got so bad a century ago that they changed the name of the town from Glendale to Witch Haven."

Charlotte hissed, "Shhh!"

We held our breath as the witches flew right over my house, so close that we could pick out the snapping rhythms of individual robes as they passed. Charlotte's eyes went wide and Ariel squeaked. She couldn't help it. The cracking of tortured fabric faded for a second, then grew louder again, moving closer.

There is a certain kind of dread that invades your insides when you hear an ambulance coming up the street and hope it doesn't stop at anyone's house you know. That's how we felt right then … times ten, or maybe times a dozen plus one.

The thrum of power from the brooms lessened. The witches' robes stopped flapping.

"It's never good," Charlotte repeated.

Ariel climbed up on the back of the couch and peeked through the curtain. She ricocheted away from the window like something had slapped her.

"They're in your yard," she whispered.

2

Witch Haven had—I guess, has—a history. One which, to be completely honest, my friends and I never gave a moment's consideration. It's not like we ever discussed it in Mrs. Kendricks' history class, though maybe we should have. The saga of local witches goes further back than Abraham Lincoln, George Washington, or the Declaration of Independence. Way further.

Witch Haven's history caught up with us that Halloween night, long after the other neighborhood kids had sorted heaping bags of candy, tossed used costumes in crumpled piles on the floor, and fallen asleep in their beds. The entire town, my parents included, lay cozy and unconscious with hand-quilted blankets pulled up to their chins against the crisp autumn night.

Not me and my friends. Loud, laughing, and sweaty, we'd been coasting down the far slope of a Halloween sleepover. A sleepover in name only. We called it a *wakeover*, because that described it better. The party officially began the instant we returned to my house after trick-or-treating and vowed not to sleep until daybreak on Sunday.

We had a good reason to stay awake. Two. Maybe three.

First, who could sleep with all that sugar coursing through their veins like high-octane gasoline in my father's vintage Mustang? Abuzz with frantic energy, fueled by st   ashes of hard-won candy, we bounced off the walls of the basement family room.

Second, Halloween came on a Saturday night this year. We could sleep till forever on Sunday. Everyone agreed Halloween should always fall on a Saturday. The grownups in charge of everything should adjust the calendar to make that happen. It just made sense.

Third, the first Sunday in November is a big moment in time-keeping according to our teacher, Mrs. Kendricks. It's when Daylight Savings Time officially ends. *Spring forward, Fall back.* At two in the morning, Charlotte, Ariel, and I made a formal ceremony of setting the wall clock back to one. We all got to relive the hour between one and two. Except for our friend, Holly. True to form, she'd set her nerdy glasses onto the end table and fallen asleep on the couch at the far end of the room before midnight.

We put our borrowed time to good use, jumping from the upper tier of a roll-out sofa-bed and landing on mattresses that my father had piled one upon the other to break our falls.

"Spring forward," Ariel said as she jumped up onto the armrest. "Aaaaannnd, fall back." She toppled backwards onto a pile of pillows.

"Look, Mama. I can fly," said Charlotte as she launched herself into space.

Ariel climbed back up on the couch. She flapped her arms frantically like a bird poised at the edge of a nest for her first flight. "Me too … I think … maybe."

She toppled off the back of the sofa. "Maybe not."

We laughed like a band of hyenas. Except for Holly, of course.

"She's cute when she's asleep," said Ariel, during a break.

"Then she's always cute," I said, "because she's always asleep."

Charlotte piped in. "I want to rub peanut butter on her face."

She produced a half-eaten, mostly melted peanut butter cup from somewhere and walked toward our sleeping friend, stiff-legged, arms outstretched like a zombie. Ariel jumped to Holly's defense. I hung back. Zombies really, truly, totally creep me out. Of all the supernatural beings in Grandma's bedtime stories, I would vote zombies off the island first.

After we cleaned up a little from the wrestling match that followed, Ariel returned to her perch on the couch.

"Geronimo," she cried as she flew halfway along the length of the bed to land on the mattresses.

"The plane is going down," I shouted. "Jump or die."

So, we became airmen—or, I suppose, airwomen—forced by engine failure to bail out of an otherwise perfectly functional plane. As the night went on, the imaginary airplane suffered an endless array of catastrophes including explosions, pirate hijackers, and—best of all—a world-wide alien invasion.

Each creative disaster required that the three of us exit the fantasy aircraft in haste. Arms and legs spread wide to catch the air, we landed with splats, whomps, and an occasional "Oof" on the mattresses. Sweat flew from us in unladylike spatters. Ariel's normally creamy complexion, typical of people with her amazing, brilliant, flaming red hair, glistened a dewy pink that overwhelmed the pale freckles on her cheeks and nose.

We rolled and bumped and piled on top of one another through the wee hours of the night, laughing at our antics until our stomachs hurt. Or maybe all the Halloween candy did that. Strewn with a thousand empty wrappers, the basement floor looked like a multicolored fairy-tale lawn.

We gasped when Charlotte made a particularly daring exit out the door of the plane. She ricocheted off the mattress, flipped head over heels, and landed in a heap on the tile floor.

All three of us went "Ouch" at the same time.

But Charlotte popped right up.

"Good thing your dad didn't see that," she said to me. "He would have pulled the plug on couch diving and made us all go to bed."

Not to worry. Dead to the world, my parents snored away in their upstairs bedroom, asleep even before Holly dropped out of the running. They'd both been airmen once. Airpeople? Airfolks? Dad flew jets off an aircraft carrier. Mom, an airwoman like my friends and me, flew helicopters overseas somewhere. They'd snooze through anything quieter than a full-scale ground attack.

Mom and Dad had taken up skydiving after retiring from the Navy. You could say they dove into it headfirst. Once a month—earlier today, in fact—they headed off to the local airfield to pursue their hobby. They always returned home happy, excited, and exhausted, except once when I'd asked my mom if I could try parachuting with them the next time and her normally rosy face turned really pale. Never mind. Jumping from imaginary planes onto mattresses with my very best friends in the world nearly equaled the real thing. It was definitely funnier.

The mayhem of an all-nighter never seemed to bother my parents. They'd probably sleep through an actual alien invasion. That's why we always scheduled our late-night slamfests *chez moi*.

Chez moi is a French expression. *Chez* means "at the house of." *Moi* means "me." If you put them together, they mean "at the house of me," which sounds stupid. It's easier just to say chez moi, or even, "at my house," especially since that's where we were, hurling ourselves through the imaginary door of the imaginary airplane toward the imaginary green island below us. Bone-white sand. A coral reef as pink as Easter. An unimaginably blue ocean. The local volcano spewed chocolate onto nearby ice cream trees whose multi-flavored fruit grew cold when ripe. No imaginary boys would ever find our imaginary island. Except sometimes, when we wanted them to.

We took a short break from our adventures, replenishing our energy from Halloween hoards, taking time to pick through the loot and savor the flavors. Charlotte lay sprawled on the couch, licking her wounds in her retro Angry Birds pajama bottoms and a white tank top as Ariel, dressed in Bugs Bunny bottoms, dropped M&Ms into her open mouth like a servant feeding Cleopatra grapes. My beloved Sponge Bob pj's stuck to my sweaty legs like pale yellow cotton candy. I figured we had one more round of flying to go before the sun came up and we could finally get some rest.

That's when Charlotte had sat up, a strand of blonde hair plastered to her cheek. She whipped her head up so fast that the M&Ms already falling from Ariel's fingers landed with little plunks on the fake leather of the sofa cushion.

"Shhh," Charlotte hissed. "Do you hear that?"

A moment or two later, Ariel peeked out the window to discover a coven of witches chez moi.

"They're in your yard," she had said. "And they're coming this way."

3

Tap-tap-tap.

We just about jumped out of our pajamas at the sound of a knock on the basement door. Ariel let out a little yelp. Odd sounds popped out of her like bubbles. She couldn't help it. Charlotte clamped a hand over Ariel's mouth and we all pretended to not exist. Holly's regular breathing sounded like wind whistling through the silence.

A voice seeped in from the other side of the door, low and raspy, like someone gargling out the words: "We know you're in there, little loves," it said. "Your ssssilence does not deceive us. We can ssssmell you."

A noise arose, halfway between whistling and static, that sounded like a hundred ghosts chiming their agreement. I tightened my arms around me as if that would somehow keep my scent from fizzing out.

"And we can hear you breathing, too."

A screechy sound came through the door, like fingernails scraping on a blackboard. I recalled how the witches in Grandma's bedtime stories etched runes and symbols on things to focus their intention and their power. She called them wards. The squealing tapered off to an eerie silence.

"Sssso, you ssssee there's no hiding from us, is there?"

The voice outside the door had a crass, vaguely British accent, like dwarves might use in some big-budget fantasy movie. It dawned on me that if you tossed in a few "arrrrs" and "mateys," it sounded a lot like a pirate talking. Yes. The witch definitely spoke Pirate.

"So, would one of you please open the door before we break it down?"

Something hard and loud hit the door at the word "break" and we all screamed. Except for Holly, who mumbled something in her sleep and rolled over on the couch.

"Eh? What was that?" the voice asked.

Excited murmurs. A conversation among the witches?

"Not that we would mmmind very much breaking the door," said the voice.

Tap-tap-tap.

"That wouldn't be Holly Jones we heard in there just now, would it? Right behind you on the sofa, I'd wager. I couldn't quite make out what she ssssaid."

My eyes went wide. How could the witches know our names?

"Such a ssssweet girl, Holly. So we hear."

The witch's unearthly cackle raised goose bumps on my arms.

"That's why we must have her."

The next slam to the door moved its hinges. It certainly moved us. We scrambled away to the far end of the room, ending up in a huddle with the still sleeping Holly at our backs.

The voice came again, more subdued this time, as if the witch meant to reassure us. "Now, wee lassssies, I think we have given you plenty of time to consider. Been more than reasonable, we have. All we want is the little girl sleeping on the sofa, and we'll be on our way. Won't harm anyone. Will we, ladies?"

Another round of murmurs sounded like the moan of wind in winter.

"See," said the voice, "I told you we could be reasonable."

The fingernails on a blackboard sound started up again, and the eerie chorus of moans rose in fervor.

"Yessss," said the voice. "As for this door here … I think, now."

The door burst into pieces as if it had exploded in slow motion. Shards peeled off one by one and dropped onto the tile floor of the basement.

Shadows darker than night billowed beyond the threshold. A low rumble, like a lion purring, rumbled from the midst of that void … the self-satisfied laughter of an ancient witch.

That woke Holly up. I could tell by her screams.

4

A witch stepped into my basement from the blackness beyond. The hiss of her robes sounded like the prolonged s's in her speech. Her figure seemed to shrink in stature, almost to shrivel, the farther she stepped into the light. By the time she stopped halfway across the room, she stood no taller than Charlotte, the tallest of my best friends—still scary as a midnight horror film, mind you, but smaller than one would imagine. The witch, hunched there in our nicely furnished suburban family room with the gurgling fish tank and brightly painted walls, didn't fit the surroundings in a way that was creepy to the core.

The remainder of her coven formed an oozing, writhing, hissing backdrop pressing against the rectangular opening of the disintegrated door like the opening itself somehow kept them out.

"You're Matilda, aren't you?" I mumbled without thinking.

The witch's cold gaze came up to meet mine. "Sssso you know me, do you?"

"Sort of," I answered. "My grandmother told me about how they drove out the dark witches years ago. You survived because you ran away."

Matilda's shoulders tensed as if my remark had hurt her feelings. Her face grew pensive. Did witches have enough feelings to be insulted?

"Flew away, to be precise, dearie. Better to fight and fly away and live to fight another day, I think the saying goes."

She scanned the room, craning her neck in an attempt to spy out the darker corners.

"But that was decades ago, wasn't it?" she said, dismissing the past with a casual wave.

The witch leaned forward, both hands resting on the head of her broom. She squinted at me. "Long before you were born, I should think."

She rubbed her hands together in a distracted scrubbing motion, as if cleaning them under running water.

"I would guess that you are ..." —she rubbed her hands again—" four years old? No, six."

I didn't answer, because it had dawned on me that I'd said too much already. Never offer a witch information. I learned that much from Grandma's stories. They always, always, use it against you.

"Sixteen?" she asked when it became clear I had no intention of responding.

I was eleven. Of my immediate friends, only Holly had reached the ripe old age of twelve.

"No matter," she said. "You mentioned something, I think, about your grandmother and some lies she told you."

As she spoke, her gnarled hands went round and round one another like a caricature of an anxious old crone. It would have been pitiful to watch except that this bent, frail, worried old woman had just destroyed my parents' basement door using only her fingernails and a word.

"Nnnnow, I shouldn't think that your grandmother, Abigail, is here in the house with us. Is she, my child?"

Why Matilda seemed hesitant to confront the kindest woman in the world, I couldn't say. The witch relaxed when it became clear that I wouldn't answer that question either.

"Thought not," she said. "I would have known."

She took another step into the room and peered around.

"Dear Abby," she said as if speaking directly to my grandmother, "rest assured that the events of the past will not repeat in the present. Oh, nnnno. I was younger then, you see. This time we are here to stay, my sisters and I. This time we were invited."

She winked at me. The fiery glint in her open eye drove me back a step. I bumped into Holly, whose legs were already squeezed against the couch she had recently been sleeping on.

"Would you please communicate that to your nnnnasty grandmum next you see her, dear?"

She smiled. At least she seemed to try, though I don't think she had much practice at it.

"If there is a next time, of course."

She moved forward with a decided limp, using her broom handle almost like an oar to push her way into each step. Step. Paddle. Step. It looked painful.

She said, "To be entirely honest, until this moment I knew nothing of your relationship to that despicable woman, young one. It was never you we were interested in."

Paddle. Step. Stop. She rubbed her hands again. Round and round. Her gaze went distant for a moment.

"Ella, is it?" she asked, somehow pulling my name out of the blue.

"Your presence here adds an interesting twist to this evening's adventure. Oh, yes it does."

Matilda rubbed her hands some more. "Is that truly your mother upstairs, sleeping like a contented child? Ooooo, this is too precious."

She winked at me again. "I shall pay you and your grandmother a visit one day soon, I will. And your star-struck mother. Shall we all plan on that, little Ella? Yessss?"

She moved her arm in a way to include the dark forms outside the open door. "Would it please you if I brought along my sisters as well?"

A hiss like the sound of a pressure cooker rose and fell in the night.

Matilda started forward again.

The four of us retreated at her advance. We inched around the empty couch and back toward the garage. I could feel Ariel's hand on my back. Holly sobbed behind her. Charlotte stood by the garage door, her back flat against the wall.

The witch's tone brightened at the sound of Holly's anguish. Speaking directly to her, she said, "Oh, hello, dearesssst Holly Elizabeth Jones. The coven has been following you for quite some time now, don't you know. You are such a sweet, intelligent, and talented girl. So much potential."

Holly's bawling only got louder.

"Precisely for that reason … and for some other more complicated ones involving your lineage … we have decided that you shall become the first new witch to be accepted into our order in a long, long time."

Holly blubbered through her tears, "N-no, thank you, ma'am. I'd rather not."

"It is quite an honor for such a young girl," the witch suggested as if Holly should be flattered at the invitation.

She smiled the way a snake smiles at a mouse.

"And, to be completely clear, you have absolutely no choice in the matter."

Leaning heavily on the cane, Matilda took another obviously painful step toward us.

We could no longer retreat. Our backs were literally up against the wall.

Behind me, Ariel eased open the door to the garage.

Matilda made a shooing motion with the back of her free hand. "Oh, go on, girl," she said. "Run away if you wish. We have no truck with you this evening."

Ariel did just that, tiptoeing through the doorway.

The witch pointed her chin at Charlotte and added, "Or with you. Go on. Scat."

Charlotte, the least obedient of my friends, slid sideways along the wall until the doorway to the garage opened wide behind her, whereupon she grabbed Holly and yanked her into the garage. I stepped forward and snatched Matilda's broom from her arthritic fingers. It's all I could think of to slow her down. The witch toppled to one knee as I dashed through the doorway after my friends.

Ariel slammed the garage door shut and Charlotte jammed a chair under the knob like they do in the movies. There was no way to lock the door from this side. We added an old car battery, my father's toolbox, and a weighted umbrella stand to the barrier. The makeshift barricade wouldn't hold for long, I knew, especially against someone who could turn a steel door into scrap metal using only her voice.

Matilda bellowed her frustration. The cinder-block wall that separated us from her rage shook. Little flakes of mortar fell from the cracks. Could my parents really sleep through this?

The abrupt silence that followed filled the space almost as much as the witch's roar.

A full minute passed, during which Matilda seemed to gather herself together.

Tap-tap-tap.

"Nicely done, girlies," she said through the door. "Very brave. You have my compliments."

Something scratched at the door, like before.

"I will admit that breaking the first door was rather fun. How often does one get to do that in a year, I ask you? But I have no intention of repeating the process unnecessarily. It takes so much out of me these days. Yessss."

Tap-tap-tap.

"Now, children," she crooned in a voice that somehow made me want to obey, "open the door and let me in."

"Not by the hair of my chinny-chin-chin," intoned Charlotte. Her eyes went wide and she covered her mouth with both hands.

I said to Charlotte and Ariel, "See if you can hide Holly somewhere while I distract the witches. It will be dawn soon."

Ariel shrugged. "So what?" she said.

"So everything. Grandma told me a lot of stories about witches."

"Stories," Ariel repeated with a total lack of confidence.

"Don't worry," I said, "I've got this. As soon as I go outside, you run up and get my parents. Then make Holly disappear. Got it?"

"Uh?" Ariel said.

Charlotte came to the rescue. "We're on it, Ella. We'll do our part."

5

My dad kept a beat-up Navy sweatshirt in the garage for those cold nights when he worked out there on his vintage Mustang. The tattered old rag might once have been a proud shade of blue. The dingy yellow letters across its chest had been bright gold long ago. After a thousand laundry cycles and more than a little engine grease, the colors had faded to pale ghosts of their glory.

The enormous garment fit me like a tent, covering me to my knees. As a little girl, I loved to throw its cavernous hood completely over my face and breathe in the mysterious smells that had permanently infused into the soft fabric. Sometimes my dad would pick me up in his strong arms, safe and warm, to tell me that I was everything marvelous in the world. Although his muffled words came to me only indistinctly through the thick fabric, it never occurred to me that every single one of them could possibly be anything but true.

I lifted my father's sweatshirt from the peg he'd hung it on and tossed it over my head knowing that it would keep me neither warm nor safe. Reaching high on tiptoes, I pulled an old, khaki-colored backpack down from an upper shelf on the back wall of the garage and threaded my arms through the it's straps.

"Help me with this," I said.

I leaned the borrowed broom against the lawn mower while my friends helped me cinch the buckles and roll up the extra-extra-long sleeves of my father's hoodie. The procedure took precious time.

I could hear a sound like buzzing bees in the room beyond the door. Matilda must have waited for the rest of the coven to fill in behind her.

"Nnnnow, girls," she sang in her sandpaper voice, "you are not going to make me count, are you?"

"Actually," I said, "I was kind of hoping you would."

My friends and I always started at one hundred and counted backwards. I would need a countdown from at least ninety-nine to make my plan work.

Apparently, Matilda had not played the same games when she had been little … if she ever had been little.

"One," she said, and the door cracked, forming a long, vertical V-shape with the point in the middle.

I grabbed Matilda's broom and hit the garage door opener with my free hand. The creaky old monster-of-a-door took its sweet time to rattle and clank open a couple of inches.

Matilda asked, "What's that horrible noise?"

I shouted at the family room door: "That's me going out the back, Matilda. My grandmother said she almost took you to the cleaners once, and I am going to finish the job. You won't be able to fly away this time because I have your broom."

To Charlotte, I said, "Close the garage door as soon as I'm out."

Charlotte obliged. She hit the close button as I rolled through the narrow slit between the ground and the partially opened garage door. The maneuver would have gone as smoothly as it always does on television, except the bag strapped to my back whacked hard against the ground and I came to an abrupt stop after a quarter of a roll. The door had already descended nearly to my shoulder, coming down to crush me as I wriggled and flopped out onto the driveway using my elbows and my butt for locomotion.

"Oops. My bad," I heard Charlotte say. "Jumped the gun a little."

I heard Matilda's cackle through the narrow opening.

"You, there," she said to someone in the family room, "give me your broom. I want to hurt that annoying little girl. The other one can wait. Hurry now, sisters."

2
Swept Up

Grandma's bedtime stories always had a witch in them. She once told me a really fun one about a young one who happened upon a broom and claimed it as her own. The girl remarked how "basic brooming" turned out to be pretty easy because the broom handled all the hard stuff. Hard stuff included, I supposed, the part where you left the ground. Even so, it took the girl in the story years of practice to master all the twists and turns of flying.

Standing there all alone in my parents' driveway with a horde of witches streaming single file around the side of the house, I had seconds, not years, to master the details of flying a broom.

"Once the girl made it into the air," Grandma said, "all she had to do was to think about flying and she was flying. The broom already knew how, you see. She could trust the broom."

I tried to recall everything my grandmother told me about the girl who had inherited the broom. How hard could flying be? The person in the story had done it.

The story. Sure, my hometown of Witch Haven had a history. Sure, Grandma's bedtime tales seemed so realistic, so alive, I never considered they might not be one hundred percent fact … maybe two hundred percent. But could brooms really fly? As much as I wanted it to be true, the assumption suddenly seemed absurd.

And yet, with thirteen bits of evidence heading my way, I had nothing left to lose by trying. So I sat on Matilda's broomstick and thought about flying.

Nothing happened.

I thought even harder about flying.

"Up," I said, and repeated the command with increasing urgency as the pack closed in. "Up, up, up!" I screamed, as if saying it louder would help.

Except for a little tickle in my tummy, like the feeling I got when I was about to jump out at someone and shout, "Boo," nothing happened. Or so I believed, until I looked down and noticed my bare feet swinging six inches above the dew-covered lawn.

This flying thing worked after all! Thanks, Grandma.

Of course, it was stretching things a bit to equate dangling with flying. Floating, maybe? Hovering? Stuck in the air above a few sprigs of wilted grass and some dead dandelions?

As I lost concentration, the broom lost two inches of altitude. The sparse autumn grass tickled my toes. Think about flying, stupid.

"Back into the air, please, broom," I said.

Up we went, several feet off the ground this time, but still going nowhere.

A lifetime of slips and tumbles taught me that no one could sit for long on anything as narrow and round as a broomstick without toppling off. If I found myself balanced perfectly on the broom's handle, it had to be … magic. My body and my mind somehow accepted the novel experience of a flying broom as normal and natural. Like Grandma told me, the broom knew how to fly and how to keep its passenger in her seat. I got it. I understood. Trust the broom.

We rose another foot.

Great, but didn't flying usually involve movement in one direction or other? I really hoped so because going forward would come in very handy very soon.

Fortunately for me, the coven of witches contained no track stars. I'd mistaken the exaggerated motions of their arms and legs as running. Instead, they waddled, and limped, and doddered at me so slowly that a pack of zombies could have passed them without looking back. I hate zombies, by the way. Yet, for all their disabilities, the witches drew steadily closer, like a line of ants or a string of video aliens in one of those antique games my father liked to play.

I know a million places around the neighborhood where someone my size could hide. If I could get my feet back on the ground — guess how well running worked with my feet not touching the ground? — I could find one and disappear until the sun returned. At the turtle speed they seemed to move, the witches would never catch up.

That's when I discovered witches possess tools more useful than mobility or speed. The one leading the herd had her talons out, pointing in my direction. She stopped in her tracks and raised her hands high above her head, preparing to hurl a spell at me. Her fingertips glowed eerie red, like embers in a campfire.

The line of trailing witches crashed over her in a black wave. Surprised by their sister's abrupt halt, they tumbled and rolled and sprawled into one another like a slow-motion replay of a traffic accident. As each witch piled into the one in front of her, she let out a grunt, a hiss, a curse, an "Ack!" or a "Drat!"

I laughed out loud at the rhythmic collision. I laughed until the witches untangled themselves and began limping and crawling toward me again.

Having a broom would be cool, I realized, only if I remained alive to enjoy it. I decided to run for it. I already knew how to use my legs.

With the witches a few feet away, I grabbed the handle of the floating broomstick to support my weight while I jumped off. The instant my palms touched the smooth wood, the broom jerked forward, a result so unexpected that I pulled my hands away like the broom had shocked them.

Whoa! What?

Something in one of Grandma's stories popped into my head. It had to do with the position of the witch on the broom. I leaned forward like the person in the tale, wrapped my hands around the broomstick again, and didn't let go. The broom began to move. An excited tingling welled up in my chest. The thrill of discovery. I would fly away, fast, and leave this nightmare behind.

The broom and I glided across the lawn and over the sidewalk at a sedate pace. Not fast. Not fast at all. Not fast enough to prevent the witches from catching up with me in about five seconds. I desperately recycled my Grandmother's stories for some inspiration.

That's when my mother, finally awake, poked her head out of the second-story window above the garage.

"Move your hands up a little more on the broom handle, sweetie," she suggested in her patient Mom voice. "Then hold on as tight as you can."

What?

Mom?

Really?

I looked up. There she stood in her bathrobe, my father beside her and, almost invisible behind the foggy panes of glass, Charlotte appeared as a distorted glint of blond hair in the shadows.

"Ella," said my mother, her voice rising in volume and pitch as the witches grew nearer, "do what I say for once. And do it now."

I spat on my hands for added grip and grabbed as far forward as I could reach. The shaft of the broom felt pockmarked. Not as smooth as I'd imagined.

The sudden rush of speed nearly swept me off its back. I let go out of reflex and the broom lurched to a stop halfway across the street. I almost fell forward off it. I'd bought a few seconds' more time to think.

"Not too bad," my mother called out.

"Mom," I shouted up at the window, "how do you know ...? How do I ...?"

Matilda drifted around the corner of the house on her borrowed broom. Even at a distance, the witch's eyes shone with the spooky reddish glimmer of two glowing coals.

I yelled something mindless, like you would if one of your friends jumped out at you in the dark. There is a certain word. One that eleven-year-olds are not exactly supposed to know and are certainly not supposed to use around their parents.

"What did you say, young lady?" my mother snapped. "When did you hear your father use that word?"

It's possible I said that word again, this time under my breath.

"Ella!"

As much to leave my mother behind as Matilda, I slid my palms along the notched broomstick to a spot I hoped would result in a manageable pace. Maybe about halfway along the shaft ....

I shot away—straight toward the old oak tree in my neighbor's front yard.

A year ago, our neighbor across the street tied a big yellow ribbon around the trunk of the tree where he said it would remain until his son came home from somewhere across the ocean. As the oversized yellow bow loomed like a bull's-eye ahead of me, I leaned hard to the right like you would to turn a bike. A soft swish of yellow fabric slapped my shoulder as I sped past the tree on a beeline toward my neighbor's front door.

I pulled the broomstick back hard, like pulling in a horse's reins, in an instinctive attempt to stop my forward motion. Instead of stopping, though, the broom took off straight up into the sky. I slid back on the broomstick until the bundle of straw at the end—I later learned that the business end of a broom is called the sweeps, go figure—caught me. My feet hit our neighbor's gutter. I half bounced, half dragged the bones of my bare feet along two dozen rows of roof shingles before clearing the peak of the house.

The house, the neighborhood, the whole world, fell away beneath my bleeding toes.

2

The hood of my dad's sweatshirt whipped and cracked behind me. Flying felt like a dream. Except that I never got this cold in dreams. The frigid wind poured through the thin fabric of my sweat-soaked Sponge Bob pajamas. My unprotected legs felt like someone had dumped a bucket of ice water on them.

I glanced over my shoulder. A gaggle of airborne witches trailed behind me like a family of geese. I have no idea where their brooms came from. I never saw them during the slow-motion chase in the front yard of my house. The nightmare vision of the witches' pale, upturned faces, straggling hair, and glowing eyes made me feel even colder than the autumn air. I watch in frozen horror as the last two witches on the driveway pushed away from the concrete straddling a shared broom.

If my eyes didn't deceive me, the highest and closest of the flying witches came at me faster than the others, gaining ground … well, air … on me rapidly. After a hundred years of practice, I thought, these witches should be better flyers than a novice with only her grandmother's bedtime stories for training. On the upside, the chilling bite of the wind had definitely diminished. At least I'd be warm when they caught me.

Then it occurred to me that those two things—the witches coming at me faster, plus the lessening of the wind—actually meant one thing. My broom had slowed to a crawl. The witches wouldn't catch me because they were older, more experienced fliers. They would catch me, and no doubt hurt me, because my broom had come to a standstill.

It made sense. I'd throttled the broom up to a point that seemed fast when moving horizontally along level ground. But that amount of power would never get a hundred pounds of girl very far in the vertical direction when gravity's doing its earthly best to prevent it. Basic physics. Thanks for the insight, Mrs. Kendricks.

Throwing caution to the wind, I slid my hands as far up the shaft of the broom as I could reach. It accelerated upwards, pressing my legs back against pointy bristles of straw as the distance increased between me and the pack of black-clad women strung out below.

3

Snap, snap, snap went my flimsy pajamas.

Flap, flap, flap the witches' thick robes answered.

I shuddered, glad for the speed but not for the chill of the wind created by it. Every so often a rogue gust grabbed at the hood of my father's sweatshirt which filled up with air and tried to lift me off the broom by my neck.

The higher we rose, the colder the air became. Icicles formed on the knob of my broom. When I glanced back again, the faces of the witches still glowered up at me.

The chase had taken us farther than I'd thought. Out past the woods that separated the small town of Witch Haven from the acres of cropland and fenced-in pastures that stretched from the forest all the way to the looming mountains beyond.

Rivers and roads stretched to forever below me. I could barely pick out the line of the eastern horizon where a gray predawn sky met the darker gray of a distant ocean. A breeze coming from the west pushed me in that direction, away from the fields below and back toward the forest at the edge of town.

I felt a crispness in the air that I remembered from the deepest, darkest winter nights. It came to my senses more as a smell than anything else. My father's Navy sweatshirt did little to prevent the freezing wind from penetrating deep to the sleeveless T-shirt beneath. My pajama bottoms afforded no protection at all from the frigid night.

When I felt I could endure no more of the cold or the climb, I slid my hands toward me, back along the length of the broomstick. The broom stopped on a dime and leveled out. I felt like a hunted animal that had given up all hope.

Unable to rein in their momentum, the speeding witches flew by, one after the other. By the time they stopped, the entire coven hovered in a flock ten yards above me. Their panting breaths formed a fog around them until the wind blew it away.

Everything seemed a little brighter way up here, I thought. The sky didn't look so black. The stars nearest the horizon appeared dimmer than they had from the ground.

The coven dispersed to fill the space overhead. They rasped and wheezed trying to draw the thin, icy air into starving lungs. I, too, found it difficult to catch my breath. It got even harder when the first shivers welled up along my spine like miniature earthquakes. What air I managed to draw, came in stuttering gasps.

Matilda cackled from the center of the swarm overhead: "A fine chase it was, precious little girl, but it's over now."

I shook with cold and fear as I chattered out my reply: "It c-c-certainly looks th-that way," I said, and then added for spite, "hag."

"Why did you stop, I wonder?" she asked, unabashed. "You are so young. Your energy is so … so fresh. And,"—she pointed a crooked finger at me as if it were a dagger—"you have my broom. With it, I think you could have stayed ahead of us until dawn. We would have been forced to let you go."

I shuddered either from the cold or the piercing coarseness of her voice. "You th-th-think so?" I asked. "What h-happens to you at dawn?"

Matilda made a growling sound low in her throat. "Ohhhhh," she crooned, "I would wager you already know the answer, my dear. But it won't help you. No, no. Sunup is an hour away yet. Plenty of margin for safety. And judging by the color of your skin, if we do nothing else but remain here discussing matters, you'll freeze to death long before then."

She was right about that. If not the cold, then the lack of breathable air would be the death of me in about a minute.

Matilda got right down to it. "Is there anything you would like to say or do before I pull the power out of your—oh, I should say my—broom, and you fall ...." She shifted on her broom and looked down. "Maybe two miles to the earth?"

"Actually," I whispered through cracking lips, "yes, there is, thanks."

Matilda looked surprised. "Ask it, then," she croaked. "And be quick. My sisters are impatient for your death. And we have other business to conduct this evening."

"What other b-b-business?" I asked.

"Our business," said the witch. "Not yours."

I sat as still as my trembling body would allow, biding time. Up here in the freezing air where no one had a right to be, time was my one friend. I needed to use up as much of it as I could.

Matilda tapped one long, gnarled fingernail on the wooden handle of her borrowed broom. The rest of her coven leaned over their own brooms, peering down like vultures as if they believed I would bolt at any second.

That wasn't my plan. Sure, a game of hide-and-seek in the distant clouds, or a suicidal slalom race through the branches of the ancient forest somewhere below might buy me more time. But the witches, for all their cunning, had missed something critical I hoped. I really, really hoped. To find out, I needed to keep them up here with me a while longer.

My own inhalations sounded like a roar inside my head. The labored breathing of the coven blended with the audible hiss of wind.

Matilda quickly lost patience. "Now, girl," she said. "Have your say, or do not. But make it quick."

I waited again as long as I dared, delaying until I saw the witch's hands move along her broom handle.

"Okay," I said, "okay. Then, c-c-could you please tell me the t-t-t-time?"

That surprised the ugly woman. She sat up a little straighter on her broom. "The time, you say, little girl? I wonder why you would ask us that at a ... well ... at a time like this."

"The time," I said. "Th-that's all I want to know."

"That has to be among the oddest last requests I have ever heard," said the incredulous witch. "And I have heard quite a few. Oh, yes. Quite a few in my day."

She wafted down on her broom, trading her superior position above me for a closer look. Matilda halted at my level not ten feet away and scrutinized me through squinted eyes. They blazed for an instant, and I felt something flood into my head like a plume of smoke. It coalesced into a buzzing cloud inside my brain. The fire in Matilda's eyes dimmed to a dull orange.

She asked, "What are all those belts and buckles you have dangling about everywhere, my lovely? Do they hold you more tightly to my broom? Or are they some kind of protection for your body?"

She leaned left, then right on her broom, peering around me for a better view.

"They d-do help to protect my b-b-body," I said.

I remembered Grandma's advice about surrendering information to a witch, but the tingling inside my head made it impossible to deceive Matilda. Weird.

Matilda pursed her lips. "Well," she said, "I sense no magic in them. And I don't see how they could possibly protect you from me."

My teeth chattered in response.

"Zena," barked the witch, "where are you?"

"I'm up here, My Lady. Above you and to the left."

A younger witch—"younger" is a relative term in this case—Zena rode shotgun behind another, much heavier woman, on a shared broom. The two witches barely fit on the one stick.

"You are the watch witch on this expedition. I presume you brought our timepiece along?"

"I did, My Lady. Of course. We can't be too careful of the hour as dawn nears."

"Yes, yes, yes," said Matilda. "Please tell this stupid girl the time before she freezes to death and we miss out on the fun of killing her."

Zena rolled up the long and cumbersome sleeve of her robe. A gold wristwatch dangled from her bone-thin arm. She examined the timepiece and addressed me directly. "It is six thirty-six in the morning, young missy."

"Six th-th-thirty, you say?"

"Six thirty-six," she repeated.

"It's starting to get light over there," I said, indicating the horizon with a quick flick of my head.

One of the other witches above me sucked in her breath. A buzz rose in the thin air like I'd thrown a rock at a beehive.

I pitched my voice to be heard over the hubbub: "When does ...." I coughed and had to catch my breath. "When does the sun come up today?"

The witches began to buzz again, but Zena silenced them, shouting, "Sisters. No. Do not worry. We are safe here."

The young-ish witch seemed pleased with herself. "The sky always brightens well before the dawn," she said.

Zena made a hideous face at me. I think she meant it as a condescending smile, but it looked more like she had swallowed bubbling lava.

"It's all been predicted," she said. "I did the calculations."

Zena paused as if expecting me to acknowledge her prowess. When I didn't, she continued.

"The sun will crest the horizon at seven forty-two local time. About one hour from now. Yesterday it rose a tad before seven forty. You simply add two and a half minutes from that. It's all on a chart I made some time ago."

"Of course," I said, "that's for the sunrise down on the g-ground."

Her smug look disappeared. She knew enough about geometry and celestial mechanics to realize that the sun would shine on us here, high in the sky, before it did on the quaint town below.

After a concerned pause, she said, "But that should amount to a difference of perhaps a few minutes."

"Yes," I said. "Good."

"Yes," agreed the watch witch, apparently content that she had fulfilled her responsibilities. "Good."

Matilda frowned. "Good?" she asked. "Good? Whatever you're up to, girl, nothing good will come of this. Not as regards to your fast-approaching fate."

"Then, one l-l-last question," I said.

Matilda's harsh whisper cracked through the icy air like a slap. "Make it quick. And know that it will be your last. It's chilly up here, and I tire of your banter."

Though I could no longer feel my fingers, I eased my broom around until it pointed at the watch witch. I looked up toward the slowly dimming stars and spoke to her as clearly as I could. "Zena, it's November, you know? The first Sunday in November. Did you remember to set your watch back?"

"Back," she replied. "What do you—"

"Daylight Savings T-time officially ended last night. Right in the middle of my p-p-party. It always does on the first Sunday in November."

"Daylight Savings Time," Zena echoed in a monotone.

The unearthly sound of murmuring witches wafted from above.

Zena looked a little flustered for an instant, but rallied with an answer. "Of course," she said, brightening as much as possible for a witch. "The watch takes care of that automatically. It is a modern watch. It adjusts for Daylight Savings Time on its own. You see, the watch has already taken the extra hour away. All by itself. That's why it says six thirty-six … uh, six thirty-seven, now … instead of seven thirty-six … drat, I mean seven thirty-eight."

Despite her show of confidence, my words bothered Zena at some level. She held up the watch. She put the glimmering metal timepiece to her ear and shook it. She glared at it with suspicion. She held it out in front of her, first at arm's length, then close up so that it brushed against her surprisingly long eyelashes. She even sniffed it.

The conversation overhead ceased while the coven held its collective breath. Even the wind stopped whistling, as if listening in on a secret.

I spoke into the silence: "It's a v-very nice watch, I'm sure. Must be, if it sets itself back automatically."

My numb fingers slipped a little on the broom and I nearly fell.

"But," I said through teeth clenched against fear and cold, "what about your chart, Zena? Your sunrise chart. Did the chart set itself back, too?"

I shivered uncontrollably for the five seconds it took her to process the information and realize that the end of Daylight Savings Time set everything back, including the hour the sun would rise.

I knew exactly when dawn would arrive because that's when my ruined sleepover—wakeover—should have officially ended and my friends and I could go to bed at last.

Zena's watched told her the correct time all right, but her precious chart had it wrong.

I could tell she had figured things out when the arm with the watch on it dropped to her side.

"Oh," she said. "Oh, dear. Oh, no."

Matilda shot her a look.

"My Lady," Zena said, "I made a slight mis—"

As the first rays of sunlight peeked over the line of ocean far to the east, Zena and six of her companions who had been floating above us in the sky burst into flames. In no time, they dissolved into puffs of black smoke that dissipated in the thin air. Their brooms fell down and away like spears, leaving the acrid odor of burning tires in their wake. I could see the dry straw of at least one broom catch fire, flaring orange and yellow against the gray predawn.

I grabbed the handle of my own broom as far forward as I could reach and pulled back hard on it. The broom bolted straight up with all the speed it could muster, shooting into a gap between the pyres that only moments before had been seven witches.

The rest of the startled coven responded immediately. Witches, at the core of their crooked, black, no longer human hearts, are predators. Grandma's stories made that point quite clear, thank you. If something, or someone, ran from a coven of witches, they would pursue relentlessly. They couldn't help it. Driven by blind instinct, the remaining witches flew to the chase, following my abrupt ascent into the higher air.

Matilda screamed, "Sisters, no!"

But her warning came too late. The remaining witches followed me up into the morning's first fresh beams of sunlight and met a fiery demise in less time than it takes to tell. Only Matilda—older, wiser than the rest—had declined the bait.

I halted my climb, leveled out in the orange glow of dawn, and peered back down at her.

Matilda watched with a curious indifference as the remains of her society rained down from above. She ducked and wove on her broom to avoid collisions with the smoking remains of one former comrade and another.

When the fallout thinned to bits of ash and wisps of smoldering something—something I probably didn't want to know about—Matilda glared up at me through squinted eyes. She seemed to take the sudden destruction of the coven rather well, considering.

"Stupid fools," she said almost kindly. "They paid a heavy price for such a tiny mistake."

The witch shook off her mood and hissed up at me with far less nonchalance: "But neither will you survive this episode, little demon. The magic in that broom can also die. Die with a single word."

She waved a hand in my direction and growled something that sounded to me like, "Gork. Ack."

Technically, that's two words, I thought.

To my chagrin, I felt the life go out of my mount. It happened slowly at first, so that I barely noticed. In a few seconds, though, the flying broom lost its magic and became just another antique household convenience with no good reason to be hanging out in the middle of the sky. I could feel the tendrils of gravity tug at my body like little threads.

"You'll die like my murdered sisters," Matilda proclaimed. "Only I will remain to tell this tale."

As I began to fall, I pushed the broom away and let the useless bit of stick and straw drop. Nothing but emptiness remained between me and the dark expanse far below. I reached out for Matilda as I plunged past her, grabbing a handful of the ebony cloak that draped the witch like a pile of curtains.

The force of my accelerating body ripped Matilda from her broom. In desperation, she dug her nails into the handle, but managed only to drag the broom through the air as we fell. Matilda's talons slid along the shaft until her fingers slipped off the end of the stick with an audible pop.

I let go of her and we fell separately. I expected a howl in defiance at this turn of events. Instead, she screamed some words at me as we plummeted earthward together. Words that I could barely distinguish over the rush of wind: "You'll soon be a bloody bump in the ground, stupid girl."

I shook my head from side to side, too frozen and frightened to speak. No. I wouldn't.

"Your life is forfeit," she hollered. "This is no victory."

I shook my head up and down. Yes. In fact, it was.

With numb, fumbling fingers, I reached behind me, feeling around for a desperate instant until … there. I found the release handle of my father's spare parachute, the one he always kept packed and ready on a shelf at the back of our garage. This is the

moment of truth, I thought, and yanked on the metal bar. "Hard,"
my parents told me way more than once, "but not too hard."

A tiny round parachute popped open behind me.

Yes!

And no.

That little thing wouldn't slow me down very much.

The miniature parachute flapped around over my head, drawing
a thin nylon line out of the pack strapped to my back. The nylon line
in turn pulled out the big main chute. I shouted my relief as a
fountain of fabric streamed out from the pack in a cascading
rainbow. When the huge umbrella of cloth blossomed like a flower
above my head, the jolt felt like a god had reached down from above
to yank me back into the sky.

I watched from my perch high above the world as Matilda, the
last witch in Witch Haven, plummeted into the darkness below my
naked, frozen, bleeding feet.

3
The Dangling Conversation

I hung from the inflated airfoil parachute like a spider from its thread.

Matilda's remains lay somewhere below. "Remains" is another word for "dead body." Often, one that's been broken into pieces. I suppose remains means something like "what's left behind." That suited me. I wanted to leave Matilda's remains as far behind as possible. I wanted them hidden forever, covered by mounds of moist dirt in the fields below.

A glance down reveled not fields, but forest. I guess the wind had pushed us a little east.

Okay, so I wanted Matilda's remains hidden by the trees of the forest below and by the lingering darkness … the remains of the night. With any luck, she had blown up during the descent like her friends had only a few minutes before. Did the bits of ash and debris left by the witches that exploded up there count as remains?

My slow, marathon fall to earth proved as cold as my panicked sprint into the sky had been. Even with my father's oversized hoodie stretched as far down over my legs as I could pull it, even with both numb hands squeezed together inside the big front pocket of his sweatshirt, even with all the wishing in the world for it not to be so, freezing tendrils of frigid air penetrated right through my clothing, stinging me like the tentacles of a jellyfish.

My eyes watered and my sinuses burned. Little tears dripped down and blew back across my cheeks. I tried to wipe the wetness away, but doing so left icy streaks on my exposed skin. I stopped trying, preferring a blurry world to a frostbitten face.

It seems cliché to say that the air whistled in my ears, although the wind moving through the rigging of the parachute and the fibers of my clothing really did whistle and thrum. When you put them all together, the noises combined to make a "woooo," like some Norse giant blowing out a mournful tune.

Grandma, I thought, you never told me a story about this.

In my mind, she shrugged and said, "They're stories, Ella. What did you expect?"

I imagined icicles growing from my earlobes like earrings. I tried to keep the sweatshirt's hood drawn down across my forehead. Since the strings that pulled it tight had long since disappeared, the stupid thing kept blowing off and the wind whooshed past my numb ears again.

The straps of the parachute harness ran outside of my inadequate clothing, plastering the sweatshirt to my body and preventing me from tucking my legs inside like I did on the bleachers at my friends' soccer games. Instead, I drew my legs up in front of me as if squatting on the floor, protecting them as much as I could from the wind. It helped a bit. Every so often, though, I had to let my legs down so that my belly muscles could rest. That made it worse again.

"Daddy," I said.

I longed for his comfort, his calm wisdom, his warmth. My own voice sounded … I don't know … pale compared to the deep drone of rushing air.

"Will I ever land," I asked him, "or will this last forever?"

Every so often, I removed my hands from the relative protection of the sweatshirt pocket to point the chute back on the most direct heading out of the forest. I needed to get past the forest and find a safe landing spot in the farmers' fields away to the west, on the other side of the woods that marked the limits of Witch Haven. I hoped I could land safely there with all that open space around me.

But whenever I took my hands out of the huge pocket, it exposed my fingers, my torso, and my arms to the chilling winds. I tried rubbing my hands together inside the big front pouch, using friction to create warmth. The parachute started to rock back and forth. Its agitated motion scared me.

2

Maneuvering the enormous parachute in the sky turned out to be exactly unlike piloting a broom. Steering my father's flying fabric toy while dangling beneath it like a yoyo proved pretty straightforward once I got the *hang* of it.

I'd learned to drive a broom … sort of … from my grandmother's bedtime stories. In much the same way, I figured out everything worth knowing about skydiving over a lifetime of Saturday brunches spent listening to my enthusiastic parents discuss their weekend flying adventures. They had explained at least a thousand times how a parachute works. I knew about toggles, risers, steering lines, and D-bags. At least in theory.

"Flying a parachute is easy," they said. "A child can do it."

We'll see, Mom. We'll see, Dad.

Parachutes have no steering wheels. Instead they have toggles, little handles on each side connected to control lines that steer the parachute. While still high up in the gray morning air, I tried a few experimental tugs on the toggles. I swerved right a little and then left a little. My parents were correct. A child could do it.

My parents also taught me that safe skydiving had everything to do with preparation, planning, and practice. Only an idiot leapt from a perfectly good airplane flying a mile in the sky without being absolutely, positively, one hundred percent confident about her perfectly packed parachute, positively fastened harness, and well-identified landing zone.

So much for preparation, planning, and practice. I'd made it this far on blind luck alone.

My father often used the forum of our lazy weekend breakfasts to pass on nuggets of wisdom about this and that. I remember him peering sagely at me over his bagel, or coffee, or a forkful of scrambled eggs, to say, "Flying never hurt anyone, baby girl. It's landing that'll get you."

True enough. Landing is both the trickiest and the most inevitable aspect of flying. Despite the roomful of fabric spread out above her like so much colorful laundry, a parachutist still falls at a pretty good rate. Even skilled jumpers could break limbs or worse on impact with terra firma. I saw it happen once out at the airfield. Ouch!

My first ever attempt at landing lay in the near future, though, according to my chattering teeth, not near enough. So, despite the cold, the dark, and my streaking tears, I practiced touchdowns while still high enough for a mistake not to matter much. Crash-landing twenty times way up in the sky is infinitely better than crash-landing once on the ground. I picked a point in the air in front of me, swooped down to it, and pulled back on the toggles—the handles that help you steer—until I came nearly to a stop. I swooped and stalled until I felt that I could repeat the process the one time it truly mattered.

Once I passed beyond the edge of the forest and back over our local farmers' fields, I could take my time and drift down far away from the dangers of trees, power lines, and other tall, pointy objects that might try to reach up and grab me. I would eventually end up—end down, I mean—on the soft, freshly plowed earth.

Thus assured, I surveyed the area for a place to alight. *Alight* is a fancy way of saying "land delicately." Butterflies alight on flowers in the garden. Goldfinches alight on twigs at the ends of branches. Big passenger jets land, but not so delicately. Falling anvils land. Witches without parachutes land. Hard.

I spent a Saturday last summer standing by the hangars at the airfield, watching a skydiving competition. I followed my father's flight as he jumped from an airplane way up in the sky and touched down inside a hula hoop target placed in a corner of the airfield half a football field away. My dad most definitely alit with a smile on his unshaven weekend face. His knees bent into a relaxed crouch the instant his jump boots tapped the earth, giving the impression that he would have gladly leapt back into the sky to do it all over if only someone had asked him.

The landing zone—the alighting zone—I aimed for measured acres in size. Much bigger than a hula hoop. A beginner should have no trouble hitting that mark. To be honest, I'd settle for any kind of landing that didn't involve serious injury.

How hard could it be?

3

This late in autumn, the local farmers had already harvested their corn and soy, stripping the earth of its bounty and smoothing out the soil. I wanted to land … to alight … in a flat patch of soft tilled dirt with nothing much sticking up to surprise me. With all that open space, even if I missed the perfect spot, the next one would do almost as well.

I couldn't say how fast I fell through the air. It felt like I was floating in the middle of the sky. Except for freezing, it felt pretty good. The more my mood improved, the warmer I felt. The warmer I felt, the more my mood improved.

It turns out that the temperature drops three or four degrees every thousand feet you go above sea level. I looked it up. That may not sound like much if you start in August and go up maybe a mile. But in November, wearing only Sponge Bob pajamas and no shoes, every rising degree felt like a warm burst of summer sunshine.

Feeling more confident and altogether better than I had a few minutes ago, I searched the ground below me for the perfect landing zone. Dad told me that it's difficult to determine your speed when you're high up and can see everything laid out below you like a map. Things get a little more obvious and a whole lot scarier as you drift down. In the growing light, I discovered that the persistent breeze had pushed me far away from a gentle landing in an empty cornfield. I saw only forest below me. I could already distinguish the tops of individual trees.

I'd somehow fallen much faster than I'd thought without getting much closer to the safety … well, relative safety … of the farmers' fields. I guessed that a west wind was trying to push me away. Hard to tell for sure because the motion of my body through the air created its own wind. The closer I came to landing, though, the more it looked like the spiteful breeze might hold me suspended over trees until I crashed into their sharp upper branches. A hundred spears of oak would finish the job Matilda had started. My confidence faltered a little—okay, a lot—when it became clear that my controlled fall from the heavens might end, not with a gentle touchdown in a field, but with a flesh-ripping crash into a tree.

Remember that word I am not supposed to know?

I pulled my hands out from the relative warmth of my big front pocket and dedicated them full-time to steering. With a pull on a toggle, I eased the chute back om the right direction. The wind worked against me, resisting my intention to land far out among the barren cornfields. Had the witches cursed the air itself, I wondered. Or did I give them too much credit?

Ahead, the branches came to an abrupt end where a fence separated wild forest from cultivated land. I closed in on both the treetops and the tree line with equal rapidity. Individual oaks and pines and the occasional white-barked beech poked up through the forest canopy.

My parents never told me how quickly everything came up at the end of your ride. In less time than it takes to tell, my altitude dropped from maybe one hundred feet to eighty. Then to sixty. High up in the sky, an hour ago it seemed, I wanted to get down as fast as I could. Now I needed to stay up as long as I could.

Something hard and sharp batted at my bare foot. Ouch! I pulled my legs as up against my chest. Twigs and stems swatted me like whips as I passed through the uppermost limbs of an oak.

A shape—big, black, and crumpled like a large trash bag—lay in the branches of the tree below me. I passed it in an instant, with no more than a glimpse. In a far corner of my mind, I wondered if bears could climb.

Something tugged at me hard, like it wanted to pull me down into the tree. The bear? I heard my pajamas rip. There goes my pocket, I thought. In the same instant I broke into clean air beyond the farmer's fence, thirty feet above an open field.

Thirty feet seems a long way if you're looking down from a cliff or a diving board. It's not nearly long enough when you're figuring out how to land a parachute for the first time.

I tugged at both toggles like I'd seen my parents do. I knew it would slow me down.

Nothing happened.

I tugged harder.

And harder.

And harder.

It looked so easy when my parents had done it.

How hard could it be?

4

In the end, I stalled—which basically means stopped—the parachute four or five feet above the ground and fell the rest of the way, landing with a plop in the soft dirt.

Rather than resist the impact, I allowed my knees to buckle and my body to roll a few times before coming to rest. The collapsing chute billowed down on top of me, turning my world deep shades of red, green, and yellow. I lay there for a minute, panting beneath the paper-thin fabric.

"Not great," I said aloud, wondering what my parents might say had they witnessed my inaugural crash. On the other hand, all four of my limbs and my only neck had survived intact. So, I added, "Not bad either. For a first try."

Digging out from under the parachute proved no simple matter. The lines that support the fabric cells of the parachute canopy in flight had collapsed to form a spider's web over me. Some had wrapped around me as I rolled. The whole bundle of string led to an unreachable place in the middle of my back. For each line I pushed or tugged out of my way, two fell in to take its place.

I escaped eventually by unlatching and wriggling out of the harness that kept the mess attached to me. Only then could I disentangle myself from the folds of nylon and cobweb of lines. I picked my way to freedom string by string, as if I was unravelling a knotted ball of yarn from the inside out, until I emerged from the heap on my hands and knees.

With mud-caked knees and a spattering of what looked like ash on the thighs, my poor Sponge Bobs had certainly earned some quality time in the washing machine. I remembered where the ash came from and made a firm decision not to think about it.

At least the air down here felt warmer. My dad's sweatshirt flopped almost to my ankles as I stood. My naked and already numb feet barely registered the nearly frozen earth as they sank into it.

I took stock of my surroundings. Acre upon acre of chocolate-brown dirt, mashed leaves, crushed stalks, and a few bits of corncob left behind by the harvester, all of it in the shadow of pre-dawn. Dim orange light reflected off fresh snowcaps on the peaks of the mountains to the west. Interesting. Still technically nighttime down here. I'd fallen faster than the dawn.

A decaying barn squatted at the far western end of the property. Its swayed roof reminded me of a retired plow horse. The uppermost timbers glowed with the light of the approaching day while its off-kilter door remained in darkness.

A long, straight road—I think the same one my bus took to school every morning—bordered the fence far off to my right. Maybe if I marched to the road and stuck a thumb out asking for a ride ... in torn, muddy pajamas, bare feet, with speckles of ash all over me (Yuck!) ... someone I knew would pick me up.

Maybe not such a good idea. Hitchhiking was never a good idea. Doubly true on a lonely country road. Triply so at this time of the morning.

Through the woods, then?

Not my first choice. Still, if a path poked out from the trees somewhere nearby, it would eventually lead east to the city park at the edge of town, on the civilized side of the forest. During a lifetime spent in an outdoorsy family, we had trekked most of the hiking paths that crisscrossed woods at one time or another. Once I started walking, I'd know how to get home. We lived only two blocks past the park's entrance, third house on the left.

I would explain what happened and have my dad drive out to pick up his parachute. I could take a quick bath and go to bed because I really wanted to get warm and catch up on missed sleep. We'd talk over the events later.

Resigned to a chilly, hour-long walk through the forest, I scanned the woods beyond the unpainted fence that marked the boundary of the cornfield. An opening in the tree line would mark the start of a hiking trail.

A leafless oak loomed over the fence like a breaking wave. The back pocket of my Sponge Bob pj's flapped like a flag from the upper twigs of the tree. Farther down, I glimpsed the dark blob that, in my terror over crash landing in the tree's branches, I imagined to be a predatory bear.

I'd have preferred a bear.

Instead, Matilda dangled upside down from a low limb, held aloft only by the corner of her robe. By some freak coincidence of wind, the dead witch and I had landed in the same place. Nearly landed, in her case. She hadn't quite made it to the ground. I didn't think so much would remain of her remains.

What to do ... other than run away screaming across the field? For starters I took in a breath to stoke my courage ... the first breath in a while, judging by the amount of crisp autumn air I swallowed. After grabbing a second lungful, I decide to creep closer for a look.

Matilda's patched and battered hat slumped in a wilted heap on the clumpy earth below her. A very-much-the-worse-for-wear belt lay coiled a little to one side of the hat. The broad belt consisted of five or six small pouches held shut with silver buttons.

The witch hung in the tree with her back towards me. Frizzy ropes of braided gray hair hung down from her head like furry snakes. One foot was bare, although I saw no sign of the missing boot. Her already-tattered robe had shredded when she tore through the limbs of the oak. Without going into the gory details, I can tell you that Matilda looked worse than her robe.

I pondered what to do next. What did that moldy old belt contain? Should I grab the hat? I could deliver them to Grandma, who no doubt would have a story to tell. Yes, I decided. She would know exactly what to do.

Taking a few more quick breaths to fortify myself, I inched forward to retrieve the loot.

The witch's leg twitched.

Without knowing exactly how I got there, I found myself flat on my back, panting with fright ten feet away. My bare heels churned up clods of dirt in an effort to put additional distance between me and the definitely undead witch.

She made a rumbling noise that resonated like a large dog's warning growl. The sound came from deep in her chest and shook the ground beneath me.

A bruised and bloody arm snaked out of her disheveled black robe. Fingers clutched and grasped at the air as she groped for something—a handhold, her broom? Her gestures grew increasingly frantic. The thick tree limb that held Matilda off the ground trembled with her efforts.

Then, without warning, the witch relaxed. Her motionless body swung from the branch like a pendulum. I thought—I wished—she had finally passed on. An instant later, though, she cocked her head to one side, either engaging some sense I didn't possess.

"Who is that?" she grunted in a voice like a talking frog.

I said nothing.

"Is that you, little girl?"

Petrified into silence, I considered running back to the deflated parachute and burying myself in it.

"Of course it is," she croaked. "Ella. The one who sssstole my broom."

The witch lapsed into a fit of coughing that I hoped would turn her insides out. But, she recovered quickly and said, "Oh, you don't have to ssssay anything. I can hear your heart pounding clear enough. Like a frightened rabbit's. Help me down, now, and I will put an end to that. Oh yes, I will. Right after you return my broom to me."

"N-no," I said, teeth chattering, though not from the cold this time. "No, I won't help you. And I don't have your broom. You killed it up in the air."

Matilda spun at the sound of my voice. I don't exactly know how she managed it, but somehow, supported only by the torn fabric of her black robe, she turned her entire body around to face me. Her upside-down glare froze me in place. Although every instinct commanded me to run, I couldn't. I couldn't breathe either. If I'd tried to blink, I doubt my eyelids would have obeyed.

The witch crooked a finger at me in a "come here" gesture. I nearly did. In Grandma's bedtime stories, witches could force people to their will using only their voice or, sometimes, gestures. But that only happened in stories.

Matilda spoke and I felt the bees buzzing inside my brain like they had when she had commanded me to answer her questions up in the sky. Her words sounded wrong, like a foreign language, but one I almost understood.

On my feet again—without knowing how I got there—I staggered toward the tree and the terrifying monster it held.

"Yessss. That's it, girl," she crooned. "Your reason for living … however temporary … is to help me down from this treeee."

She hacked once and groaned. "After that, we'll see. We'll seeee."

I stood at attention only a yard from the witch. She smelled like rotting meat. I swear I could feel the heat from her red, glowing eyes.

"There is a thing I would have you do for me. Yessss."

I nodded.

"You will retrieve my belt from the ground over there. Immediately. You will hand it to me. And my hat. The hat is mosssst important Hurry, now. Hurry."

I moved like a zombie, which felt totally wrong, because I really, truly, absolutely hate zombies. I watched as if from a distance as my reluctant feet shuffled toward the objects on the ground. In my best effort at defiance, I picked up the belt first, not the hat, and brushed the dirt and ashes from it.

"Sssss," hissed the witch.

Before I knew it, I had the hat in one hand and the belt pinched between the fingers of the other. The ancient leather of the belt felt slimy. The fabric of Matilda's hat nearly crumbled in my grasp.

"Goooood," she crooned. "Now hand them up to me quickly. The hat firsssst."

I watched my arms stretch themselves up toward the inverted witch.

"Quickly, girl."

Matilda hung there like an oversized bat, too high to reach. I stood on my tiptoes. I jumped up and thrust the objects in her direction at the top of my leap. I jumped again. She strained downward at each attempt, her stiff, claw-fingers extended like a vulture's talons.

Matilda's face swelled red with blood. Her eyes bulged twice their normal size. Prominent ropey veins pulsed in her forearms. I could barely distinguish the flesh of her outstretched hands from the bark of the oak tree that held her.

I wanted to run or to collapse and cry. Instead, I tried with everything I had to push the hat and the belt into Matilda's skeletal fingers.

"That's right," she rumbled. "Harder, now. Higher. Up a little higher." She seemed to lose patience all of a sudden, and screamed, "Do it already, you evil brat! Right n—"

Without a whisper of warning, without a chirp from a bird or the flicker of an autumn leaf, dawn finally reached us there on the clotted earth of the abandoned field.

Matilda erupted in a ball of fire, a hot spherical core of yellow and orange light that morphed into a mushroom cloud like a miniature atomic bomb. The cloud dissolved into wisps of inky black smoke that threaded their way skyward through the barren branches of the hibernating oak. A wave of searing heat flashed over my face like a slap and I found myself on my back again, tossed aside like a love letter from a boy with cooties.

5

My father's sweatshirt, soaked through with dew and mud and who knows what else, clung to me like a wetsuit. The dry branches that had recently supported Matilda sputtered as if they'd catch fire and burn. Her black hat lay on the earth beside me, wisps of white smoke wafting up from it into the chill air. The hat smoldered for a second, before the tiny ember at its tip went out with a hiss. I'd lost track of the belt.

My sinuses burned with the same scorched rubber smell that had accompanied the destruction of Matilda's coven high up in the sky, a horrible odor so strong it made me retch. My body shook with shock and cold. Freezing isn't a sensation you ever get used to.

I heard a car horn in the distance and Charlotte's voice shouting, "There she is. There she is."

Damp earth muffled the sound of someone running, coming closer. It was over. I thanked my lucky stars. For the second time in a single day, I'd been saved from a witch by the dawn.

4
Off On the Wrong Foot

"There she is," said Charlotte. "There she is, staring off into space again. I thought we were all supposed to be looking for flying brooms."

"Flying brooms would be too easy to spot," said Ariel. "No, we're looking for buried ones."

Charlotte said, "Right you are. We've been searching for buried flying brooms for the last couple of hours, but some of us aren't doing that right now."

She shuffled up to me, dragging her feet methodically through layers of leaves as if ploughing through surf on a beach. A little deeper in the woods I heard Holly and Ariel also sliding through the detritus, heading our way.

Detritus is a Mrs. Kendricks word. It basically means "decaying junk on the ground." Cold autumn winds had long since blown the branches above us bare. Fallen leaves and other debris covered a maze of tangled roots with a thick organic carpet. What were the odds of finding a broom beneath all that detritus when we could barely find our own feet?

Charlotte, Ariel, Holly, and I had scoured the woods for hours, kicking our way through the leaves, hoping to find a broom or—was it so much to wish for—maybe two. I knew at least two had survived my morning's encounter with the witches. Neither Matilda's broom nor the one she claimed after I'd grabbed hers had suffered any obvious damage during our battle in the sky.

I'd cleaned up and slept a little after returning home from my overnight adventure. Mom woke me up around lunchtime.

"Call Charlotte," she'd said. "Then call Ariel. Then hang up and call them both again. One or the other's been on the phone for you every fifteen minutes since we got home."

Before eating lunch, I took my mother's advice and spoke with my friends, Charlotte and Ariel and Holly, too. Half an hour later, hands on hips and eyebrows raised, my mother stood between me and the door.

"Going somewhere?" she asked, clearly implying that I wasn't. "I think you need to rest and recuperate."

"We're all getting together," I said. "To talk about what happened last night."

She folded her arms across her chest.

"Ella, do you even realize how close you came to … to …?"

I made an exaggerated show of rolling my eyes.

"Of course, Mom. My friends were there, too. That's why we need to go over it all and figure things out."

I don't think my mom believed the half-truth. To be clear, what I told her was completely *true*, but only *half* the story. True, my friends all wanted to talk about what had happened last night. But, I wasn't about to let my mother in on the other fifty percent—that, during our flurry of phone calls since I'd awakened, Charlotte had convinced me we needed to find those brooms, and fast.

Mom stared at me for, like, two hours. When she finally uncrossed her arms, I knew I'd won.

"Okay, sweetie," she said. "It's good to get back on the horse that threw you."

Whatever that meant.

She stepped aside and held the door open for me. I wrestled my bike through the doorway, my gateway to freedom.

2

My friends and I began our search for the brooms with enthusiastic kicks that lifted dead leaves high off the ground. We hoped to get lucky and literally stumble across a broom that had nosed its way into the debris.

Those brooms had to be somewhere but, after long hours of looking, we'd found a lot of places where they definitely weren't. Over time, our animated motions had deteriorated into little slides and shuffled steps. As the muscles in our legs tired and faltered, the optimism went out of us like air from deflating balloons. If the sound of Charlotte's voice was any indicator, it made the same whining noise, too.

"How hard can it be to find a stupid broom?" she asked.

I filled my lungs full of forest air. It smelled like a Saturday morning at the farmers' market, rich with the odors of vegetation and dirt and a little bit of ground pepper tossed in. The spicy part tickled the back of my nose.

"You're staring at nothing, by the way," she said.

"I'm not staring at nothing," I lied. "I'm staring at the place where I landed this morning."

Having said it, I then had to do it.

A split-rail fence, much in need of repair, separated the four of us in the woods from the recently harvested cornfield to the west. Earlier this morning, before the sun officially rose, I'd plopped to the ground in a half-frozen heap on the other side of that fence. I could see the little indentation where my father's rainbow parachute had collapsed over me in brightly colored folds.

"What's so interesting over there?" Charlotte prompted.

"Nothing, I guess, Maybe I'm still a little confused."

"That's new, how?" Charlotte asked.

"I'm confused about last night … I mean this morning," I said, "I think Matilda muddled my brain a little. Not all of it makes sense."

"Inconsistencies," said Ariel as she shuffled up.

Her amazingly red hair belonged in this world of leaves and fall colors. She should have been born a fairy, I thought, and lived in these woods all her life. If witches had turned out to be real, why not fairies?

"When things still don't fit together after you have examined the evidence, they're inconsistencies," Ariel said. "It's a Mrs. Kendricks word."

Whatever you called them—nagging thoughts, confused memories, or inconsistencies—this morning's events refused to add up. They tugged at me, nibbling at my attention the way my pet guppies ate their breakfast.

"You might as well get the inconsistencies off your chest, Ella," Ariel said. "It's not like we've been doing anything super useful here all afternoon. I mean, great, let's find a flying broom and all. A buried flying broom. But seriously, how long do we have to kick these stupid leaves around before—"

Ariel stopped in mid-sentence. She must have seen the disappointment on my face.

She shrugged, and said, "Sorry, Ella. We can all see your heart's not in this. Or maybe your head. Why don't you tell us what's bothering you?" She couldn't help but add, "You're going to do it anyway."

I looked to Charlotte for support.

"Ariel's right," Charlotte said. "We're going to hear all about it eventually. You never keep anything to yourself for long, so don't grow up to be a spy or a lawyer, okay? Maybe if you let us all in on your dark secret, it'll help us figure out where the brooms are and we can get home before midnight this once."

"There are a couple of confusing things," I admitted.

"Inconsistencies," said Ariel.

Charlotte rolled her eyes and said, "Fine. So there are a couple of confusing things ..." She glared at Ariel daring her to interrupt. "... that have you stumped. Let's get it over with."

"Okay," I said. "The first confusing thing—"

"Inconsistency," said Ariel.

Charlotte tried to kick Ariel in the shin, but her half-hearted effort amounted to nothing more than an eruption of leaves.

"—is how you all found me so quickly."

"What do you mean?" asked Charlotte.

"How far are we from my house right now?" I asked in turn. "Three miles?"

"Straight through the woods?" said Ariel. "I don't know. Maybe two. But it's a lot farther when you drive it."

I held my hands up. "Two miles or ten. It doesn't really matter. I wasn't on the ground for that long before Matilda went nuclear and all of you showed up. How did everyone get here so fast? How did you know?"

How could they have known where I'd landed, a soft, shivering heap alone in the mud?

"And the second confusing thing—"

"The second inconsistency."

"Okay, Ariel! The second inconsistency is my parents. I mean, what were they doing here? They should have been fast asleep. They're always asleep. They'd sleep through the end of the world."

My friends looked a little confused themselves.

Ariel said, "Obviously, we woke up your parents the instant you left the garage with all those witches in tow. Your mom yelled at you from the window. Remember?"

I shrugged.

"We were standing in the room right behind your parents when you flew off into the sky."

I shook my head. A vague image of my mother's face in the window above the garage wafted into my head like a transparent ghost in one of those old black and white movies.

"She explained to you how to make the broom go faster. Good thing, too."

I nodded. "Sure, I suppose." Mom flew helicopters. What did she know about flying brooms?

"Then we all hopped in the car and drove here as fast as we could," Ariel concluded.

"Exactly," I said. "That doesn't make any sense to me. Why precisely here?"

"I think that's your third inconsistency," said Ariel. "You told us there were a two."

"It's her second, second one," said Holly. "Either way, it's inconsistent."

"I don't care how you count it," I said. "How did everyone already know where I'd landed when I was none too certain myself?"

Charlotte responded with typical sarcasm, the same way she would explain a math problem to an idiot or to a boy, which amounts to the same thing.

"We followed the first rainbow-colored parachute we spotted flying over the middle of nowhere at the crack of dawn on a Sunday morning, Ella. Just lucky it turned out to be you, I guess."

"Hmmm," I said, unconvinced, and then added, "but there's another second-confusing thing ...."

After a few seconds of silence, Ariel asked, "Why is everybody looking at me?"

"The other second-confusing thing, something that doesn't make sense at all is ... it seems silly when I say it, but ... why you were all in your pajamas? I mean, who in the world goes driving around in their pj's?"

Put it down to my muddled state of mind. Even after a full morning's rest, cobwebs still clung to the inside of my skull. For some reason, the pajama thing bothered me more than first-confusing thing or the first second-confusing thing. Counting confusing things turned out to be confusing in itself, which, I think, made it the third second-confusing thing or maybe the fourth second-confusing thing.

"Halloween, maybe?" I suggested. "Everyone still had their costumes on?"

But I knew before I opened my mouth that my explanation didn't make any sense at all.

Charlotte and Ariel looked embarrassed on my account.

"You really don't remember, do you, Ella?" Charlotte asked.

"Remember what?"

"The all-nighter? Jumping onto the mattresses? The witches at the door?"

"Of course," I said. "Sort of. I remember the witches."

Ariel said, "The witches came and we hid in the garage. You put on your father's spare parachute and flew away on Matilda's broom. Once you were in the air and out of sight, your folks got all cool and calm. Your mom especially. It was kind of creepy. My parents would've flipped out at that point."

"My mom flew helicopters somewhere," I said. "Somewhere dangerous, I think. She never talks about it. Whenever her military career comes up, she goes all James Bond and kills the conversation. It's her way of acting not-scared."

Ariel said, "When the fireworks started up over toward the edge of town, your dad actually brighten a little. He said, 'That's my baby girl,' and told us to keep our eyes open for a tiny rectangle in the same part of the sky as the fireworks. You were easy to find at first. The parachute lit up like a rainbow, I guess because you were in the sunlight for a while. Then you went dark. When Holly finally spotted you again, your dad stared up at the sky for a second and said, 'She's headed for the biggest, flattest landing zone she can think of. That's my baby girl! But, the wind's against her.' We all jumped in the car and zipped off down the road going a million miles an hour."

"Mom must have been driving," I said.

"When we got to the field over there …" Ariel nodded at the bare earth on the other side of the split-rail fence, "… the tree was smoking and you were lying on your back."

Ariel held her hands up in a questioning attitude. "What's so confusing about that?"

"Inconsistent," said Charlotte, Holly together.

3

We put our backs to the split-rail fence and returned to our task, shuffling through years' worth of fallen leaves as the autumn sky steadily darkened. I still had some … inconsistencies … in my memory of events. Absolutely nothing I could remember shed any light on the whereabouts of the missing brooms.

Charlotte kicked a particularly tall pile of leaves. Its contents flew into the air and spiraled down around her like a hundred little dragonflies.

"How hard can it be to find a stupid broom?"

"Charlotte," I said.

"What?"

"Please, please, please stop saying that."

"Stop saying what?" she asked. "I didn't say anything."

I halted in my tracks, feet buried in the multihued carpet.

"Yes you did," I insisted. "It was, like the thirty-seventh time."

"No," she said. "I was definitely thinking it. But I never actually said it."

"You did, Charlotte. You said it out loud. And I was counting. That's exactly thirty-seven."

"No, I …" She folded her arms across her chest and asked, "Anyway, how hard can it be to find a stupid broom?"

I sighed. "Thirty-eight."

"We need to think this through a little better," I said. "If Matilda landed right around here this morning—"

Ariel said, "She didn't exactly land, Ella. You said she got stuck in a tree until the sun blew her up. I'd guess she was hanging right there where all that black goo is."

Ariel pointed, but I refused to look.

"Okay. If Matilda almost landed right here this morning," I said, "then where's everything else that fell out of the sky with her?"

"What everything else?" asked Charlotte.

"A bunch of brooms, for starters," I said. "And all sorts of other paraphernalia, too."

Paraphernalia is one of Mrs. Kendricks bigger words. It means stuff.

"Belts, hats, rings, shoes. Whatever didn't burn up with the witches, I suppose. Some of the brooms caught fire. But not all of them. Mine didn't."

Not finding a broom was bad enough. We also failed to find remnants of robes or hats, or, thankfully, the remains of half-toasted witches. I grew more and more convinced that, if any items had survived last night's disaster in the sky, they lay beyond reach, a mile away in the deep woods.

I balled my fists and asked the sky, "How hard can it be to find a stupid broom?"

Charlotte smiled and said, "Thirty-nine."

Ariel held up a finger like a teacher making a point.

"You have to admit, it's pretty hard finding a broom made of straw and wood where we're looking, They don't call it 'the woods' for nothing."

"If only the brooms had come from Walmart," Charlotte lamented.

"I know, right?" said Ariel. "We could each pick a color to look for. I claim purple."

But we were absolutely not looking for brightly colored brooms with perfectly straight, plastic covered shafts and sweeps cut by a machine. Witches didn't buy their brooms at Walmart.

According to Grandma, witches made their brooms from scratch, using natural materials and ancient instructions. Somewhere in the process, they infused magic into the brooms. Infuse means seep, like flavor infuses from a teabag into hot water.

My grandmother told me a bedtime story once about the way witches put their brooms together. I asked her if it wouldn't be easier to buy one somewhere, toss a little magic at it, and off you go. She cocked her head to one side and said, "Perhaps in the stories you tell your grandchildren, Ella, modern witches will fly around on pink, plastic brooms."

Grandma went on to describe how the witches spent hours, or maybe days, sifting through piles of straw for undamaged stalks of exactly the right dimensions and texture. She told me how each witch then went alone into the forest—perhaps into the same forest as my friends and I—seeking the perfect fallen tree limb with the proper shape and specific properties needed to make her flying broom's handle. Grandma explained that the wood's grain had to orient just so in order to conduct the energy without overheating, exploding, or doing one of a dozen other horrible things that happened when someone got magic wrong. We came up with a week's worth of bedtime that included laughable scenarios in which a magical broom did something horrible and unexpected to a witch. Remember Mickey Mouse in The Sorcerer's Apprentice?

I didn't find the stories so funny anymore. I'd seen the kinds of very real and very serious magical disasters that befell a distracted witch.

Speaking of distracted, I almost jumped out of my skin when Holly tugged at my sleeve.

"You know," she said, "the color of the broom doesn't really matter if you aren't looking where what you're searching for actually is."

As often happened with Holly, I had to run the sentence past my brain several times to get at its meaning. Whatever Mrs. Kendricks might say about its grammar, Holly's statement contained some good advice.

I asked her, "You think the brooms might not be in the woods? You think they're somewhere else?"

She said, "Remember you told us how the wind blew you and your dad's parachute away from the fields and back into the forest, how you had to turn around and come back, and how the tree almost got you because of it?"

"Sure," I said. "I barely made it out onto the field. I nearly crashed into the same tree as Matilda."

I gestured back up into the oak where my Sponge Bob pocket still waved from a twig like the last leaf of autumn. I thought about how close I'd come to sharing that tree with a not-dead-enough witch.

Holly said, "If the wind blew you and your big, floaty parachute so far in the wrong direction, then maybe Matilda's floppy robes pushed her toward the forest, too, but a little less. Well, probably a lot less … but not zero less. Maybe her robes billowed up and slowed her fall like a small parachute. Barely enough to save her life. Just enough for the wind to push her back here to the edge of the woods."

"And," I added, "brooms aren't billowy at all. They're sticks, not parachutes."

"Exactly," she agreed. "They came straight down—"

"Like arrows," I said. "If that's true, the brooms must have landed—"

"In the cornfield," shouted Ariel and Charlotte from behind us.

They sprinted off toward the field but their run quickly degenerated into a comical hopping dance as fallen branches and tree stumps forced them to leap and dodge along the way. Holly and I barely kept up, following in their leafy wake.

4

We climbed over the wooden fence and out of the forest, then ran as fast as the soft earth allowed. I passed the dent in the dirt where the impact of an exploding witch had tossed me and caught up with Charlotte and Ariel halfway across the cornfield. They'd stopped to examine a toppled corn stalk that looked quite a bit like the handle of a wooden broom.

Behind us, Holly yelled, "Hold it, you guys!"

She bent over to pick up something dark and glistening from the ground. It looked like a dead bird.

"I found a shoe," she said.

Holly held it up high, pinched between her thumb and a finger. An odd-looking leather boot, quite small, like a child would wear, dangled from her hand. Little globs of gray-brown earth clung to the boot like those alien-looking nests mud wasps make.

"It smells really bad," she said.

Holly held the object up for us to see, or maybe to get it as far from her nose as she could. Although sized for a little girl's foot, I could tell the tiny shoe was never meant to be worn by a child. Black and shiny, except where the dirt from the cornfield had sullied it, the narrow boot ended in a long, pointy toe that curled toward the sky. It looked ancient and strange, like a discolored mitten you found half in and half out of the ground after the deep snow has finally melted back for the spring.

I caught a whiff of something foul.

"Maybe you should put that down," I said.

But, shy and cautious Holly did something completely unexpected.

"Holly," I shouted. "No!"

Before my words could register, Holly shucked off her left sneaker and the sock beneath. My jaw dropped as she slipped the black boot over her bare foot. I heard a little pop when her heel hit the bottom of the shoe.

Holly sucked in her breath. "Oh my," she said, and toppled over.

She rolled over on her back, arms and legs flailing like she was making a snow angel. Or a mud angel, I guess. Charlotte and Ariel assumed Holly had lost her balance and landed in the dirt. They laughed like hyenas. Soon enough, though, they realized that nothing laughable had happened to our friend and scurried back to find out what had gone wrong.

Holly's face turned pale as we watched, then blue. Panted breaths came close together. It sounded like the air couldn't get past her throat on its way to her lungs. Holly darted glances from one of us to the other and back again, apparently unable to move but for her panicked eyes.

My mom knew a lot about first aid. As a helicopter pilot in the Navy, she had trained to fly missions where people could get hurt or worse. She flew a medical rescue chopper these days, like the ones you see at car wrecks on the interstate. Over the years, Captain Mom had passed some of her medical knowledge on to me. It gave us something to do on rainy days and boring weekends. "You never know when you'll need to use this, Ella," she had said. "And the one time you do, it might save someone's life." We practiced together, taking turns being the victim, until we both had confidence in my ability to respond in a crisis.

I dropped down beside Holly and went through the checklist. Was she choking? I examined her for a blocked windpipe, found none of the obvious signs, and recalled that she had spoken to us before she collapsed. I rolled her onto her side and asked if something was stuck in her throat.

Still unable to voice a response, her eyes shouted, "No!"

"Then what is it, Holly?" I asked.

In the asking, the answer became clear. Like a character in a bad movie, I smacked my forehead with an open palm. "It's the shoe," I hissed. "It's Matilda's shoe. It's got a spell on it or something. Get the shoe off her."

The three of us immediately turned our attention to Holly's left foot. Ariel put both hands on the boot and tugged. Her hands slipped off the shoe's shiny surface and she fell on her butt with a dull flop. Charlotte tried next, making certain she had a firm grip. She dug her fingers in between the shoe and Holly's ankle. Hanging on for dear life, she tugged once. Then again. Then again.

"It's like the boot is fighting back," she said. "Look."

As we watched, the leather boot molded itself to the shape of Holly's foot like some soft and pliable living material. It had already closed around her ankle like a thick sock.

"Get it off her," I shouted.

Ariel and Charlotte tried to pry the boot off together. They succeeded only in dragging Holly along the ground for a yard or two.

"Ella," Charlotte cried in frustration, "help us."

So, I sat on Holly, grabbed one of her legs in each of my hands, and dug my heels into the ground to brace us.

"Okay," I said. "Got her."

Ariel and Charlotte one-two-three-pulled. On their third or maybe fourth attempt, the boot finally gave up its grip and flew off with a short sucking hiss. We sprawled around Holly in a rough circle with Charlotte holding the shoe.

In another situation, she might have said something funny like, "If Holly was a Thanksgiving turkey, I just got my wish."

Instead she shuddered in disgust and flung the boot far away like she would a snake or a big spider she found crawling on her neck. Charlotte being Charlotte, though, she regained her equilibrium after a few deep breaths. Brushing her hands together to clear off some of the mud, she said, "That was easy." But I could hear the edge in her voice.

Right then, Holly let out a wail that would have made a fire engine jealous. Ariel covered her ears, but I took the sound as a positive sign. It meant Holly's throat had cleared.

Holly spoke through a fit of coughing. "It's like … cough … there's a feather … cough-cough … stuck in my throat," she stuttered. Her voice sounded soft and fuzzy, as if the sounds came out through a cotton ball

Ariel asked, "Holly, geez, what happened? One second you were there, standing like a normal person … well, like Holly anyway … then you were up on one foot pretending to be a ballerina trying to put on that stupid shoe. I think Ella told you to stop. Or at least she should have. Then you fell over and started acting like a zombie. And we came running and the shoe was trying to eat you. Geez, Louise! What happened?"

Holly coughed again and looked like she wanted that question answered, too.

5

I'm pretty sure I knew what had happened. At least in general.

I knew because my grandmother's bedtime stories contained all the clues.

It's a theme in those stories that every living being subtly influences whatever they touch. Some of our energy, our aura, rubs off on things, forms a bond, and makes it ours. The longer we have something, and the more precious it is, the stronger the bond. Certain people have trouble getting rid of stuff. Charlotte's mom is a packrat. That energy bond is one of the reasons.

Grandma told me the effect is especially true of witches who, by their magical nature, have strong and active auras. When a witch's clothing comes in contact with the witch, it can't help but take on some of her witchiness, especially if she wears the clothes over an extended period of time. The fabric, or animal skin, or whatever she's got on, picks up the witch-essence that oozes from her all day and all night long.

It's the same for you and me, believe it or not, except, not being witches, there are important differences. The first difference, according to my grandmother, is that normal people don't so much ooze energy as emanate it. Grandma says people vibrate. We shine. Our auras consist of bright colors that depend a lot on the situation, including our mood, our health, and even the food we eat.

Witches, especially old ones, carry around a lot more power than ordinary people. That power is what makes them witches. Only, it's icky power, malicious and destructive. It makes witches' auras thick and black like sludge if they're old, or muddy brown if they're still young.

Grandma says if a witch can't rid herself of the evil power by expending it in spells, or by shedding it like a snake does its skin, the energy backs up and engulfs her. It can cause her psychic or even physical pain. If the blockage goes on for too long, the weight of her own aura eventually suffocates the witch, turning her into something horrifying that my grandmother refuses to discuss.

Grandma also says that bodily cleanliness is never more than a talking point for a witch—something on her to-do list that she never quite gets around to. I don't exactly understand how Grandma knows this, but she says if witches bathe at all, it is rarely and reluctantly. A witch's clothing may never lose contact with its wearer's cold, pale skin. It can't avoid storing some of that gooey, dark energy in its fibers. Revolting, I know, but remember who we're talking about.

So, according to my grandmother, anything a witch owns over the course of her supernaturally long life has probably accumulated an essence not very different from the witch herself. That's especially true of the shoes on the bare flesh of her disgusting feet.

Matilda, an ancient witch, had possessed more than her share of creepy, dark energy. Wherever she went after she exploded, she left Planet Earth with one foot bare. I was certain the shoe that tried to kidnap Holly belonged to Matilda. And I knew that dead Matilda's evil power had a hold on my friend.

6

"We need to get Holly home and into a bathtub," I said to the others. "and wash the witch off her foot."

Ariel nodded her agreement and added, "What's that terrible smell?"

"Smells like pig poo," said Charlotte. "But worse. Which is actually impossible."

We all looked around. The foul odor of a long-dead animal— times ten, or maybe twenty—swirled around us like a fog.

Charlotte sniffed her fingers, gagged, and almost fell over backwards herself. "Ugh," she gasped, holding her arms out in front of her. "Disgusting beyond all imagining."

What did she expect? Her fingers had been wedged deep down in a shoe that spent most of the last few decades wrapped around an old crone's scaly foot. Thank goodness Charlotte had kept the half-alive leather from closing entirely around Holly's ankle. Had she not taken that risk, I don't think we would have ever managed to get the bewitched boot off our friend.

Ariel's hands twitched like she wanted to repeat Charlotte's finger-sniffing experiment, but thought better of it. Instead, she picked up a handful of plowed earth and used the tiny granules of dirt to scour her fingers. When she finished, she extended her hands far out to the side like a bird drying its wings.

She made a face and said, "I can still smell it."

Charlotte, in turn, rubbed her own hands in the dirt.

"I'm stinkier than you, Ariel. I stuck both hands all the way in there."

Ariel's already milky complexion got a little paler.

"My hands reek," Charlotte said, wrinkling up her nose. "I think I'll go over there and puke for a while."

Thankfully, she didn't.

7

Charlotte lived in an old farmhouse not far away. Her parents' property stretched for what seemed like a mile in every direction. We slung Holly across the handlebar of Ariel's bicycle and pedaled to

Charlotte's house. The bike belonged to Ariel's much older brother and sported an extra-large handlebar, otherwise, I don't see how we could have managed.

An old plastic tub sitting on the back porch fit Holly's tiny feet perfectly. We filled the tub from a hose. Holly flinched at the cold water, so Charlotte went in the house for a couple of minutes and brought back some hot water.

Charlotte and Ariel cleaned their hands a dozen times each. We washed, and scrubbed, and dried Holly's left foot. At Ariel's suggestion, we did the same with the right one, just in case. We used soap, shampoo, alcohol, and cleanser—anything we could think of to take away the yuck of her contact with Matilda's shoe. Holly alternately laughed, cried, and went silent as we worked.

At first, she complained that my hard scrubbing tickled. In the next instant, when no one touched her at all, she said, "Ouch. Not so rough, Ariel." The odd behavior made me wonder how weird I must have seemed to my friends when the whys-and-wherefores of people in pajamas had completely occupied my attention.

Our concentrated scrubbing had a certain feel to it, like the performance of some kind of cleansing ritual. Holly's voice, initially distorted like a crow that had only recently learned to speak, sounded better, more natural, the longer we spent. She probably got the most thorough footbath in human history although I doubt anyone keeps records on that sort of thing.

When we finished cleaning up Holly, my friends washed their malodorous hands twice more. Malodorous, by the way, is one of those big Mrs. Kendricks words you can keep in your back pocket and whip out when you're really trying to impress someone. Mal basically means "bad." Odorous, you can probably figure out. Put the words together and you get one bad—in this case, one terrible—smell.

After a half hour of ritual cleansing, we dried ourselves with some clean rags, emptied the used water onto a rubble heap far away from the house, and tossed the tub in after it for good measure.

Holly's feet had turned into pale wrinkled prunes, hideous to behold. Her left foot, the one the witch's shoe had latched onto, appeared petrified, which bothered me but, for Holly's sake, I didn't mention it. She walked without a limp and seemed mostly fine. I hoped nothing had gone permanently wrong during the time she wore the witch's shoe. Or had the shoe worn her?

Holly would definitely lead the list of discussion topics the next time I saw my grandmother. Grandma would let me know how concerned I should be. Also on that list were questions about other people close to me. My mother, for example, seemed to have a more than casual knowledge of flying brooms. And, given events of the last day, I had growing misgivings about the person closer to me than anyone else, myself.

The questions kept piling up. I needed to speak with the expert.

Time for a sleepover at Grandma's.

5
Chez Grandma

I explained to my parents why I absolutely had to spend the night chez Grandma. They put on the not-quite-willing-to-look-me-in-the-eye expressions they get when they think they're keeping a secret from me,   or when they're working as a team against me.

We met in our living room, me on the couch, my father in his favorite chair, my mother pacing aimlessly about. Dad squirmed around a little in his seat and tried to cover their hesitation.

"No way, baby girl. It's Sunday and you've got school in the morning."

"I'm sick tomorrow," I said. "I have been traumatized beyond my ability to cope. Call it a mental health day."

"Nope," he said. "I'm teaching and your mother has to—"

"But Daddy …" I whined.

I wasn't too old or too proud to whine if I thought it might help me win my case. Sometimes … not this time, apparently, but sometimes … it worked.

"… I really need to talk with Grandma."

"Ella, sweetie," said my mother, "I think it's too late to call Grandma now. She's probably getting ready for bed."

I dropped the childish whine. It never worked with Mom.

"Did I mention that I've already asked her?"

I watched my mother deflate.

"Want to know what Grandma said when I did?"

I didn't give them time to answer.

"She said, 'Bring it on.' That's a quote."

"Oh, come on, Ella," my father objected. "Your grandmother doesn't talk like that. She's too … old."

"No. She actually said it, Dad. You understand what 'That's a quote,' means, right?"

My father let out a little puff of air. Mom tapped her palm on the fireplace mantel.

"Seriously, guys? After everything that happened today? You know how much I need to see Grandma."

Still nothing. So, I took a firmer stance, deliberately omitting any reference to the word "please."

"One way or another," I said, "I am going to speak with my grandmother tonight. Face-to-face. That's a quote."

I needed information that only Grandma could provide. Enough information to guarantee me a good, long life—one lasting at least into my teens. That information simply had to come from my grandmother who, it seems, had been drilling basic survival skills into me since she first held Baby Me in her arms at the hospital. I'd always thought her bedtime stories were just that. Stories. I understood now that they were lessons.

My mother said, "Why don't we give her a call later and set something up for this weekend?"

I shook my head in slow motion. "Nope. It has to be tonight while everything is still fresh."

That look passed between them again.

"I'll call her in the morning," my mother promised. "It's nine thirty. She's getting ready for bed."

"No, Mom. She isn't."

"Ella!" snapped my father. He sat up straight-backed in his chair.

He seemed surprise at my belligerence. Belligerence is absolutely not a Mrs. Kendricks word. It's an Ella word. I looked up belligerent myself so I could call Charlotte something other than "stupid" the next time we got into one of our hissy-fights. I also looked up cantankerous.

As belligerently as I'd acted, my father's tone of voice stopped me. In our house, we decided things rationally and democratically whenever possible. Sometimes, though, in the middle of an argument, my dad got all stiff and formal and followed with a proclamation—basically an order—that closed down any further conversation. His Navy job once required him to give orders. Lots of them. So many orders, in fact, that they promoted him to honorary admiral when he retired, which meant Admiral Dad officially outranked Captain Mom, though the flow of command usually ran in the opposite direction at our house. Admiral Dad was one inch from shutting down my bid for a Grandma sleepover.

Instead of issuing an order, though, he fell right into my trap, bless him.

He asked, "How can you be so sure she's not already in bed, Ella?"

"Because," I said, "she's right here on speakerphone."

I held up my cellphone for Mom and Dad to see. A picture of my grandmother beamed out from the screen. Her phone number shone below it. The caption read "Grandma !!!" in bold, white letters. I swung the phone back and forth between my parents pretending the image of Grandma on its tiny screen exuded the stern-yet-compassionate look she had perfected during her thirty-some years as an elementary school teacher. To my surprise, it worked. The room went quiet. My parents seemed at a loss for words. They must have wondered what the witches in the sky had done to their precious, well-behaved, and seldom belligerent child.

A tinny, digital voice spoke from the little box in my hand. "Bring it on," it said.

The little bird inside the phone chirped again. "I'll make sure Ella gets to school in the morning. All you have to do is drive her over here. It's getting late. Your little girl and I need to talk."

2

"Of course, they know why you wanted to see me," said my grandmother as we watched my parents back out of her driveway. "And they don't like it very much."

I clinked two porcelain cups down on an ornate lacquered-oak table—the focal point of Grandma's parlor and the bullseye of Grandma's social circles. She used it for everything: dining, writing, thinking, and chatting with her favorite—well, her only—granddaughter. I sat down on one of the four hand-painted chairs.

I said, "I can't remember a time without your bedtime stories. But when I try to talk about this stuff with my mom and dad, they never come clean."

Grandma poured boiling water into our teacups. A delightful aroma wafted up into the room. It smelled fresh, like a winter night, and felt cool at the back of my sinuses. The peppermint tea came from Grandma's vast selection of handpicked herbs. She'd dedicated about half of her basement to their drying and storage.

"I understand, dear. Your parents have their reasons for not discussing matters with you. Poor reasons, in my opinion, but reasons nonetheless."

"What's there left to hide after everything I've been through?" I asked.

"Oh, plenty," she said.

Her shiny metal tea ball made tiny slurping noises as she dipped it in and out of the hot water. The thin liquid in her cup grew a shade darker each time. "There's plenty left for them to hide and plenty left for you to learn. A lifetime's worth and more."

I shrugged.

"Understand, Ella, your parents were not so much hiding things from you as hiding you from things."

Grandma saw my confusion and said, "You encountered some of those things last night, I hear."

"I could have died last night," I said. "Twice."

I drummed my fingers on the solid table. Its wooden top made my tap-tap-tapping into a surprisingly loud sound.

"Technically, once last night and once this morning, I guess. But it still works out to twice."

My grandmother continued slurping her tea ball.

"I made it all up as I went along, Grandma. I got lucky. The sun was about to come up and you told me that witches and sunrise—"

"—go together like origami and flamethrowers," she said. "True enough. You were very lucky. You were also very smart. Of the two, I think you owe your life to the latter."

She let the tea ball sink to the bottom of her cup and reached across the table to take my hands, as much to stop the drumming, I think, as to offer comfort.

"And I would never have forgiven your parents if any real harm had come to you." She squeezed my palms to emphasize how much she cared. "This whole episode proves that I was right all along. As far as I'm concerned, it would be irrational and dangerous not to pursue your … let's call it your alternate education … more aggressively."

"Really, Grandma?"

My anxiety over the day's events and the lingering anger I felt toward my parents transformed into anticipation.

"Alternate education? Are you going to teach me about witches now? I mean, more than telling me stories?"

"We've been going over the basics since you were born, child. It's time for more hands-on instruction, I think."

"Really, are you going to train me to use actual magic?"

"Perhaps," she said. "Eventually. Much of what we do from now on depends on your attitude and dedication."

"I'm in, Grandma," I said. "Bring it on!"

She broke out her smile, the one that warmed up entire rooms.

"But," I had to ask, "how would you know anything about magic? The real stuff?"

I mean, obviously, Grandma had some stories to tell. Stories that I now understood contained useful truths. But magic? Grandma had nothing in common with Matilda and her brood.

"You can't be a witch," I explained. "First off, you're definitely not evil. And you can go out in the daylight."

She laughed. "One needn't be a dark witch to know a few things about magic, Ella Why don't you let me worry how I came to know what I know and I'll promise to let you in on the secret someday?"

She released my hands and we shook on the deal. Grandma had offered to teach me what she knew about magic. All I had to do was not ask her how she knew.

"Good," she said. "The first step is to reconcile this with your parents. That part is entirely up to you."

What? I pulled my hand back.

They'd argue that I already knew more than I should about the world of witches. They'd claim that my grandmother had interfered with their plan to keep me safe. They'd tell me this morning's events was proof they hadn't lied hard enough. They'd say I had risked my life in a misguided attempt to show off in front of my friends. My parents would dig in their heels, claiming they'd hidden an entire reality in order to protect me from forces beyond my understanding or control. Before dinner this evening, when my parents thought they were out of earshot, I overheard my father say we might have to move again.

Now Grandma told me I'd have to change my parents' minds about all of that before she would talk to me any more about magic. My mother and father had lied to me about magic all my life. Whatever hopes I'd had of learning witchcraft or of flying again crashed to the ground like an unmagical broom.

Grandma chuckled, guessing the reason behind the look on my face.

"Oh, I wouldn't be too concerned about your parents," she said. "I think you'll find that your mother, at least, is on board even if she doesn't share your enthusiasm."

I shrugged.

Grandma lifted her steaming porcelain cup and peered over it at me. The tea hadn't yet cooled enough to drink. She inhaled deeply enjoying the aromatic steam, then lowered the cup into its saucer.

"I've been wondering about today," she said. "My notion of this morning's events isn't entirely clear. Why don't you let me know what happened up there?"

I closed my eyes and thought for a second. Grandma took my hands in hers before I could start drumming.

I blurted out the first thought that came to mind. "I flew, Grandma! I flew. And it was the happiest thing I've ever done. Even with witches chasing me."

She acknowledged the fact with a squeeze of her hands. "Of course, you did, Ella, although you didn't know the first thing about how to fly and it was second nature to the witches that were chasing you. Still, of all the people flying around up there last night, only you made it back down. I need to understand how that happened."

She stopped and waited. An old trick, but one that worked every time. She knew I couldn't not keep talking. Grandma let the pressure build for a few seconds.

Then I burst out, "You're mostly right. Only I made it all the way down. Matilda almost did. Almost. An old oak stopped her a few feet short of the ground. That tree probably saved her life. For a little while, anyway."

Grandma accepted this clarification. "So how did all that come about? The rest of the coven, I mean. No witch would willingly fly into the sunlight. Can you explain it so even an old grandmother would understand?"

Grandma was not old at all. Well, maybe a little old, but she didn't act … you know … elderly.

"They made a mistake," I said. "A huge mistake."

Grandma raised her eyebrows.

"I got lucky," I admitted. "I tricked them and they fell for it."

She nodded.

"We were awake all night, Grandma. Me and Charlotte and Ariel and … well, not Holly. We called it The Post-Halloween-Daylight-Savings-Wakeover—like a sleepover, but with no sleeping— and we made a big ceremony out of turning the basement clock back at two in the morning."

"The clock on the wall by the stairs?" asked my grandmother.

"Right," I said. "We set the hour hand back from two o'clock to one o'clock. That's what you do in the fall. We did a section on daylight savings with Mrs. Kendricks. Anyway, I knew what the real time was. And I knew from your stories, witches don't do all that well in the light."

She interrupted. "They don't do well in daylight, Ella. Not all light. You need to understand the difference."

"Right," I said. "Of course. I already know that. When I realized the witches had the time wrong, I figured my best chance was to keep everybody around, as high in the air as we could go, until daybreak. The higher I flew, the harder they chased me. We all ended up in sunshine. It happened a lot quicker than I thought it would."

She thought about that. "How did you know when the sun would come up? I certainly didn't."

"Like I said," I explained, "my friends and I knew what time it really was. We also knew to the minute when the sun would come up because we all had to wait for sunrise before we could go to bed. That was the rule for the wakeover. Except that Holly always falls asleep. Thing is, with daybreak right around the corner, I couldn't understand why the witches were still out."

My grandmother spoke flatly. "Oh, I know why they were out. And I know what they were after. Halloween is traditionally the time when witches take on initiates."

Her eyes went kind of blank for a second.

"But that's for a later conversation," she said. "Go ahead with your story."

"I'm pretty sure Zena's digital watch reset itself from Daylight Savings Time to regular time automatically," I said. "She was proud of her modern watch. But her sunrise chart must have been wrong—still using Daylight Savings Time. I don't know exactly why. Maybe she took a shortcut, just continued her calculation from the day before instead of looking the time up in the newspaper, like we did. I can't say for sure. Anyway, that mistake left the witches prowling around an hour after their bedtime. All I did was hang out with them in the air until the sun came up."

I shrugged. "That's about it," I said in conclusion. "I just got lucky."

Grandma pondered my words. She held her teacup in front of her. "I agree that circumstances worked in your favor, Ella," she said, finally. "I agree that you were very lucky indeed. And I agree that the witches made a serious mistake."

She tapped the side of her cup with a fingernail. "But I don't agree you were *just* lucky."

"What do you mean, Grandma?"

"I mean you were also insightful, creative, and more than a little bit devious, child. All quite laudable qualities."

I must have looked confused again, because Grandma's eyes twinkled.

"In a hundred years, Ella, I don't think I would have ever noticed the difference between Zena's chart's time and regular time. Or how to turn it into an advantage. In all likelihood, had I been in your shoes, I would have died up there."

"Bare feet," I said. "I wasn't wearing any shoes."

"Had I been in your feet, then," she said.

Grandma sniffed her tea again and decided to risk a sip.

"I want you to use your brains to think about something else with me for a moment, Ella. Something you probably didn't notice during last night's events, but I most certainly did."

"Okay, Grandma. Sure."

She asked, "Can you tell me how this whole episode began?"

"I don't think I understand the question," I said.

"Do you really think that Matilda and the other witches in her coven came to your house and broke into your basement to have a confrontation with you? Specifically with you? Was Matilda out too late on Halloween night gunning for Ella Roberts?"

I replied, "They landed on my lawn and used magic to get into my house."

"So they did," said Grandma.

"They broke down my basement door," I added.

Grandma nodded. She obviously knew the details of the encounter.

"And once they were in, what happened?" she asked.

Well, a lot of stuff had happened that my grandmother must already know, I thought.

It surprised her when I said, "We talked for a while."

"Talked?" she asked. "Talked about what?"

"About …"

Grandma raised her eyebrows.

"We talked about you, actually, Grandma. Matilda asked me if you were there, in Mom and Dad's house. She seemed a little wary of you for some reason."

"Matilda is—or I should say, she was—inclined to be cautious in her dealings with me," my grandmother said. "For good reasons."

I wanted to ask her more about that. It sounded like my grandmother already knew a great deal about Matilda. And Matilda about her. Even so, why would anyone, let alone an evil and terrifying witch, fear my grandmother, the least frightening person on the planet?

Before I could voice the question, Grandma said, "We might have avoided the whole fiasco if I had anticipated Matilda's mood better. Instead, I was sound asleep in my comfortable bed, like the doddering old fool I pretend not to be."

I tried to protest. My grandmother, my personal hero, had never erred in my entire life as far as I knew.

She raised a hand to ward off my objection. "What else did you talk about with Matilda?"

"Well," I said, delaying my response, "we talked … about …"

"Holly," she and I said together.

My eyes widened.

"Holly Jones," she repeated.

"How did you know that, Grandma?" I asked.

"That coven of witches was not really looking for you, Ella. Oh, Matilda might have known you'd be there. But, when the coven came to visit, I think Holly was foremost in their thoughts. It was an accident that Holly happened to be at a sleepover—"

"So-called sleepover," I said. "A wakeover, in fact. Chez moi. Anyway, Holly was ..." I wanted to argue her point, but when I thought about it, I realized that Grandma was absolutely right. As usual.

To save face, I said, "They didn't come to *visit* Holly." For emphasis, I added air quotes around the word visit. "She was sound asleep on the couch when the witches broke down our door. They were there to kidnap her."

Grandma tapped her cup and waited, eyes twinkling.

After a second or two, I got it and giggled despite myself. "They were kidnapping a kid napping," I said.

We sat back and sipped our tea in silence. I thought through Grandma's suspicions and admitted that the witches may have actually come for Holly, not me. I'd put myself in their way and, without meaning to, brought a heap of hurt down on my own head.

My grandmother patted my hand. "I see you've had a bit of an insight?"

I nodded.

"Do you want to know why I brought this up?"

I nodded again.

"Here it is," she said. "The first thing you have to realize is that before last night's attack, your parents' plan to keep you in the dark and out of trouble had worked perfectly."

"No way," I said. "If it hadn't been for all those stories you told me, I'd have been a splat on someone's roof this morning. I never would have confronted the coven."

She replied, "Precisely, Ella. If I hadn't filled you with ridiculous stories since you were a baby in diapers, you would never have considered standing up to Matilda. You would never have tried to lure the witches away based on some silly, half-remembered tales told to you by your wacky grandmother. You would have been safe."

"Wait," I said, "I—"

"Although I disagreed with your parents' reasoning," Grandma said, "I can't deny their strategy had worked until this morning.

They got you through your early years without a hitch. You should thank them for that."

I didn't exactly want to.

"And second," she said, holding up two fingers, "I'm worried about your friend, Holly. Very worried."

Huh? I thought. "Why Holly?" I asked. "Why not me so much?"

"There's exactly one reason Matilda's attention would be drawn to such a young girl."

She lowered her teacup into its saucer with a click and stared down at it.

"I think Holly has a secret life, a magical life, and she's emanating magical overtones."

Emanating? Didn't emanating mean something like broadcasting?

Grandma continued. "What I mean to say is your friend has been actively practicing magic. Practicing at a level beyond simple child's experimentation. She doesn't know, can't know, how obvious and vulnerable that makes her. When someone uses magic like that, it creates a vibration others can feel."

I must have looked confused.

"When you drop a pebble in a pond," she explained, "it makes ripples."

That didn't exactly help.

"At any rate," my grandmother said, "Holly has almost certainly been dabbling in magic. Real magic, borderline dark magic. Probably for some time now. Holly came to Matilda's attention through her own actions, innocent though they may have seemed to Holly at the time."

I thought about what Grandma said.

"So, you're telling me that my painfully shy, mega-intelligent, weirdo friend is really an evil witch in the works? And Matilda somehow figured it out?"

"If I understand what you're saying, then yes. Matilda had no special interest in you, Ella. At least not until you crossed her in your parents' basement. The target of the coven's interest was Holly. Whatever happened up in the sky this morning was a grand mistake. Something that should never have happened."

It didn't make sense. Holly, an evil witch? She had always been the goody-est of Goody-Two-Shoes.

"Matilda took no notice of you before today, Ella, because you've never toyed with magic," Grandma said. "I would have known long before she ever did. Your parents made sure it couldn't happen. They protected you from … from yourself, as a matter of fact. You should thank them for that, not blame them."

I didn't want to hear this. Not about Holly, not about my parents, and not about myself. I definitely did not want to hear it from my grandmother, the one person who had always taken my side.

"But, Grandma, you said that you were right to tell me all those stories about witches even though I didn't know until today that you were teaching me something real."

"We no longer have any choice in the matter of your education," she said, "whether it was or wasn't the best course before this morning. From now on, you must learn, you must progress. And quickly."

"Why?" I asked. "Why now, all of a sudden?"

"Because, now they know about you," she said. "The cat, to use an apt metaphor, is out of the bag."

"Now who knows about me, Grandma?"

But she wouldn't say.

6
Nighty-Night Insight

Bedtime chez Grandma always meant stories about witches. Entertaining, enchanting, impossible stories. I remember falling asleep to Grandma's fantastic tales ever since I could understand the words she used to tell them. Maybe even before that, because some of what I know about witches I don't remember learning. I've known it since forever. And, since forever, I'd assumed it all to be, a fun, fictional, make believe world. One hundred percent made up. Maybe one hundred and ten percent.

My forever ended the instant Matilda's pointy-toed boot touched down on my front lawn last night.

I lay on my bed upstairs in Grandma's house all snuggly beneath a shiny, silk comforter that spread like a cloud over me. The tallest, and the best, bed in the universe. Even at the ripe old age of eleven, I still had to jump off the floor to climb in. Grandma used a step stool.

"I love these pajamas, Grandma," I said.

The new Power Puff Girls pajamas she'd handed to me a few minutes earlier felt crisp and clean. The pattern on the bottoms had action images of Bubbles, Blossom, and Buttercup on a navy-blue background. The short-sleeved top sported a picture of the determined superhero trio. The words "Saving the World" floated in the air above them and "Before Bedtime" swam beneath. A new scrunchy, still in its plastic package, sat on the night table beside the bed.

"The Sponge Bob pj's are soaking in a tub next to the washing machine," Grandma said. "Your mom dropped them off along with your father's disgusting old sweat shirt. There's hope for them, I suppose. I've picked up a few tricks for removing spots along the way."

Grandma definitely had a knack for cleaning. I wondered if her laundry skills involved anything more than special soap.

"Still," she said, "I can't promise they'll ever come clean. Kerosene and a match would be a better option for your father's sweat shirt. You say you know where the pocket of your pajamas is? I could sew it back on later, if you'd like."

The gnarly old oak out by the cornfield could keep my pocket, I decided. My bad memories of that tree and of the witch dangling from its branches far outweighed any need to repair my pajamas. I stretched the new Power Puff Girls top to my nose and knew that Grandma had already worked her laundry magic on it. The fabric smelled like spring.

"Why don't we go ahead and pitch the Sponge Bob pajamas, Grandma?" I said. "Thanks for trying, though."

I pushed the bottom of the shirt back over my belly, wriggled down a little farther between soft sheets and warm comforter, and said, "But remember, that sweat shirt of Dad's is his single favorite article of clothing."

Mine too, truth be told. It had saved me from freezing to death. I owed that sweater my life.

"Right," said my grandmother.

We settled in to a comfortable silence. But, not for long.

Grandma had already decided on tonight's tale. I could tell and I hoped she would hurry it up. Should I start taking notes like we did in school? We took notes to help us sort out the facts and prepare for a test. What sort of test would I have to take on this material, I wondered? Then, I realized I'd probably already passed one. Barely. And only by cheating.

"My mother knows more than a little about flying a broom?" I asked, "doesn't she?"

Without missing a beat, Grandma conceded, "Yes, dear. She certainly does."

"I guess that makes a ton of sense since she's been a pilot all her life."

My grandmother nodded. "Your mother loves nothing more in the world than you and flying."

"But I don't see how that happens all by itself," I said.

"How what happens, Ella?"

"How flying a broom is possible all by itself. You don't learn to fly a magical broom without learning a lot of other stuff, too."

She waited for me to finish the thought.

"Other … magical stuff, I mean." My voice cracked a little when I said it. "So, I wonder what secrets she's been keeping from me all these years."

After a moment's consideration, my grandmother countered. "But you flew a broom, too, Ella. On your first try. Without, I might add, knowing any magic at all."

"Not true. I had your stories to go by. Maybe, I knew at some level that flying a broom was possible. Matilda and her crew proved it when they landed out front. If they could do it, I guess I knew a little bit about how I could do it, too. Otherwise, I would never have tried. But I'd barely managed to get my feet off the ground until Mom poked her head out of the bedroom window and offered advice—expert advice—on how to make a broom go faster."

"So," Grandma said, "maybe, as a safety measure, I prepped you for flying. That doesn't mean your parents have been keeping secrets from you or that they don't adore you."

"What I am trying to say, Grandma, is that driving a broom is one of a million things people—no, not people exactly, I mean, witches—do in your stories. None of them just fly a broom without being able to do everything else, too. Flying on a broom only makes sense with all of the other stuff happening around it. The rest of the magical stuff, I mean."

"Magical brooms occur in a magical context," she said. "Keep going."

I thought about how to say what I meant. "I can believe brooms fly only if I believe in everything else that's magic. It makes no sense otherwise. All of it has to be true, or none of it is."

She pondered my words and said, "I don't think I could have said it any better."

"So, my mom, and maybe my dad, too, must know a lot more about all of this than they've ever let on."

She tucked the covers around my shoulders.

"You're right," she agreed, "and warm and tight."

Those words, "warm and tight," signaled that the time had come to get down to some serious storytelling. She was putting an end to the conversation.

"But Grandma," I blurted, "you can't leave it at that. You have to tell me more."

She pushed a curl away from my forehead. It bounced right back, of course. Where other girls were born with actual, human hair, I came into this world equipped with a head full of unruly, brunette springs. My grandmother lay down next to me on the bed, and I rearranged myself so my head, curls and all, fit perfectly on her shoulder.

After a little more jostling to find the most comfortable position, Grandma said, "You're right. There's a lot more you should know. Ready?"

I nodded.

"Bring it on."

2

"Once upon a time …" she said, and we laughed, having agreed years ago it was a ridiculous way to start a story.

With a wink, she began again.

"A while ago …"

I nodded my approval.

"… there were some young girls living their own little lives in their own little town."

"How many girls?" I asked.

"Three, maybe four," said my grandmother. "At least two."

"Four," I decided.

"Four, then," she said. "These four girls were not so young, but not so old, either. They were friends who did everything together."

I cut in. "Where did they live, Grandma?" I asked. "Where was their little town?"

"Doesn't matter," she said. "But since you asked, they obviously lived someplace. In fact, Someplace was the name of the town."

I nodded.

"Better than Nowhere," she said, "which was the name of the next town down the road. Only mean, angry people lived there."

"Or Anywhere," I added. "How would you ask directions to those places?" I imitated a lost traveler. "Excuse me, ma'am. Can you tell me how to get to Anywhere?"

My grandmother answered, "Sorry. Can't help you. I'm not from Anywhere. Nowhere's where we're headed."

We laughed.

"So," she said, "Someplace was a far better place than Nowhere or even Anywhere. It was, in fact, better than Most Places."

"Which was far, far away," I said. "Over in the next county

"The next state, I think, Ella. You'll have to check your geography."

She gave my shoulders a squeeze. "Now, be quiet and listen."

She stared out the room's only window as if looking beyond it to the stars.

"Four not-so-young friends were walking in the woods by a pond, talking about something that doesn't really matter."

"Boys," I said, forgetting my promise to keep quiet.

"Precisely, Ella," said my grandmother. "They were talking and laughing about boys—"

"—who are boring and stupid and definitely don't matter."

"Who, at this stage in their young lives, the girls pretended were boring and stupid. Nevertheless, for some ridiculous reason none of them would admit, they couldn't stop talking about boys."

"Yuck," I said.

She put a finger over my lips to short-circuit my reply.

"But one boy in particular matters very much in this story as you'll soon hear.

"The oldest of the girls spotted a dark blob floating on the water near shore. Black, crumpled, and shiny, it looked like an old plastic trash bag, the kind you put in your garbage can for men in sleeveless T-shirts to pick up and toss into big, stinky trucks. A few minutes later, they spotted the blob again sitting high in the water, drifting along the bank almost like it was following them."

"Ooooh. Creepy," I said.

"It gets better," my grandmother replied.

She populated her tales with improbable scenes and unlikely creatures, but they never seemed to frighten me much, or give me nightmares. In fact, I kind of liked the scary parts. The creepier, the better. Except for the zombies, of course. I really hate zombies.

"The blob appeared to be perfectly dry although the girls knew that it should have fallen to the bottom of the pond like tons of other waterlogged debris had over the years."

"What was it, Grandma?" I couldn't help but ask. "Un-sunk junk?"

"The girls were as stumped as you, Ella," she said. "And not half as witty with words. So, they stood there on the path by the lake and tried to guess.

"The girl who first spotted the blob said, 'It's a bag, I think.'"

"Duh," I responded.

Grandma held up a finger for patience. "Don't be so quick to judge," she said. "I already used the word bag in my story, so naturally you think it had to be a bag."

"Sorry."

She ignored my apology.

"Another of the girls guessed it was a life jacket fallen from a boat. Another said it was definitely someone's raincoat, with air trapped in the pockets keeping it afloat."

"That was a pretty good guess," I said.

"Inventive," she agreed. "But incorrect."

She patted my arm. "The fourth girl wasn't content with questions. She snatched a stick from the ground, tromped through the underbrush to the edge of the pond, and fished the blob out of the water. Her friends gathered around as she flung the shapeless thing down on the path and spread it out with the stick."

Grandma opened her arms a little wider than her shoulders.

"It was a greasy, black triangle of fabric … felt, in fact … about two feet long. The pointy end was aimed along the path. The other, wider, end was rounded with two overlapping layers that implied and opening."

"Weird," I said.

"Want to guess what it was?" Grandma asked.

"Nope."

"As they watched," she said, "the blob did something exceedingly strange."

I squirmed a little closer to Grandma, and asked, "Which was?"

"It inflated like one of those long balloons that clowns blow up and twist into shapes. The opening at the big end expanded into a circle with a wide lip—a brim—all the way around. The blob grew into a cone as if some invisible hand was pushing it up from the inside. The girls watched, entranced, as it blossomed into its full size and conical shape, like a black traffic cone, then lay there on its side for a moment, as if resting. Just as the girls let out the breath they hadn't known they'd been holding, it began to flop around like a fish out of water before toppling upright with the pointy end toward the sky.

"That's all the clues you need, Ella. Care to venture a guess what it was?"

I shook my head no. I'd seen something like it this morning, lying on the ground below a half-dead witch. Grandma certainly knew this and had decided, for reasons of her own, to include it in her tale.

"The girl who'd pulled the thing from the pond pointed to it with her stick. 'Obviously, it's a hat,' she said. 'A dunce's cap. That's where the stupid person's head goes.'

" 'A hat,' the girls agreed. One of them picked it up, and gave it a shake. Dust, twigs, bits of leaves, and one or two bugs slid off like its surface was made of Teflon. She turned the hat over and shook it again to be sure nothing would jump out from inside. Satisfied, she lifted the hat high over her head and peered in.

" 'Ummm …,' the girl with the stick warned, but it was too late.

"The hat writhed in her friend's hand. It vibrated. It shook. It pulsed along its length like it was trying to break free of the girl's grip. In less time than it takes to tell, the hat fell, or maybe leapt would be a better way of describing it, straight down onto the girl's head. A whoosh of air squirted out from the brim as the hat sunk down, covering the girl to her shoulders. She yanked and clawed at the hat trying to pull it off. Muffled by the hat's thick fabric, her cries for help sounded like they came from a great distance.

"Her friends backed away in horror. But the girl with the stick—"

My grandmother went silent and tapped her chin.

"Why'd you stop, Grandma?" I asked.

"It's a bit cumbersome to keep saying, 'the girl with the stick, Ella.' I think we need to come up with a better name."

"Right now? In the middle of the action?"

"Will there ever be a better time?"

"Then, how about Buttercup?" I suggested. "Like the girl in The Princess Bride."

Grandma thought about that for a second.

"—but Buttercup didn't abandon her friend. Instead, she got a two-handed grip on the hat's pointy tip and yanked until it popped free with a slurpy, sucking sound. Buttercup tossed the hat over her shoulder and shook her friend.

" 'Are you alright?' she asked.

"The girl looked sheepish. Her hair pointed everywhere at once, like she'd been playing with that static generator you have in science class.

" 'It really stinks in there,' she said.

"Buttercup wrinkled her nose at the foul air clinging to her friend. The girl needed a shower, and fast. Their pleasant walk in the woods had come to a putrid end. Buttercup was about to mention this as politely as she could, when her friend's eyes opened wide and she shouted over Buttercup's shoulder, "Hey! No!"

"Buttercup spun around to find that another of her friends had inexplicably retrieved the hat from the ground and tossed it on her own head. The hat seemed to fit the second girl better, either because she had a larger head or, perhaps, because she had placed the hat on herself at the right angle. For whatever reason, the hat didn't sink down to her shoulders like it had on the first girl.

"She gave Buttercup a thumbs-up and said, 'I don't see what the big deal is, you guys. It's just an old hat that … odd … it's tightening around my forehead.'

"The girl wiggled the upper part of the hat in an attempt to jostle it loose.

" 'I feel funny,' she added, 'like the world is getting farther away.'

"That was enough for Buttercup. She grabbed at the hat but it refused to budge. The hat felt greasy and seemed to push her hand away when she tried to wedge her fingers between the hat and her friend's head. Buttercup had the good sense to force her friend to the ground where, by a combination of pushing, pulling, and shouting, she and the other girls somehow managed to remove the hat without also removing their friend's skull.

" 'Whew,' the second girl said with some relief. 'Weird. It's like the hat was talking to me. When I picked it up, it told me that, if I tried it on for just a second, I might be able to …'—she shrugged and looked puzzled—'… I don't know. I forget.' "

This sounded a lot like Holly's encounter with the predatory shoe. I waited for the part where they all went home and scrubbed themselves clean. No real harm to anyone. End of story.

But Grandma went on.

"Buttercup barely heard her friend's explanation. This time, she picked up the hat."

"What?" I asked. "How stupid was that?"

"No, dear," Grandma said. "Buttercup was too smart to put the hat on her own head. The thing had already attacked two of her friends. But she did want to know what was going on with the weird hat, how it could have jumped out of one girl's hands and onto her head, and how it spoke to another. So, she held the hat out at arm's length and peered at the darkness within. A rancid odor oozed like fog.

"Buttercup noticed something strange at the far end of the hat. Something dark that seemed to move against the pitch black of the hat's depths. Something she couldn't quite focus on. Something coming at her fast! Before Buttercup could even flinch, the hat flew out of her hands, all on its own, and leapt onto her head with a plop.

"The next thing she remembered, two of her friends were sitting on top of her in the middle of the path. The third had run away in terror."

Here my grandmother paused to ask me if I was okay. She'd felt me squirm a little at the idea of sentient clothing.

I shrugged.

"There's more, you know," she said. "But if you're too tired …"

"Does the story get any worse?" I asked.

"It does," she said, "in the middle. Then it gets better again toward the end."

"Maybe you can hurry it up a bit," I said, "and get to the end without so much of the middle?"

She chuckled and fast-forwarded her tale.

"The girls buried the hat and went home. Burying the hat was not altogether a bad idea, by the way, although burning it would have been preferable. Anyway, they stuck the hat in the ground, covered the hole with some dirt and rocks. Time passed without much happening and they forgot about the hat until, one day—"

"Wait," I interrupted. "Forgot about it? That seems unlikely."

"When I told you that the girls forgot about the hat, it was because quite a bit of time passed. It's not that nothing at all happened, Ella. I've deliberately skipped over the details so you could get to sleep before midnight for once."

I peeked at the clock on the bed table.

"Too late, Grandma."

She sighed.

"We can stop here if you want, Ella."

"No, we can't. But get to the good part as quickly as you can, okay?"

Grandma plowed ahead.

"A good bit of time passed. Everyone grew up a bit. They went to school, of course. And Buttercup found she liked a terribly intelligent, shy, and painfully geeky ...

"Dare I say it?" she asked.

I giggled.

"Boy!" She shouted the word the way someone would shout "Boo!"

"I don't know if I like geeky boys, Grandma," I said. "Joey Jackson is kind of cute. And he's good at everything. He's smart, too, but he doesn't act like a geek. Once, someone dared him to throw a rock over the fence at school and he broke a neighbor's window. The school made him pay for a new window, so that was kind of sad. But it was, like, two hundred feet to the fence. Maybe three hundred. I was impressed."

"Do I know Joey?" she asked.

"No, I don't think so," I said. "But I guess my dad's kind of a geek. And I like him okay."

"So do I, Ella," said Grandma. "I like him very much. Even if he thinks I'm too old to use expressions like 'Bring it on.' "

She let out her breath with a "Humph," then returned to the story.

"As I've said, enough time had passed that the girls all but forgot about the incident with the hat. They lived their normal lives in a normal town, going to school, playing sports, meeting at the mall."

"Sounds pretty boring to me, Grandma."

"Other people's lives often seem that way, Ella, as yours may seem to them. In this case, two of the girl's lives grew far more interesting when an odd woman began showing up unexpectedly."

"What was so weird about the lady?" I asked.

"The woman herself wasn't exactly odd. What was odd is that she seemed to appear out of nowhere wherever the group of girls got together."

"That's a lot of alliteration, Grandma," I said. "The group of girls got together."

Alliteration is a Mrs. Kendricks word, of course. It describes words in a sentence that repeat the same letter sound. Like, "Peter Piper picked a peck of pickled peppers."

"Did she actually come from Nowhere, the town? Or was it from nowhere, the concept?" I asked.

Grandma ignored my interruption.

"The plain-looking woman seemed familiar, they agreed, but no one could attach a name to her."

Grandma tilted her head toward mine like she had a secret to tell.

"You understand that when I say that the woman was plain-looking, it's just a polite way of saying she was downright ugly. Nothing on her face lined up properly. Not even the warts.

"The woman's presence seemed innocent enough at first. If the girls were shopping, they saw the woman coming out of one store and going into another. If they were at a movie, they'd see the woman entering a different theater down the corridor. Or they'd spot the woman walking her cat at the park after dark. A cat on a leash did seem a bit odd, maybe, but not necessarily suspicious. And, somehow, all the dogs in town seemed to know better than to fuss with this particular feline.

"One Saturday evening after dinner, Buttercup and one of her friends—the girl the hat spoke to when she'd tried it on—were sitting together at the edge of the fountain in the center of a mall when the odd woman approached them.

" 'Hi, young ladies,' she said, sounding amiable enough. 'I couldn't help but notice we've bumped into one another a lot lately. Too often to be a coincidence.'

"Buttercup had come to the same conclusion weeks before.

"The woman said, 'I'm Matty. Pleased to finally meet you both.' She stuck out a gnarled, leathery hand for the girls to shake."

"Wait a minute," I said. "Matty sounds a little like—"

"Shush," said my grandmother. "Let me finish the story before we both fall asleep and I have to start over tomorrow night."

I nodded. Tomorrow was already here.

"Against her better judgement, Buttercup took the woman's hand. As she did, a strange tingling sensation shot up her arm. Cold, sharp, and uncomfortable, like the woman had sprinkled ice chips on her bare flesh.

"Still holding tightly to Buttercup, Matty said, 'I bet the next three men that come out of the store across from us will have a red shirt, a white one, and ...' her face went lifeless for an instant, like she had gone far away '... and something confusing. Maybe a Hawaiian shirt.'

"The woman dropped Buttercup's hand like you would let a dirty napkin fall into the trashcan. Before Buttercup could even challenge the woman, three men left the store opposite the fountain in rapid succession. As you have certainly guessed already, Matty was dead right about their clothing. The men were dressed exactly as she had predicted, except that the last one wore a tie-dyed T-shirt, not a Hawaiian shirt.

" 'How did you do that?' Buttercup's friend asked.

" 'Oh, you could do it too,' explained Matty, 'with a little practice. I can sense the ability in both of you.'

"Buttercup was intrigued.

" 'I can teach you both to do what I just did, right here, right now, if you have a few minutes to spare,' the woman claimed.

"The girls had no plans to speak of, and hours to kill before their parents returned to pick them up. With a glance at one another, they agreed to hear Matty out.

"She had them guess all sorts of details about people's clothing, their conversations, their behavior. Anything that could reveal its truth or falsity in short order. She'd stare into the girls' eyes occasionally, or point them in a certain direction, or wave her hands mysteriously above their heads. Before long, the girls were guessing right some of the time, then half the time, then most of the time. Buttercup could tell when she was on the right track by a weird tickle in the pit of her stomach accompanied by a feeling of certainty, like she was describing an event she had already seen.

" 'Good,' Matty crooned. 'Good, good, good. Both of you. Better than I had hoped.'

" 'Now, my child,' she said to Buttercup, 'I'd wager you could do something more interesting if you're willing to try.'

"Flushed with her success, Buttercup said, 'Sure. Why not.' "

"This delighted Matty. 'I want you to try and make that young lady over there trip,' she said.

"With a gesture of her absurdly pointed chin, Matty indicated an attractive teenager on the other side of the fountain. She was modeling clothes outside one of the fashion boutiques.

" 'It's a wonder she can walk at all in those impractical shoes,' Matty added.

" 'I don't think I really want to do that,' Buttercup protested.

"But Matty cut her off, saying, 'Oh, shush, child. A little stumble will bring her down a notch … teach her a little humility. She's far too pretty. Here. Give me your hand and I'll help you.'

"The woman grabbed Buttercup's hand before the girl could object. Without exactly meaning to or fully knowing what she was doing, Buttercup half-imagined and half-willed the model to lean a little too far to the left, then a little more, and a little more until she eventually lost her balance. The instant she had the image firmly in mind, Matty wrenched Buttercup's hand up, palm pointed in the model's direction. Something shot out of her hand like a puff of wind.

"The pretty girl's weight shifted too far out over her high heels. She tilted like a chopped tree beginning to fall and, with an embarrassed little scream, she toppled to the ground. Half a dozen onlookers, 'oooohed,' as the girl fell. Buttercup heard a crack but couldn't tell whether it was a shoe's heel or the model's ankle that snapped. The crowd, 'aaaahed', at the sound, but Matty clapped her hands, saying, 'Wonderful. Marvelous, my dear. Good control. And on your first attempt, too. You will go far. Oh, yes.'

"But Buttercup wanted no more to do with this woman. She had humiliated the model in front of all those people. Maybe worse. She felt terrible and wanted to apologize.

"Matty would not allow it. 'She'll be fine. She'll be fine. Why would she believe a word you say, anyway. Nothing permanently damaged but her pride, and she had a tad too much of that to begin with, I should think.' "

My grandmother stopped the story again to tell me that we'd reached the middle, the part I had asked her to skip over. She confessed that she'd summarized events so far because she knew I didn't want to, or particularly need to, hear the details right then. She asked if I'd prefer to continue the story tomorrow or, actually, later today, since it was already after midnight.

I rubbed my sleep-deprived eyes to moisten them, and said, "In for a penny, in for a euro."

Grandma smiled, because that's what Grandpa used to say.

"Despite her reservations," she said, "Buttercup arranged to see the odd woman again. She and her friend met with Matty often in the following days, and weeks, and months. The two girls found reasons to meet at places without their friends. They practiced the tricks the strange woman had taught them, even when Matty wasn't around. Magic turned out to be fun and interesting.

"Matty explained that the skills they were beginning to master — 'Just beginning, mind you!' — weren't especially difficult or noteworthy in and of themselves. They seemed unusual because only a certain kind of person could perfect those skills even if they worked at it all their lives. This magic, she admonished them, was both a gift and a responsibility. She encouraged the girls to, 'Practice. Practice. Practice." and to use their magic whenever they could, for whatever purposes they desired, as long as they used it."

"So, what does admonish mean, anyway?"

Grandma pursed her lips.

"It means, 'advise,' or 'suggest.' It sometimes means, 'warn.' Buttercup, took that last meaning of admonish to heart. She was cautious with her newfound talents and made every attempt to use what she was learning, to improve situations for others. She resisted the temptation to utilize her powers for personal use. She refused to try some of the more obviously malicious spells. And before you ask, Ella, malicious means 'mean-spirited'.

"On the other hand, Buttercup's friend became an especially keen student. She practiced every trick, spell, or potion Matty was willing to teach her. More daring and reckless than Buttercup, her friend's actions became increasingly self-centered and spiteful. Things around her got broken and people got hurt. Sometimes they ended up in the emergency room.

"Matty, for her part, seemed not to care at all what the girls did with their knowledge and abilities, only that they pushed themselves to use it. She taught incantations, of course, but she also schooled them in what she termed 'animalinguistics,' the art of communicating with animals. Mostly cats since there are a lot of cats around. 'Dogs,' said Matty, 'are too stupid to notice that they can't talk.'

"And yes, before you ask, they learned to fly on some spare brooms Matty kept lying around. Flying was Buttercup's favorite bit of magic in the whole world. It's what kept her coming back.

"It's a wonder Matty managed to keep the training sessions going for as long as she did. Shielding the girls' parents from the obvious changes in their daughters' lives was masterful witchcraft, as we will discuss some other time. I can't tell you how she did it."

Can't or won't, I wondered. But I knew how Matty had done it. I'd had a witch inside my head earlier today. Well, earlier yesterday now that midnight had come and gone. If Matilda had commanded me never to speak again, I'm not sure how I would have ever found my voice.

"Over time," my grandmother said, "Matty encouraged the girls to introduce some distance from one another, instructing them to spend more of their apprenticeship apart.

"This suited Buttercup, as she was increasingly uncomfortable with the style of magic her friend practiced. It almost always involved unnatural control over her environment or over other people. And it usually resulted in some sort of trouble."

"Then there was ..." — my grandmother let the silence draw out before adding — "the boy."

"Oh, yuck," I said.

"Well, Ella. Time passes for boys, too. And the geeky one Buttercup had liked years ago turned out to be not so bad. He'd grown up tall and smart and quite handsome. There was also something special about this particular boy that maybe we can discuss another time."

Interesting, I thought. What could possibly be so special that it made up for him being a boy?

"By the end of high school, Buttercup and the geeky boy were head over heels in love."

"Double yuck," I said a little louder than before.

"Prom time came around. Graduation. They were enjoying themselves at the dance. Yes, Ella, boys can dance. Some of them, at least."

"Was dancing the special thing about him?" I asked.

"A dancing boy is indeed special," she said. "But no, it was not the especially special thing. I'd like to leave that discussion for another day. It will distract from tonight's story."

Without a pause to let me argue, Grandma dove back in.

"When the band took a break, Buttercup excused herself and headed for the restroom. She returned to the lobby a few minutes later but couldn't find the geeky boy. Her friends said they had no idea where he went, but they wouldn't meet her eyes.

"Reasoning that everyone needs to pee, Buttercup waited for the boy in the lobby outside the men's room. It soon became clear that Buttercup's young man wasn't inside. Rather than waste her time on a fruitless search of the gym, she muttered a simple finding spell she'd learned from Matty and let her intuition do the rest.

"The young witch was surprised to discover that her boyfriend was no longer among the crowd in the gym. Instead, for some reason, he had wandered away, down one of the classroom corridors.

"Buttercup tiptoed down the corridor, checking all the shadows and hidden corners until she found her boyfriend in one of the alcoves. He was fighting with her one-time best friend. Their arms were entwined as they pushed and shoved against each other with heavy breathing and muffled grunts. It took far longer than you would think before it dawned on Buttercup that her boyfriend and her best friend were kissing. Kissing like they meant it."

I sat straight up on the bed.

"Oh, gross, Grandma!" I yelled. "Triple yuck! That's disgusting! You promised me you'd skip over the bad parts." Clasping my hands to my ears, I said, "And now you tell me this? It's ... it's ..."

I flopped down on my back and pulled the pillow over my head.

"I don't think I want to hear any more tonight."

Grandma somehow made out what I said through the thick down pillow. She slipped it off my head with a tug. "I think you do, sweetheart," she said. "Take a few deep breaths. This is one part you should definitely pay attention to."

She tucked the pillow back under me and I collapsed down on it. Three full inhalations and some calming thoughts later, I told her to go ahead.

With a nod, she continued. "You can imagine the emotions that went through Buttercup's head and heart when she found her boyfriend in the arms of her best friend."

"Relief, maybe?" I mumbled.

"Not quite, Ella. No. The poor girl's feelings ricocheted between disbelief, heartbreak, outrage, denial, and back again in rapid succession. She settled on furious. Anger burned in her chest like a hot ember.

"I trusted him with my heart, she thought.

"Her rage demanded an outlet and, in a flash, she realized how to give it vent. Want to guess what she decided, Ella? What would be the worst, the cruelest way to punish the kind, shy, intelligent boy she knew so well?"

"She made it so he couldn't dance?" I asked. "Because that's the only interesting thing you've mentioned about him so far."

"Hardly, dear," she said. "Bodily coordination and a sense of rhythm, while attractive, weren't what made him special. Want to try again?"

"Not really, thanks," I said.

Grandma tossed my sarcasm aside. "Without thinking it entirely through, Buttercup determined to take away what was most essential to the boy—his intelligence and wit, his insight and his humor, his kindness. In short, she would make him as boring stupid as all the other boys she knew."

"Shouldn't have been too hard," I said. "They're all already boring and stupid. I thought we'd agreed on that."

"Without his best qualities, thought Buttercup, why would she care if he liked another girl? So, as Matty had taught her, she imagined the desired result, found the right words, and said the spell out loud. There's more power in a spell if you say it out loud."

Which I already knew, even though I didn't know any actual spells.

"Buttercup felt hot energy accumulate, flowing into the pit of her stomach from the earth below the floor, from the sky above the ceiling … from everywhere. She held on to the magic, allowing the power to bounce around inside her. It mingled with her fury until she could no longer contain the pressure. Oh, she wanted this! Her hands flew up to cast the spell.

"At that moment, the geeky boy turned to face her. He must have heard her speak the incantation. Only then did Buttercup notice a distant, slightly cross-eyed gleam in his eyes. She realized with a jolt that the boy wasn't in love with the other girl. Quite the opposite. He was under her spell. If you knew what to look for, the signs were unmistakable. None of this was his fault. He was not to blame.

"But the pent-up power was already streaming out of her, burning the palms of her hands in the process. She tried to pull back, but only succeeding in diverting her aim a little. The other girl, the young witch who had once been Buttercup's best friend, managed to get both hands up before the spell hit her. Even so, the force of it knocked the girl back against one of the solid, classroom doors then bounced her ten feet across the hall. She slammed into the lockers with a metallic clang. The sound of the band starting back up masked the noise that otherwise would have had people running to investigate.

"Buttercup's spell was far more powerful than she had intended or even imagined possible. She watched in horror as her former friend's eyes rolled up and she melted down onto the floor."

"Whoa! Hold on, Grandma," I said. "You mean she melted onto the floor like the Wicked Witch of the West in The Wizard of Oz? That was totally cool."

My grandmother snorted. "Oh no, dear. My goodness. I was using a figure of speech. I only meant that she slumped to the floor, unconscious."

"Too bad," I said.

"Buttercup knew that her incantation would have put an end to anyone but a practicing witch. She saw that her rage gave the spell tremendous power while, at the same time, robbed her of any control over that power.

"The spell's intent had been to purge its victim of something that was essentially them. In the case of Buttercup's boyfriend, it would have been his intelligence, his native kindness, and the memory of what he had shared with Buttercup. In the case of the devious young witch, the result was quite different. Intelligence had never been her strong suit and, since she met Matty, there was precious little kindness left in her to steal. Instead, the spell took away what was most important to her."

Grandma raised her eyebrows. "Care to guess?" she asked.

"Well," I said, "if the spell was meant to take away whatever defined her, then I would say it had to be her evilness. Did she end up all sweet and nice?"

"No," said my grandmother. "She didn't end up very nice at all."

"So, what was it?" I asked.

"Remember that the girl had spent a good part of her young life practicing to be a witch. Night and day for years. For her, everything else paled in comparison. Magic, in particular a flavor of magic in which she used her powers to manipulate and even harm people, had become her life."

"So the spell un-witched her?" I asked.

Grandma nodded.

"Exactly, Ella. Very good. The spell ripped every scrap of magic out of her friend. All of it. The capacity to perform magic she was born with and everything she had learned since. By the time the girl bounced off the lockers and sprawled on the floor, she had ceased to be a witch."

"Wow," I said after a moment. "That's pretty impressive."

My grandmother didn't respond.

"Can witches do that, Grandma?" I asked. "To other witches?"

Instead of answering, she jumped back into the story.

"Buttercup was horrified at the obvious pain she had caused the girl. But, when she thought about it for a second, she understood in her heart that, by casting the spell, she really *had* meant to hurt someone. The spell she used was intended to do damage. As her anger had increased its power, it had also blinded her to the spell's consequences.

"On the upside, her former friend wasn't dead. Her fingers twitched, she moaned softly and, a few seconds later, her eyes fluttered open. Buttercup's geeky boyfriend snapped out of his daze in the same instant, rubbed some leftover slobber off his lips with the cuff of his shirt—"

"Arrrrrgh! Absolutely, totally, disgustingly revolting, Grandma!" I said. "That image will haunt me the rest of my life."

"Sorry, dear," my grandmother said. But I don't think she meant it because she continued without a pause.

"Kindhearted person that he was, the boy dashed over to the girl on the floor and helped her up. He propped her, half-conscious, against a locker and asked, 'What's your name, where are you, and what year is it?'

"She got two out of three right.

"Buttercup helped her boyfriend pry the girl off the wall and they shuffled back down the hall supporting the woozy ex-witch between them.

" 'I didn't mean to—,' he began.

" 'I know,' Buttercup said.

" 'We were just talking and she—'

" 'I know.'

" 'I would never—'

" 'I! Know!'

" 'She said some funny words I didn't understand, then—'

" 'I know,' said Buttercup. 'Please shut up about it.'

" 'But, I—'

" 'Or you could shut up about everything forever as far as I'm concerned.'

" 'Okay. So, when can I—'

" 'I'll let you know. But you can definitely start shutting up right now.'

" 'But—'

" 'Nope.'

" 'I only wanted to—'

" 'Now!'

"She reached around the ex-witch's back and took his hand firmly in hers but she didn't look at him, or say another word to him, for the rest of the evening."

"So, to sum your story up," I said, "there's a sort of happy ending ... if you don't mind gross stuff involving kissing, slobber, and holding hands with boys. Which I kind of do."

She smiled.

"There is a happy ending to the story, Ella. There is. But not yet. Because, when Buttercup left the prom an hour later, Matty was waiting for her outside in the parking lot, dressed in full black vestments. Vestments means robes, if you don't already know that. Only her pointed hat was missing."

I guessed that a group of young-ish girls had buried Matty's hat years before.

" 'Look what you've done,' Matty screamed from far end of the lot. 'The time I've invested in that girl. And you, you little cretin, destroy it all in seconds. Oh, I'll have my revenge on you, I will. You will pay me back in blood!'

"Buttercup yelled back at her, 'She was kissing my boyfriend. What did you expect me to do?' "

I opened my mouth to protest against Grandma's repeated references to kissing, but she held up a finger to silence me.

"Matty raised her hands to cast a spell," she said, "a deadly spell that young Buttercup knew she would never be able to deflect or resist.

"Buttercup saw it coming and braced herself for the worst. She took one last deep breath, inhaling the simple scent of blossoming flowers and the musty odor of newly planted fields behind the school. A thunderstorm rumbled, coming in from the northwest as they always did. Roiling clouds blocked out the shimmering stars near the horizon, but not the full moon overhead.

"She loved this place, she realized. And her friends. And her parents. And the geeky boy, too. Unwilling to give it all up, she raised her own hands to defend against Matty's attack, knowing full well that her very best wouldn't be nearly enough.

"Matty's incantation sounded all wrong to her, like some long-forgotten language. The old witch's hands glowed with an angry red aura. She lifted them high above her head and shouted out a stream of words that were indistinguishable from the thunder. With a downward sweep of her arms, Matty hurled destruction toward the defenseless girl."

Grandma paused.

"Want to know what happened, sweetie?" she asked. "Or are you ready to sleep now?"

I didn't especially want to hear what happened next, truth be told. It couldn't be good.

I said, "I'm listening."

Grandma patted my arm.

"The spell came crashing through the air like a cannonball. It smelled of sulfur and burning iron. Red sparks trailed behind it like a comet. The girl felt the heat press against her. Buttercup never suspected that Matty held so much raw power inside. She wanted to duck but knew it wouldn't help. Instead, she pushed back against the oncoming fireball with all her will.

"The sum of Buttercup's power was like a gnat to Matty's flyswatter. She sensed, more than saw, the magical bolt rushing closer like an oncoming train.

"Then, maybe a yard from the girl, the ball of fire simply vanished. No sparks. No smoke. No explosions. No special effects of any kind. Nothing very exciting at all. Except for the disagreeable odor, it was like the spell had never been cast.

" 'What?' Matty asked no one in particular. 'How ... how can this be?' She stared at her hands in dismay.

"That's when, one by one, a group of women appeared around the parking lot as if they had suddenly emerged from nowhere."

"From Nowhere?" I asked, relief at Buttercup's reprieve obvious in my voice. "You mean that town up the road from here?"

"From Someplace, then. We've already determined Someplace is a better place than Nowhere. The point is that, except for Matty and Buttercup, the parking lot had been completely empty a moment before. At least it had seemed empty. Perhaps the women had been there all along, but unnoticed. The critical point for you is to understand exactly who emerged and who had the mastery to dismantle some very dark magic in mid-spell."

Grandma stopped talking and slumped back on the bed a little.

"Sooooo?" I prompted.

"So, who do you think was there in the high school parking lot," my grandmother asked. "Care to guess?"

"No," I said. "I don't want to guess. I'm really tired. This once, Grandma, please just tell me."

"Certainly, dear. The women who appeared out of nowhere ... sorry, out of Someplace ... were Buttercup's relatives. Her mother was there, both of her grandmothers, and several women she'd never met but recognized from the family album."

"The oldest of the women spoke to Matty. 'You've exactly one option, witch.'

"Matty hissed like a cornered racoon.

" 'There's a price due for the evil you've created here in recent years. Release your claim on this one—this one meant Buttercup—and leave the area for all time. In exchange, we'll grant you a ten-second reprieve.'

"When Matty hesitated, the old woman said, 'To be clear, I lobbied for five.'

"Matty wanted to argue the matter, but the woman said, 'Nine,' then, 'Eight.'

"Much as Matty had a minute before, the woman raised her hands in front of her. Her palms glowed pale blue. The other women followed suit, each shining with a different hue. Together, they formed a rainbow of magical light around the witch. Matty was clearly outmanned—"

"Out-womanned," I interjected.

"Out-womanned," Grandma said. "And outgunned. Understanding her life and death predicament, Matty produced a broom from somewhere within the folds of her robes, mounted it, and shot straight into the air.

"The women stared after her, seemingly content with the result, all but the oldest of them who clearly wished Matty had lingered for that extra second to test her fate. Buttercup collapsed onto the curb, head slumped onto her satiny prom dress. Her mother brushed the young girl's shoulder, but Buttercup pushed the hand away.

" 'Momma,' she said, 'I want to go home, please.'

"She glanced around at each of the women, family who had appeared in a perfectly mundane high school parking lot as if by magic—no, thought the girl, not 'as if'—in order to save her life.

"Buttercup stood, brushing the shape back into her dress with distracted flicks of her wrists. She said to her mother. 'You have some serious explaining to do.' "

I know exactly how she felt, I thought.

"The beginning," said Grandma.

I smiled. Grandma never said "The End" because every story's end is the next one's beginning. There's always another chapter, and one to follow that.

Grandma went through the motions of tucking me in. I'm kind of too old for that, but tucking-in has always been part of our bedtime ritual, and no one ever grows too old to appreciate special attention.

She tried to smooth my hyper-curly hair. It did no more good than Buttercup brushing her prom dress. Probably less.

"Wait," I said when Grandma started toward the door.

She stopped and turned to face me. "What, Ella, my sweet? You can't possibly want to hear any more tonight."

"No, Grandma. But … who was the girl in the story? Buttercup? Was it you? That kind of makes sense."

She pondered my question for a second and said, "I recall more than one girl in the story."

"Okay, who were the two girls, then? The two young witches, I mean? You were actually in this story, weren't you, Grandma? This one's real."

Instead of answering, she put her finger to her mouth, made a soft "Shhhh," and turned to leave. Lacquered pine floorboards creaked as she tiptoed out of my room, pulling the door behind her, leaving it open a crack as always.

On any other night, Grandma would have walked seven squeaky steps straight to her bedroom. Instead, she stood very still in the hallway on the other side of my door. A full minute later, her voice, low and muted, came from the yellow glow of the corridor.

"Yes, I was there, Ella," she said. "I was there in the parking lot at Buttercup's school."

That didn't make sense. If Grandma was Buttercup, as I'd assumed, then she was everywhere in the story, not just in the parking lot.

"But Grandma," I said, "I thought that—"

She interrupted me with a question, two actually, that, when you put them together, gave me my answer and more.

"Would you have been as proud of your mother as I was, if you had known her back then? And how do you think you'd feel about Holly's?"

7
They're There!

Monday morning.
Yuck.
I found Charlotte and Ariel waiting by the curb at the end of the bus loop when my grandmother dropped me off at school. I always felt rested after a night at Grandma's, but had never given the reason why a moment's thought until this morning.

Ariel shrugged when I asked about Holly. "She's home, I guess."

Charlotte added, "Barely surviving an attack by a foul-smelling, magical shoe apparently upset her."

I'd been chased all over the sky by a whole flock of murderous witches—not just by their footwear—and still managed to show up for class. Call me a complainer, but after my traumatic weekend I really felt I had earned a day off from school, too. Life's not always fair.

Charlotte once said that a day in school felt exactly like a day in prison. Long and boring, with no way out. Add bad food for lunch, bullies at recess, the occasional grumpy teacher, and I think you get the picture. If you really wanted to be somewhere else that day, multiply the feeling by two or three or maybe ten. Okay, I always wanted to be somewhere else, but this time I had a lot of stuff to do and limited daylight hours in which to do it. This time, I needed, not wanted, to be somewhere else. I needed to find a flying broom.

As the class settled in after morning recess, our teacher, Mrs. Kendricks, announced, "Homophones are words that sound the same but are spelled differently and have different meanings."

We all knew the definition would appear on our test at the end of the week, so we scurried to write it down.

"Homo is Latin for 'same' and phone is Latin for 'sound,' " she said. "Put them together and you get homophones, words that sound the same."

We wrote that down. One of the stupid boys in the back row asked if only Latin words could be homophones, or if it worked for English, too.

Mrs. Kendricks shook her head and went on. She explained how homophones are used in literature, stage, and humor. How, sometimes, they are confused with homonyms, which are words that are both spelled and spoken identically, but have different meanings, like tire, to become exhausted, and tire, one of the four rubber donuts that cars roll around on.

"In contrast," she said, "wind, air that is moving, and wind, to roll a string around something, are not homophones because they are pronounced differently. Not the same sound."

"Now, listen carefully," she said, "because this next part is a little confusing."

"A *little* confusing?" squawked Jimmy Richardson, the self-appointed class clown.

We all laughed and so did Mrs. Kendricks.

"We'll go over it all again later. But this can be fun. Trust me. I need your attention. Are you ready to listen?"

We all nodded our heads.

Mrs. Kendricks said, "Hetero is the opposite of homo. It means 'different.' Graph essentially means 'writing' or 'spelling.' So, heterographs are words that are spelled differently, like giraffe and spaghetti. Homophones … words that sound the same … that are also heterographs … words that we spell differently … are fun. Think of words like joy (happiness) and joey (a baby kangaroo) and you're on the right track. These kinds of homophones are what we are going to spend our time with today."

My classmates and I scratched this into our notebooks. One or two scratched their heads in confusion.

"The opposite of all these types of words, as you may guess, are synonyms—words that sound nothing at all like one another, but mean the same thing. Car and automobile are synonyms. Got all that?"

I looked over my notes for a second and nodded along with the rest of the class.

We talked about write and right. And rite. With and width. Two, to, and too, too! Four, for, and fore, for that matter. I raised my hand to add which and witch, but reined (rained) in (inn) my enthusiasm before Mrs. Kendricks called (cawed) on me.

Mrs. Kendricks made it clear how very disappointed she would be if any of us ever mistakenly substituted a homophone—like their for there, or hear for here—in place of the correct word in a written assignment.

Ariel, who had an aunt (ant) named Beatrice, asked if Bea counted along with be and bee, but she never got a straight answer from Mrs. Kendricks whose (who's) basic position seemed (seamed) to be that Bea is not (knot) a complete name.

One (won) of the nerdy boys (buoys) on my row (roe) asked, "Then, what about Glen with a capital 'G' and glen with a lowercase 'g'?"

Care to guess what (watt) the nerdy boy's name was?

Mrs. Kendricks said that glen and Glen together formed a perfect example of capitonyms. It's up to you to figure out what she meant. Seemed pretty obvious to us.

I looked up the word glen, with a small "g". According to the dictionary, it's "a narrow and deep mountain valley, esp. in Scotland or Ireland". I wondered why you can't have a glen in, let's say, Spain. Are valleys in Scotland or Ireland that different from valleys everywhere else?

According to my own definition, Glen, with a capital "G", means "a skinny boy with big glasses who sits near me in school and asks stupid questions". He is one "glen" that I dearly wish *was* in Scotland or Ireland.

The best of my best friends, Charlotte, has always had a special relationship with words. They kind of bounce around in her head for a while and then squirt out all at once. Homophones are right up her alley. Without raising a hand, she blurted, "Since be is a homophone with bee, and four and for and fore are, too, then how about "be for" and "before"? Like in the sentence, 'I decided to be for the president before he was even elected.' "

Mrs. Kendricks evaded the question. "Why do you assume the president must be a he? Our current mayor is a woman."

So, another of the other geeky boys, Justin Grieves, asked about a flower pollination experiment in which one of the buzzing subjects was referred to as "Bee Four". Bee Four only wanted to be with others who were bee width. Mrs. Kendricks rolled her eyes (ayes, I's) at that one.

"Dam," he said and the classroom went silent. Mrs. Kendricks folded her arms and raised an eyebrow. "A dam is a big wall with a lot of water behind it. What did you think I meant, Mrs. Kendricks?"

Maybe school wasn't so bad today.

Except that I really, really, really wanted one of those brooms.

2

Ariel, Charlotte, and I agreed to meet as soon as possible after school to continue our search for witch paraphernalia. I itched to go back to the farmer's field before it got dark. The sun went down a lot sooner, I knew, with Daylight Savings Time only a memory.

Lots of the witches' possessions must have fallen to earth after Matilda's flying sisters turned into cinders. Some of the items had survived in better shape than the rest, no doubt. I knew for a fact that at least one witch's boot made it to the ground intact because it tried to eat Holly. If that stupid shoe hadn't interrupted our search, would I have found a broom by now? I hated to waste the time that riding the school bus home would steal from our search.

But our plans for the afternoon fell by the wayside as we stood in line to board the bus. I heard a car horn toot.

"Ella," called my mother from the nearby parking lot.

She beckoned me over to the rolled-down window of our family's minivan. The bus driver shrugged at her through his tinted windshield. My mother shooed him away. Ariel and Charlotte stared from their seats near the front of the bus as it eased along the yellow-painted curb and rolled out of the circle. I made the universal "call me" sign at them by wiggling a hand at my head, with the thumb near my ear and my pinky near my mouth.

"Ella, sweetie," my mother said as soon as I slammed the passenger door closed. "I know you've wanted to talk about … things … for a while. Since the other day. And I guess, given all that has happened recently—"

"Yeah, Mom," I said, "a chat would be great, but right now I have something I need to do with my friends. And they just left for home. Can't it wait until after dinner?"

Rude of me, I know. But, gosh, I had important things to accomplish and only a limited amount of sunshine.

To my surprise, Mom took my atrocious manners in stride.

"Maybe we do both at the same time," she said, and put the car in gear. "I could use your help with something, too."

Great, I thought. Add some chores to the most important afternoon of my whole life.

"Mom," I whined, sounding exactly like Chloe Anderson, the spoiled, blond princess who sat between Glen and me in Mrs. Kendricks' class. "I really need to do something with Charlotte and Ariel before it gets too dark. I promised to meet them right after school."

She smiled to herself but offered nothing to me.

"My mom is mum," I mumbled under my breath and realized that Charlotte's knack for alliteration might have rubbed off on me over time.

"What's that, sweetie?" she asked.

I said, "You embarrassed me in front of my friends again. You always do that. I promised to meet them and now you won't let me."

"Of course you can play with Charlotte and Ariel and Holly," she said.

My mother glanced at me and added, "Well, maybe not Holly."

I shrugged.

"We can talk about Holly a little later, Ella. There are some other … other matters … that you and I have to discuss. Matters that have waited far too long to see the light of day."

"But Mom," I protested, "later is later. And there's not much 'light of day' left. I have something important to do with Ariel and Charlotte."

She challenged me, saying, "What is it you were going to do that's so important it can't wait a short time?"

A fair question, actually. So I told half the truth, both fifty percent better and fifty percent worse than the whole thing.

"Holly left her bike when she got … uh … hurt yesterday. We're going to pick it up before somebody steals it."

"Oh, don't worry about that," my mother said. "Your father and I found Holly's bike this morning. It's safe in the garage at home. She can pick it up whenever she's feeling more like herself."

That stopped me. How did my parents know where Holly left her bike?

3

The farmer's fields usually shot past in a sixty-mile-an-hour blur during the ride home from school. This time, though, not two minutes after our conversation in the car left me pouting out the passenger window, my mother pulled to the side of the road in a haze of dust. She skidded the van to a halt only inches from a drainage ditch that ran all the way into town.

"Hey, Mom. What's up?" I asked.

She took in a big breath, emptying the car of about half its air as she steeled herself to speak.

"Mom?"

My mother turned to look at me with half a smile and half a grimace.

"I think this would be a good time for a little walk together," she said. "And a private talk."

"No," I said. "Actually, it's a terrible time."

I appreciated that my mom wanted to discuss events. I really did. But what promised to be the best conversation I might ever have with my mother—sorting through the millions of mysteries and countless confusions in my life—threatened to interrupt the most important afternoon ever. The one that ends with me flying my own broom. The longer my mother delayed the search, the less likely finding that broom became. Given the choice between a heart-to-heart with my mom, and the broom I really, really, really wanted … well, the chat could wait until tomorrow. I turned to complain some more.

But before I could get the words out, I realized something. Several somethings.

First, I noticed that, if Mom had chosen the worst possible time for this discussion, she'd picked the best possible place. The van's engine clicked and creaked as it cooled. My mother had parked us at the edge of the field where I'd agreed to meet Charlotte and Ariel in fifteen minutes. The very field that my panicked friends and I had raced away from the day before with a dazed Holly slumped across the handlebars of Ariel's oversized bicycle.

In a rush of insight, individual bits of information fit themselves together in my mind like a self-assembling jigsaw puzzle.

My mom just said that she and my dad had stashed Holly's bike in our garage. I saw the place inside the fence where we all leaned our bikes yesterday. Nothing there. That meant my parents already knew about Holly and the witch's boot. Enough, at least, to find her bike in an otherwise anonymous cornfield. Next, I recalled how uncharacteristically dusty the car's fenders and tires had looked when my mom picked me up at school. The same rust-colored dust swirled in little puffs outside my window. I noticed clumps of mud and leaves on the floor of Mom's normally clean car. They weren't there last night when my parents had dropped me off at Grandma's. My mother had gone for a walk in the woods recently. Today. During school.

My parents had already visited this field today searching for something. They couldn't possibly know that my friends and I spent half of yesterday combing through the same shallow furrows looking for fallen brooms … could they? And I'd not spoken about Holly and the shoe attack to anyone.

Except my grandmother.

My heart sank all the way down to the leather passenger seat of the minivan. If my parents knew the whole story, they would put a quick end to my search for a broom. I would never be allowed out of the house again, let alone get to fly.

Count my life as over.

That's why my mom brought me here, to the side of a lonely, two-lane, country road overlooking the farmer's field where so much had already happened. We would have our little talk and I would learn precisely how over my life was.

She took another deep breath.

Here it comes, I thought.

She pointed her chin in the direction of the cornfield and said, "I need your help out there, Ella. Your father and I looked all morning and never even found a sign of one. Not a stick. Not a straw."

I stared at her open-jawed. "One what?" I had to ask.

"Don't look so surprised, honey," she said. "If you want me to teach you to fly, we've got to find you a broom. And maybe, if we're lucky, a second one for me." She smiled at the thought.

4

My mother let herself out of the car and leapt across the drainage ditch by the side of the road. She all but levitated over a split-rail fence that marked the boundary of the cornfield. Only then did she turn to look back.

I sat immobile, my seat belt clamping me to the seat. I noticed the moisture from my breath fogging the passenger window. A crow's annoying caw-caw-caw sounded once, then again from the top of a tree a football field away. As if in echo, a pickup truck honked three times as it zoomed past us, heading toward Witch Haven. I could see neither the driver nor the passenger through its tinted windows. Judging by the truck's speed, though, it had to be Jamie Parr and his dad, the high school football coach.

"Come on, Ella," my mother called out. "Your father and I spent the entire morning picking this field apart. It's empty, as far as we can tell. Like nothing was ever here."

In all the years of my life ... okay, eleven isn't that many years, but eleven still counted as all of them ... in all those years, my mother had never once hinted that brooms could fly or that witches were more than myths. She'd saved my life yesterday when she offered some tried and true advice on how to work a broome. Did that make Captain Mom a witch? Or, like my grandmother, did she merely seem to know a good deal about them for no particular reason?

I thought about it for a second, recalling no signs or symptoms that suggested my mom might be a witch. No black robes in her closet, no all-nighters away from home. No stinky shoes, thank goodness. No potions or charms. No spells or incantations murmured in the middle of the night. And no magical flying brooms.

Did my mother command any supernatural powers? Did she currently cavort with demons? If she did, how could she possibly keep all that from me? Me! Her one and only daughter and the center of her universe.

"Mom?" My voice sounded distant and ethereal even to me.

Through the half-opened car window, I saw my mother put her hands on her hips.

"Sweetie," she said, standing close to the fence, "I know you must have some questions. I promise a full confession now that the cat's out of the bag. I have to … I want to … tell you everything. I went through the same thing with my own mother when I was a little older than you."

Wait.

She went through the same thing with her mother? Her mother? Her mother was my—

"But," she said, "I'm asking for your help with this first." She swept an arm toward the field in an inclusive gesture.

As my surprise at my mother's deceit faded, and a sense of betrayal washed in to fill up the space and I felt less and less inclined to cooperate.

"I know more or less what went on here, Ella," my mother said, her laser stare keeping my attention. "Close enough, anyway. And I think Holly might be in some danger if we don't clear this area of any and every witchy thing before she starts feeling better and comes back to look for it herself."

I hadn't thought of that.

"And the power in the brooms, if there are any brooms left at all, is diminishing. They're like living things, in a way. They need to be continuously cared for and empowered. If we don't find them and bind them to us … well, to me, for now … they will be of no use to anyone before long."

Even though her argument made sense, I noticed that my arms had folded themselves across my chest in an obstinate gesture of refusal. My body had decided, all on its own, that it would not move from my seat in the car. Ever. Under any circumstances. For as long as I lived.

My mother sighed loud enough for me to hear.

"Honey," she said in as tender a voice as she had ever used with me, "if we don't find those brooms today, right now, they will die. You'll never fly on one again. Nor will I. This is our one and only chance."

Her gently spoken threat stabbed deep into my heart, opening a chasm that boiled and churned like a volcano. Instead of lava, though, grief welled up. Don't ask me how, but the magic in the broom had woven its tendrils into me during my brief encounter in the sky. Tearing them out would be akin in its violence to ripping a seedling from its roots in the earth.

When my mother told me later about her own coming of age—how the same choices had forced themselves upon her at a similar point in her own past—it became clear that she knew exactly the effect her words would have on me. My mother must have ached to fly no less than I did right now. She knew precisely how I would respond to her words because the same thing had happened to her long before she ever had a daughter.

Although my anger at my mother's insensitivity and secretiveness had a life of its own, it couldn't compete with my urge to fly. I unfastened the seat belt, shoved the heavy car door aside with an extended creak of hinges, and followed her into the field.

We had to find those brooms, whatever it took, so I could fly like my mother had before me. And, I realized with a start, like my grandmother undoubtedly had before her.

"I am so unbelievably mad at you," I said.

"I know, sweetie," she said. "We'll talk about it all later. With Grandma, too. I promise. Right now, though, we need to find those brooms before dark."

5

I told her everything as we walked across the field.

I told her how my friends and I had already searched the woods for hours and found nothing. I told her how Holly figured out that the brooms almost certainly fell someplace else.

I told her how we ran across the field searching right and left for anything that looked like a stick.

I told her about our encounter with the witch's shoe and what happened to Holly.

Mom's face contorted with disgust.

"Where is the shoe now?" she asked.

But I had no answer. "Charlotte tossed it away over there somewhere."

I pointed to the middle of the field.

"Then that's where we start," she said, and stalked off in the direction I'd indicated.

"Wait, Mom," I said, trotting to catch up. "What are you going to do with the shoe when you find it?"

I didn't want whatever had happened to Holly to happen to my own mother. Especially with no one around to help me if it all went bad again.

By way of reply, my mother pulled a large, dark green, plastic trash bag from the leg pocket of her camo fatigues. One of those heavy-duty, double-thick ones meant for leaves and yard stuff. A pair of cooking tongs, the ones you use to toss salads or grab hot things from the frying pan, materialized in her other hand. She'd come prepared. I gave her that.

Our determined march came to an abrupt halt when we reached the midpoint of the field.

"Right about here?" my mother asked as if she knew we were close.

I nodded.

She turned in a slow circle once, then again.

She sniffed the air. "Aha," she whispered, and marched off in a new direction.

I followed closely behind her for a dozen paces and nearly ran into her when she came to a sudden stop. On the ground before her lay a black blob crushed low into a rut. It looked like a half-buried dead animal.

"Is this it?" she asked.

I had to look twice.

"I think so," I said. "It doesn't look so much like a shoe anymore, does it?"

"Don't know how your dad and I could have missed it this morning," she said, and tapped her foot in agitation, "unless it was hiding from us."

With two quick clicks of the tongs, my mother leaned over to pick up the witch's old shoe.

"Mom," I cautioned.

"I know what I'm doing, honey," she said, and clicked the tongs. "Plastic," she added, as if that should mean something to me. "Nonconducting."

Without further ceremony she snatched the misshapen shoe with her tongs and held it up for inspection. Both the shoe and the ground upon which it had lain reeked with the stench of death.

"Whew," said my mom. "Fruity."

Quite an understatement.

She glanced at me. "Are you sure this is it?"

At a distance of five or six feet, I walked around my mother and peered at the object. Half hidden within a dark-brown crust of dirt, I saw the same tiny black leather boot that Holly had somehow managed to pull on over her own larger foot. It looked like the left one of a pair. I noted the curled toe.

"Yup," I said. "That's it. Can you please make it go away?"

She handed me the bag. I waved it in the air until, with a pop, it inflated like an oversized balloon. My mom reached out, dropped the stinky black thing in it, and took the bag back from me.

Before tightening the drawstring, she turned away from me and whispered a few words into the bag. She made some kind of sign with her free hand and then plunged it into the bag for a second, as if the gesture would seal the spell.

"Better safe than sorry," she said.

Almost as an afterthought, she reached behind her to pluck a spray can from a little holster on her belt. She emptied half the can into the trash bag before cinching it shut at last.

"Deodorizing disinfectant," she said. "That should help with the smell."

"Could you spray some of that onto the dirt over here," I asked. "It stinks as much as the shoe."

She said, "Help when you can, Ella, but trust the earth to heal itself. That's one of the first things you are going to have to learn."

Interesting, I thought. I want to learn. But I want to learn to fly a broom first.

I really, really, really wanted to do that.

My mom held the bag away from her, at the far end of an outstretched arm. It still smelled pretty ripe even with all the disinfectant. I could tell she wanted to set the bag and its contents down and move as far away from the smell as she could. I know I did. But I don't think my mother felt comfortable letting the magical shoe out of her control. It had already demonstrated a capacity for mayhem.

In the end, she said, "Oh, well. We can take showers when we get home."

She tossed the bag over her shoulder like Santa Claus' sack of toys.

"Where to now?" she asked me.

"Definitely not the woods," I said.

I looked back toward the woods, where Holly, Ariel, Charlotte, and I'd wasted the better part of yesterday. Following Holly's advice, my friends and I eventually left the trees to search the freshly harvested cornfield … until the witch's shoe put a halt to our search. Although we might have overlooked smaller items, I felt certain we would have discovered anything as large as a broom lying in our path.

"And probably not this part of the field, either."

So I turned toward the west again and pointed. "That way. If we don't find anything, we can double back later. Ariel and Charlotte will be here any minute to help."

With that, we marched off across the desolate patch of dirt. My mother fell into pace at my side. She put an arm around my shoulder—thankfully, not the arm with the stinky bag at the end of it—and brushed her cheek across the top of my head.

"Let's try that old barn by the far fence," I said on a hunch. "My friends can search the field more systematically once they get here."

"Systematically," said my mother. "Where do you learn all those big words, Ella?"

I smiled. "Miss Kendricks is all about words, Mom," I said. "She says we probably know more interesting words than most college students. You should hear Charlotte's vocabulary. She's the princess of language."

"Well, you are my princess of everything," she said, and squeezed my shoulder.

I told you I was the center of her universe.

6

The decrepit barn had once been painted red. The same vivid blood red that always covers barns at some point in their existence. Maybe they are born that way. Maybe there was a law.

My mom guessed that ten years had passed since the barn's previous owner, an eccentric old man named Maximus Hatcher, sold his cattle and property and bought himself a warmer home somewhere down in Florida. The new owner grew corn and soy but kept no animals. After purchasing the farm, he built a modern storage facility for his equipment and abandoned the ancient barn to the elements.

The elements had not treated the barn kindly. A decade of rain, wind, and snow stripped away the paint and stole the building's brightness. Whole sections of shingles had blown off and the spine of the roof sagged. At the barn's south end, the heavy wooden beam of a hay hoist canted at a funny angle over the open loft door. Above it, an arrow-shaped weather vane had somehow survived the years. It remained prominent in its position at the apex of the roof despite the deteriorated condition of the building.

The pasture around the barn hadn't been mowed in a long time. My mother and I waded through thigh-high tufts of grass that hid the barn's concrete foundation. This late in the year, the cold-blooded snakes had already hunkered down for the winter, thinking slow thoughts in their hidden holes. We hoped.

Charlotte and Ariel crisscrossed the field behind us. They plodded their way from end to end and back again, shouting and laughing at each other like they always did. I couldn't make out what they found so funny. It must have been very funny because they continued to laugh an hour or so into the search.

Mom, on the other hand, grew more serious, even a little glum as the daylight waned. Shadows already darkened the nooks and crannies created by the barn's outcroppings. Dusk crept up on us and we still hadn't stumbled across a single artifact—which is a fancy, Mrs. Kendricks' way of saying "thing"—let alone a broom or two.

"Ella," said my mother, "are you certain that the wind was blowing this direction the other night?"

I opened my mouth to tell her, yes, in fact, the wind had absolutely, definitely, for sure blown the same direction as tonight. It almost blew me and my oversized parachute into the trees. I had a pocketless pair of Sponge Bob pajamas to prove it.

Before I could answer, my foot tangled in a tree root or a stick, and I fell flat on my face with an "Oof!"

"Are you okay, Ella?" my mother asked.

"Yeah, Mom," I said. "I just tripped on this stupid ..."

I looked back at my trapped foot.

"... broom handle."

She appeared beside me before I'd taken another breath. I had literally stumbled across the thing we had been searching for. How often does that happen in real life?

As I scrambled to my feet, my mother gently lifted the broom from the weeds. She stood there holding a dark stick with some tufts of straw hanging off its back end. Why so black? I wondered. All of the brooms I remembered came from blond wood like oak or pine. It took a second before I figured out that when a witch blew up, it left a mark.

Mom's excitement at finding the broom ebbed as she examined it more closely. Charring from the intense heat of the exploding witches covered most of the broom's handle and continued along its trailing end. Even the straw brushes that formed the broom's sweeps looked burned.

"The scorching along the handle might not be as serious as it looks," she said. "We can sand it smooth. But I don't like what the heat has done to the straw."

She shook the broom and a dozen shafts of blackened straw fell to the ground. We stared at the pile for a second. Then Mom ran her hands through the rest of the bristles. Another dozen pieces of straw fell to the ground. Not all of them were discolored, though.

"I guess it could be worse," she said after half a minute of silence. "We won't know until I can get this home and test it where no one is looking. I wonder, though, what kind of shape the rest of the brooms will be in."

I chimed in, "I know that at least two of the brooms came through the fight without being touched by fire."

"Yours and Matilda's," she said. "Of course! Nobody exploded on them. I hadn't thought of that, Ella."

I couldn't tell you how my mother knew so much about what happened in the sky above the forest near the fields outside of the quaint little town in which we all lived. Nor had it really occurred to me that the smoke and fireworks in the sky represented people dying gruesome deaths. I would have to think about that later.

"Wow, cool," I heard Charlotte say. "You found one."

She and Ariel came over to investigate.

"We did," my mother acknowledged. "But there are more still to find. Likely as not, most of the other brooms burned up entirely. But we know of two that should be in good shape."

That struck my friends as good news.

"It is officially nighttime," said my mother.

The sun had dropped below the tree line to the west a while ago.

"We have to be as efficient as possible," she said. "Ignore the field for now. Let's concentrate our attention here."

My mother asked Ariel and Charlotte if they had any insights or opinions or even hunches about the best place to look. She mentioned that two nights ago the wind blew out of the west. Like tonight. It had affected the location of the brooms, but since everything had started so high up, no one could predict exactly where any particular thing had come down.

My friends already knew that, of course. Holly figured it out yesterday, before the creepy shoe got her.

"No clue, Cap'n Mom," said Charlotte. "Sorry."

Ariel stood stock-still, peering at the roof of the old barn. "Wait a minute," she said.

We followed her gaze upwards. Twilight still brightened the western sky. The barn loomed in the foreground, barely more than a silhouetted hulk.

I saw the sag in the timber at the crest of the roof. It looked like the back of an old horse. I saw the damage to the oak rafters from the rain that could had penetrated the roof. I saw the weather vane that had somehow survived the years and noticed that it pointed south.

South?

"Mom," I said.

"I see it, Ella," she whispered.

"That weather vane is ancient," said Charlotte. "Maybe it's stuck."

"No," said my mom. "It's too big to be a weather vane."

"That's a broom," Ariel said. "Maybe, one of the good ones.

"I'd be willing to bet you're right," my mom said. " We have to get up there."

I began to look around for a ladder or a pole. Anything that would get us closer to the broom. Ariel was a born climber. She could shinny up anything. I'd seen her climb trees to places squirrels feared to go. Ariel would laugh at the rickety roof and have the broom down in an instant.

Risky, but …

I caught a motion out of the corner of my eye and turned to face something I'd never expected to see in all my eleven years. Or in the eleven million years that followed.

Accompanied by a low, rumbling hum that may not have even been a sound, my mother rose into the air astride the blackened broom.

7

My friends and I watched in awe as my mother coasted up along the east side of the barn. When she got to the eaves, the part where the roof met the wall about twenty feet up, the broom gave a little cough. A puff of black smoke belched from its tail and the broom dropped three feet before regaining its lift.

My mom said that word I am not supposed to know yet. The one she accused my father of teaching me.

I yelled up at her, "Double standard, maybe, Mom?"

She just looked worried.

"Ella," Charlotte asked in all innocence, "I'm wondering if your mom might be a witch?"

Ariel interrupted before I could frame a sarcastic response.

"I hear that Holly's mom was a witch once. But she got better."

"Yeah," said Charlotte. "Something happened when she was younger. A long time ago. Something that my dad says saved her from being a witch. An evil witch."

Ariel said, "Does that mean Holly is …"

"An evil witch?" they said together.

"Oh my," said Charlotte.

My mother reached the sloping part of the roof.

If the broom she rode had not been damaged, if she had any confidence in its ability to remain airborne, I suspect she would have flown straight up to the apex of the roof and snatched the second broom down before Ariel and Charlotte finished their brief conversation.

Instead she took it slow and safe, half-hopping, half-gliding across the tattered shingles. She bounced lightly along the roof, using her untrustworthy broom only to lessen the impact of her steps on the structure of the weatherworn barn. I'd ridden a broom exactly once in my life. But even I could appreciate the skill and control my mother demonstrated in each of those little leaps. No newbie, my mom. She had long ago mastered the art of flying in a way that few conventional pilots would ever experience.

Ariel piped in again: "My mom said I don't have to worry about what happened to Holly's mother because witchcraft is hereditary."

Charlotte responded, "My dad told me the same thing. I mean, seriously, the pressures a girl has to deal with growing up these days, who would want that sort of curse on her head?"

Intent on my mother's progress up the roof, I still felt the embarrassed heat of their sudden gazes.

"Oh, Ella," Charlotte said, "I didn't mean that you were necessarily a ...."

"Right," said Ariel, "I mean, not everyone grows up to be an evil witch, right? Sometimes things work out. Take Holly, for example. Her mother was a witch. Once. But then she wasn't anymore. And then, Holly ... then she ... oh, dear ..."

Meanwhile, my own witchy mother had reached the pinnacle of the roof, where she stood straddling its peak. I watched her ease her weight down onto the exposed planking. The rotting wood creaked a little, and she said that word again.

I shouted, "Geez, Mom!"

In slow motion, she swapped her partially burned broom for the undamaged one. After tucking the scorched broom under an arm, she pushed up from the roof and ... she couldn't help it ... zoomed skyward to perform a double loop right there above the barn.

Only then did I respond to my friends.

"I don't know what I am anymore," I said. "I'll have to get back to you on that. But I know that you are my best friends in the world. And that won't change, whatever happens to me. Ever."

I finished my little speech just as my mother landed next to us.

"That's two out of thirteen," she said. "Not great, but good enough for one day. Your father and I will come back tomorrow to look for the rest. We know a little better where they might be, thanks to you girls."

Ariel and Charlotte stared at my mother as if they had just met her for the first time. And, I guess, that was pretty much the case.

"Let's get these brooms safely home," she said. "I think the damaged one can be saved but I'll need to work on it."

With no more fuss than that, she hefted the brooms onto one shoulder, slung the bag with the witch's shoe in it over the other, and stalked off in the direction of the van. After a few steps, she turned back around and addressed my friends.

"Go get your bikes, girls. We can toss them in on top of the brooms. You shouldn't be riding home after dark and it looks like rain. Don't you all have homework or something you have to do?"

Five minutes later, all packed into the van, our seat belts on, we waited on the side of the road for a herd of cars to pass. I rode in the front seat. In the back, Charlotte and Ariel were talking about Holly. Even with all the windows in the car wide open, they held their noses shut against the lingering odor.

For the first time since she qualified for a driver's license a thousand years ago, my mother kept to the speed limit all the way home. She told us it wouldn't do to get pulled over for speeding, given the contents of the car. Said contents included three girls, three school backpacks, one mom, two bikes, a couple of magical witches' brooms, and an odoriferous green trash bag. You can look up odoriferous if you want, but you probably don't have to.

All seemed right with the world.

Except that my mom was a witch and, probably, so was I. Holly surely had to be. The car reeked with the nauseatingly foul stench of a rotting shoe. To top it off, just as we were finally merged onto the unusually busy country road that led home, I spotted a pair of dark figures in the shadows that blanketed the opposite side of the field.

I hadn't thought about Matilda's pointy hat and leather belt with all the pockets since my parents and friends had rescued me from the cornfield early yesterday morning. I left them there beneath the tree that had held Matilda immobile until the sun blew her up. Where were the hat and belt now? Should we go back and try to find them?

As I watched, the two shadows—one quite large, the other quite small—slipped over the distant fence and into the woods.

"Mom," I said.

"I saw them, Ella. There's nothing we can do about it. The only safe place for us right now is home."

I knew then that all was not right with the world. It would soon get a lot scarier.

8
Chez Grandma Encore

A black-and-white police cruiser nosed itself onto our sloping driveway like a beached killer whale—if orcas happened to wear a rack of flashing red and blue lights on their backs.

"Mom!" I squeaked.

"Already on it," she said, and rolled past our house without slowing down.

We drifted along a curve in the road and out of sight of the house before my mother snapped the van into a squealing right turn. We coasted to a stop on the cross street at the end of our block.

The presence of a police car, especially one with its emergency lights in full bloom, would make a saint panic. So how do you think I felt at that moment? The highlights from my last two days included the fiery demise of thirteen witches, the theft of a magical broom—three magical brooms, if you included the two in the back of Mom's van next to a dead witch's reeking shoe—and a whole lot of suspicious behavior. We had no way to explain the brooms or the horrendous smell if a policeman ordered us to open the van's doors: "Oh, that's just some roadkill we scooped up on the way home from school, Officer. We do it all the time. Wanna see our basement!"

My mother's pilot instincts had saved us, though I didn't know from what exactly. Something about the police car in our yard seemed wrong ... okay, duh, obviously ... and she had reacted. In the time it took me to squeak, the flustered, barely organized soccer mom who greeted me every morning for breakfast became a cool, efficient, and determined machine, self-assured and in control. She had flown secret military missions somewhere back before I was born, though she never ever talked about them. That's what "secret" means, I guess.

"What did you see, Ella?" she said in a clipped voice of command. "I didn't get a good visual."

I wouldn't have been surprised if she'd followed up with a "Report, Marine."

"I saw Dad," I said.

She nodded curtly. "Go on."

"He was standing on the front porch. A couple of people were coming up the sidewalk. One of them was a police officer. A big one. Dad was talking to them. He looked up as we drove by, but didn't wave or anything. I think he was speaking to the woman."

That made her frown. "Go back," she said. "How do you know it was a woman?"

Her officious tone annoyed me. "Because, Captain Mom, unless it was a very short Scotsman with a ponytail wearing a flower-patterned kilt, the person next to the policeman was a lady in a knee-length skirt."

"Ah," she said, and deflated a little.

"The policeman was big," I explained, "but I don't think Dad looked especially worried or anything. He and the woman were chatting, not shouting."

How I absorbed all that information between the stabbing splashes of police lights in the half-second before Mom flung us around the corner like a roller coaster, I can't say. The brain is an amazing organ.

Mom nodded, inhaled a deep breath, and patted my knee. "Let's stop by the supermarket and pick up some groceries," she said. "Would you please pass me my phone, honey? I need to call Grandma."

Wondering how many different personalities she could go through in two minutes, I rummaged in her knapsack—Mom didn't exactly carry a pocketbook—and dropped the phone into her waiting palm. At least my friends weren't there. We'd dropped them off on our way home.

Mom tapped the phone's screen and held it to her ear. I could tell it was my father on the other end, but I could hear only my mother's half of the conversation.

"Hi, baby," she said. "I've got Ella and some other things here with me in the van. What's up with you?"

A pause.

"Uh-huh. We were heading home and remembered we needed to do a little shopping first. Is anyone there with you?"

She listened.

"Really? The mayor? In person. How do we rate that honor, I wonder."

Mom's eyebrows went up. "Why do you think she cares about some fireworks?"

I opened my mouth to speak. My mother put a finger to her lips and shook her head side to side.

"No. I don't know exactly when we'll be back," she said. "I'd suggest they go home and we can all have a civil conversation sometime tomorrow."

Mom listened.

"I see," said my mother. "Well, please let them know I'll be home in about an hour. Only me. I have some errands to run and Ella's staying at a friend's."

"Oh, really?" she said. "Then tell them an hour and a half. No, make it two."

She tapped the screen to end the call.

"You're staying at your grandmother's tonight," she said to me. "I hope you don't mind."

She knew I didn't.

"And you might be sick for school tomorrow," she added.

Even better.

"But first we have to find a place to stash that disgusting shoe."

"And deodorize the van," I suggested.

"We could set fire to it," she said.

"The shoe or the van?"

"Maybe both. But I doubt even that would completely eliminate the stink. Let's see if Grandma has anything that will do the trick. I could stop by the pharmacy and pick up some chemical deodorant. It'll smell worse than the shoe, but at least it'll smell different."

"I'll call Grandma and tell her we're coming over," I said, reaching for the cell phone on the seat between us.

My mother put a hand over mine. "I don't think so, sweetie," she said. "We're going to have to be spies for a little while."

I nodded and said, "Spies don't make phone calls when they can be intercepted or traced."

Mom patted my hand.

"What did the policeman want?" I asked, and congratulated myself on the casual tone in my voice.

"Apparently, the department received reports of fireworks out over the woods a couple of nights ago," she said.

I knew about the flashes, of course. I'd been hovering on a stolen broom smack in the middle of them. As I thought things through, something about what my mother had said bothered me.

"Why are they asking us about it?" I wondered aloud.

My mother smiled with no hint of humor. "Exactly," she said.

2

Grandma answered the front door in her bathrobe. It took a second for the obvious delight on her face to turn to disgust.

"What is that smell?" she asked. "It would repel a skunk."

One look at my mother and she took the question back. "I don't want to know, do I?"

Mom shrugged. "You probably do," she said, "but later. For now, it will be enough to get rid of the stink and the thing that's making it."

"How can I help?" Grandma asked.

My mother shook her head. "I'll take care of it," she said, "if you take care or these."

She eased the two brooms out from behind her back.

My grandmother's eyes lit up.

"Oh my, oh my, oh my," she said. "You found them."

Grandma held the ornate front door of her three-story Victorian home open to us.

"Only these two," my mother said. "And only with the help of Ella and her friends. Holly figured out where they came down."

"Holly? Hmmm."

A shadow flashed across Grandma's face for some reason. When she turned to me an instant later, the look was gone.

"Well, good for you and your friends, Ella," she said. "Now, go get a trash bag from the kitchen. Put those foul-smelling clothes in it and toss the whole thing outside to rot. After that, jump right in the tub and scrub that stink away."

I headed down the corridor leading from the foyer to the kitchen.

Behind me, Grandma said, "I took your new Power Puff pj's out of the dryer ten minutes ago. Grab them before you go up the stairs."

I nodded.

"And try not to touch anything on your way," she added. "Not even the floor."

3

A lingering whiff of the witch's shoe greeted me in the foyer when I went back downstairs, but I didn't think the smell came from me anymore. My Power Puff Girls pajamas smelled fresh and clean.

I found Grandma in her living room, half sitting, half kneeling on a cushion beside the mahogany coffee table. The two brooms lay side by side on its polished surface, somehow purged of any offensive odor. Wearing a pair of old, white silk gloves, Grandma brushed her fingers through the bristles of the scorched one. She shook her head in dismay with each stroke.

"Where's Mom?" I asked.

"Your mother left already. She had to get rid of that stinky shoe and then drive back to meet the mayor. She'll be in touch when it's safe."

I plopped down on the couch. My grandmother caressed the broom again.

"Do you think these are the only ones to survive, Ella?" Grandma asked.

"Nope," I said after a second's thought. "At least two of them came down without anyone exploding on them."

I remembered kicking my powerless broom away. I remembered the sensation of falling. I remembered the feel of Matilda's coarse robe as I grabbed it and pulled her off her own borrowed broom.

"We found these two by the barn at the old Hatcher farm." One deep breath later, I added, "I don't know anything about the others."

Grandma said, "If a broom was badly burned or if it fell nose first and cracked its shaft, the magic would have been broken. No matter what shape they were in when they landed, none of them will be of much use in another day."

The magic in the brooms eroded with time. That's exactly how my mother had explained it.

"Can we fix the burned one?" I asked.

"Perhaps, dear. It will take some time, though. I'm going to bind it to me so I can better care for it. Your mother and I will try to rebuild it later."

And how would you know anything about repairing magical brooms? I wondered. Oh, right. I already knew the answer, but it'd take some getting used to.

Grandma laid the burned broom on the table and picked up the charcoal-free one. She held it out in front her, on the palms of her gloved hands.

"What can you tell me about this, Ella?" she said. "Is it Matilda's broom, do you think?"

I looked the broom up and down, comparing the object in her hands with my memories of the fight against a coven of witches. I knew nothing about any of the brooms except for the one I'd snatched from Matilda and flew away on after a few unsuccessful attempts. That one had notches all up and down the handle. I remembered feeling the bumps as I ran my palms along it trying to find the best balance between speed and control. Matilda's broom also had a gnarly knob at the end of the shaft. The broom Grandma held was smooth, shiny, and free of blemishes. No knob to speak of.

"That's Zena's broom," I concluded. "I'm pretty sure. It's the one that Matilda was riding after I boosted hers. The rest would have burn marks on them, right?"

"Boosted?" Grandma asked.

"Stole," I said. "Right out of her arthritic hands."

My grandmother laid the broom on her lap.

"I see," she said. "It makes sense. That's how you managed to stay ahead of them. By chance, you grabbed the oldest broom around."

"What do you mean, Grandma?"

"You're still quite small and light," she said. "That helped some. Physics matters, even with magic. But Zena was young, by witch standards. And her broom"—she patted the stick in her lap—"couldn't have had many years on it. It was still a little green and sluggish. Matilda would have caught you in seconds if she had been riding her own broom instead of Zena's.

"Quite by accident, though, you took—you boosted—the one magical item that made a difference. Otherwise you would have been at Matilda's mercy before you ever left the ground. It was a close thing, Ella. You … we … were very, very fortunate. More so than anyone could have expected."

I didn't actually want to know that. I wanted to believe that my own cleverness, not dumb luck, won the battle over Matilda's coven. According to my grandmother, I should never have confronted the witches in the first place. I should be dead.

What long-departed person had claimed, "The truth shall set you free?" I'd have to look that one up, because they lied. The truth made me feel small and scared and not at all free.

But, I thought, where would Holly be now if I hadn't been so naïve? So overconfident? So lucky? Would tiny, timid Holly be the fourteenth witch in the coven, riding on her own broom in the sky above Witch Haven? Would we be able to pick out Holly's hollow cackle as she and her "sisters" terrorized the town? Who would the coven have come for next? Would my friends and I have formed the next batch of evil witches? A little club of preteen demons? Generation W?

But I'd lived and the witches had died. I had blended a heaping helping of stupidity with a little good fortune in exactly the right combination. Thanks to my ignorance, our town was rid of a bunch of evil beings they probably never even knew existed. Thanks to my ill-conceived arrogance, Holly lay at home, sound asleep in her own bed with a fluffy blanket pulled up to her nose. Thanks to my underserved luck, a flying broom rested three feet away in my grandmother's lap.

"Grandma," I asked, "is it even possible for a coven to have fourteen witches in it?"

I think I surprised her with my question.

"I mean," I added, "it has to be possible. You don't count eleven, twelve, thirteen, and stop. But a coven of witches that adds up to anything but thirteen doesn't seem right somehow."

Instead of answering the question, she said, "I spoke with your mother while you were upstairs. It seems that you're mine to entertain until at least tomorrow night. So let's make good use of our time together."

I nodded.

"For starters," she went on, "we have to heal these brooms. Then we start feeding and caring for them so they won't dribble their power away and die."

Broom maintenance was a new concept to me. I sort of understood how magic could fade over time. It had to, when you thought about it. If magic hung around forever, so much of it would remain from all the magic done in the past that ... I don't know ... the world would explode or something.

But I'd never heard of anyone having to feed something magical. On the other hand, I'd never heard of anyone not feeding something magical.

I guess I didn't know much about magic except what my grandmother had woven into her bedtime stories over the years. Stories I'd assumed to be no more than fairy tales constructed from her imagination.

She seemed to have overheard my thoughts.

"Ella, dear, I've been cramming as much of this information into you as I could since you were born. Much of it against your parents' wishes, I must admit. The knowledge has to reside in your body, not your head. Magic is not something you think your way through. Does that make any sense?"

Her eyes twinkled.

It did. There are different kinds of knowledge. If I knew anything about magic, I knew it like I knew how to walk, not like I knew a fact from Mrs. Kendricks' geography class.

Grandma said, "I may have even crossed a thin line upon occasion. A witch's training isn't supposed to begin until she shows certain definite signs. Things can get confusing otherwise."

I'll say.

She continued. "But that first few inches of air you put between you and the ground the other night was absolute proof of your magical ability. All the evidence anyone might need. None of your friends could have done that if they spent the rest of their lives trying."

"Except Holly?" I asked.

"Except Holly, who is a special case. She never had your secret training." Grandma drew air quotes around the word secret. "Nor will she. I put everything I could think of into those bedtime stories. Every one of them is absolutely one hundred percent true."

"Wait a minute," I said, "those stories couldn't all have been true. There's no way. We made most of them up together."

She shrugged. "Some were exact accounts of events that I myself experienced and some were described to me by trusted friends. Oh, I'll confess the occasional plot was a complete fabrication. But the truths inside the story lines were solid gold. Even the made-up stories were about things that are entirely possible."

"I'm not sure that 'entirely possible' is exactly the same as true, Grandma."

She spoke right over my objection. "So let's go ahead and assume that I haven't been lying to my only granddaughter all her life, and that we both had better things to do with our time than waste it in fantasy."

"Okay. Sure," I said, because in my heart I wanted it all to be true. I wanted to believe in magic and brooms and flying. Who didn't?

Then Grandma surprised me with a pop quiz.

"Ella, I want you to tell me everything you know about bindings and about brooms."

Tests never bothered me much in school. I took detailed notes in class and always knew in advance what an upcoming exam contained. This time, though, I had no warning. I had no notes. I had no topic. I'd never had a class about brooms or about bindings.

My mother says a child's mind is a sponge. Sometimes she says it about me and sometimes, more sarcastically, about my father. She's right, of course. Think of all that a baby learns in the first few years of life. Walking. Talking. Playing. Millions of facts about the world we live in. Who to trust. How to act. That information finds its way into a brain through the back door. It's absorbed without question. Absolutely none of it acquired in order to do well on a test.

That's how I already knew how to ride a broom the first time I ever tried it. That's how I learned about magic.

I said to my grandmother, "All I know about brooms is how to make them go faster and slower."

"That little bit of knowledge saved your life once already," she said. "So far, pretty good."

"But I'm not so great with right and left or up and down."

"No matter," she said. "That's more of a practical concern. We'll get you up on a broom very soon and see if you inherited your mother's flying gene along with her witch gene."

Witch gene? Is being a witch something you get from your parents? I mean, parents were invented way before flying, so I seriously doubted that the love of flying worked that way.

"What about bindings?" she asked. "That's what we need to discuss tonight."

"Ummm …" I mumbled, trying to remember if my grandmother had ever used the word bindings in any of her stories. I decided that she hadn't.

"I don't think I ever heard you talk about bindings, Grandma."

"How about: 'The magic works the witch as the witch works the magic'?"

She quoted the moral of a bedtime story in which a basically good magician spirals down into evil after dabbling with a forbidden spell, while, a hundred miles away, a very young and very bad witch invokes Good Earth magic for all the wrong reasons and ends up the beloved warden and protector of a magical forest.

"Right," I said. "I remember that. So?"

"People seem to think that magic is what someone does to something," Grandma said. "They think magic is imposed on the world to create a specific result."

I shrugged and asked, "Isn't it?"

"Magic is a relationship between the magician and the object of her attention," she told me. "It's cooperation at a most fundamental level. A back-and-forth of energies and will." Her hands moved in front of her as if she was pleading a court case.

"Can you think of any time when you thought you were using magic, but the magic also influenced you, Ella?"

Easy question, since I had used magic exactly once in my life.

"I flew on a broom," I said, "and I really want to do it again."

My grandmother's eyebrows went up, indicating I should continue with that thought. She rose from her cushion on the floor and sat next to me on the couch.

"And now all I want from life is to fly on a broom again."

"The magic works the witch as the witch works the magic," she confirmed. "How about that?"

"How about that?" I echoed.

"It's a good thing, though, that the broom we have here is not Matilda's," she said. "The residual evil in it would take you over before long."

She tapped her foot. "You're absolutely certain that this one was never hers?" she asked.

"It's not the one I was riding the other night. It's not one that I took from her." I asked my grandmother, "If the magic in the broom is so awful, why didn't it take me over then and there?"

"Who said it didn't?" she replied, sounding a lot like Mrs. Kendricks. "Remember, you pulled Matilda off her broom without a second thought the other night, even though you had to know what would happen to her if she fell from that height. In fact, I bet at some level you are proud of what you did."

An unfamiliar and decidedly uncomfortable feeling blossomed deep down in my belly.

"And," she said, "the fact that you don't feel terrible about it worries me."

But I did feel terrible, now that I thought about it. Grandma saw it on my face and pulled me close to her. The uncomfortable feeling expanded inside me. A deep sense of sadness and guilt and self-loathing welled up into a knot that blocked my throat like something half-swallowed. It burst out of me as choking sobs that wouldn't stop.

"That's my girl," she said as she wrapped herself around me for comfort.

After a minute or two, she spoke again.

"I know, and you know, that you did what you did in order to save yourself and your friends."

Still …

"And that black and evil witch," —she almost spat the words— "was no more human than a roach. You did the right thing, Ella. You did the best thing that anyone could possibly have done. You did the perfect thing."

Her words did nothing to convince me.

"But I want you to remember this."

I gasped, "What's that?"

An ocean of regret and horror enveloped my world. It felt like a thick black blanket falling over me, squeezing out light. I had ended a person's life! And I'd meant to do it. I'd even planned it.

"I need you to remember right here and right now that when you did what you had to do, when you did the only thing you possibly could to stop that evil vermin, you did not succeed."

"Oh, yes I did." I'd killed her. A pointy hat and maybe a really stinky shoe were all that remained of Matilda.

"Ella." My grandmother sounded as stern as I'd ever heard her. "Think it through. Matilda didn't die when you pulled her from her broom. She survived the fall. Remember? You told me that. She was hanging upside down in a tree, very much alive and still trying to kill you. But the morning sunshine claimed. Not you."

"No," I said. "I pulled her off that broom right there." I pointed to the one sitting on the cushion. "And she fell. But I cheated. I brought a parachute and I didn't die."

"Yes, she fell. But you know full well she didn't die. Not from the fall."

Grandma gently shook my shoulders for emphasis. She had never done that before.

"And—you have to believe this—Matilda was a very bad witch. A black witch. Not a person at all. Not anymore. Not like you and me or anyone else you know."

Grandma put a hand on each side of my face, like blinders on a horse, forcing me to stare straight into her sky-blue eyes.

"Ella," she said, "Matilda … was … not … human. None of them were."

A power behind her words brought me up short. Grandma was absolutely right. Humans didn't regularly vaporize before breakfast. That quickly, I stopped crying. Like someone had turned off a faucet.

Grandma held my chin between the thumb and fingers of one hand. She peered into my eyes with serious intensity. Whatever she saw in there apparently satisfied her and she let me go with a caress across my cheek.

"The parachute was a brilliant idea, by the way," she said.

She hugged me a second time.

"The magic works the witch as the witch works the magic," she reiterated. "And all you ever want to do is fly on a broom again."

I wiped a tear away. "Yup, that's what I want. To fly and fly and fly."

I felt refreshed and inspired. What had Grandma done just then? Had she manipulated my emotions the same way Matilda had my actions? Is that something she could even do?

It didn't matter.

"I really do want to fly," I repeated.

"Then this may be your lucky day," she said.

4

I grabbed a cushion and joined my grandmother on the floor by the coffee table. She held Zena's broom in her hands.

Grandma said, "I want your full attention, Ella. You're going to need this information."

"Bring it on!" I said.

She smiled and, handling the broom with surprising reverence, set it down on the table.

"You seem to recall my old bedtime stories readily enough," she said, "but what we're doing now is no story. It's real. Do I need to remind you that reality is more important than a lifetime of tales about amazing things?"

She'd made her point. Grandma's stories had a high fun factor. Real life, not always so much. I preferred the fantasies in my head over the realities outside of it.

"Okay. Good," she said. "Let's get started."

Sitting there with our backs against the couch, she asked me to recite a little nonsense rhyme that had played an important role in many a bedtime story.

"But I thought we were going to talk about reality," I said.

"Sing," she said, and started in with the tune.

The silly syllables never made sense, exactly, but I remembered them easily enough. We'd sung them together so many times over the years that they had worked their way into the fabric of my being. But Grandma took me through the verses again, several times, correcting my pronunciation once or twice.

"Now, dear," she said when I'd gotten it right, "think about those stories I told you, the ones where people recited these words or sang them."

Okay. Given enough time, I was sure I could retell each story line by line. Then I realized what Grandma had said.

"They're words?"

"They are indeed. But what matters right now is for you to notice what else the characters in those stories were doing when they sang this little song."

I'd never thought about that. I'd always assumed the nonsense rhymes were simply the glue that stuck the stories together. Something Grandma threw in so I could participate in the adventure.

I shrugged.

"Then let me ask you this," she said. "What were you doing, what were you feeling, when the characters in the stories spoke those words?"

Nothing, I thought. I was all about snuggling under downy covers on a soft bed.

Grandma smiled at my confusion. "Well, you were certainly not idle," she said. "More times than you would think, I had to cut a story short because you were on the verge of doing something that would have surprised us both."

I blinked. "Like what?" I asked. "Like when?"

She tapped her chin. "Do you remember the story where a band of evil rock-elves captured and imprisoned a young witch named Janie?"

I did. "Janie and the Elves" ranked high on my list of favorite stories.

Janie, a young and beautiful witch, had been cornered by a tribe of rock-elves. Rock-elves looked and acted like tallish dwarves— without the unsanitary facial hair. At their ruling council's command, they tossed Janie into a bleak and dreary cave whose depressingly bare and monotonous walls were the stuff of legend. The elves used the cave as a bland kind of torture that left their captives sense-deprived, mindless heaps after only a few days. The elves meant to force Janie into marrying their prince, Janus, out of sheer boredom.

This wouldn't have been so bad, I remembered thinking, because in Grandma's story Janus was as kind and handsome an elf as his ministers were cruel and ugly. Besides, the couple would have been known as Prince Janus and Princess Janie, which I thought sounded kind of nice.

Instead of giving in to the elves' pressure, though, Janie used her magic to brighten the world around her. She sang colors and pictures into the walls of her cell when the elves weren't paying attention. Because she kept her spirits up, her wardens couldn't convince Janie to marry the elven prince whom she had never even met.

As often happens in this kind of story, a strong and handsome knight with very white teeth showed up to rescue Janie and claim her as his wife. She had one foot out a fifth-story window when a retinue of elves led by Prince Janus burst into the room. Janie took one look at Prince Janus, thanked the handsome knight very much for rescuing her and, after some three seconds of consideration, told him she would prefer to hang around the castle a while longer and maybe have dinner with that other guy over there by the door.

Unfortunately, her rescuer, who turned out to be stupider than a sleeping rock, also proved to be a rude guest. He grabbed Janie by the waist, lopped off one of Janus' arms, and leapt from the window into the moat below. A waiting horse, the cover of night, and before you knew it, Janie was again a captive awaiting a forced marriage, this time in an elegant room high atop a gray stone tower.

She didn't wait around for a second go at it, however. The night before her involuntary wedding to the Neanderthal knight, Janie sang the little nonsense song that people always sing in Grandma's stories. A magical window opened in the wall. She scurried through it, clawed her way down a magical rope, and ran from the handsome knight's castle and right into Prince Janus' waiting arm.

Janus and Janie did get married, as it turned out. But only after many years had passed. Years in which they laughed and played, and occasionally fought like junkyard dogs. Years in which they matured into adults and grew quite fond of one another.

As a wedding present, Janus' mother, the Elven Queen of All That Is Known, banished the evil rock-elf counselors to the sky realm, where a family of giants out for a picnic lunch promptly ate them as hors d'oeuvres. Oh, and Janie helped Janus win his arm back. But that's a different story.

I loved the Janus and Janie story. What school-age girl couldn't relate to imprisonment in a boring place? But I didn't see why Grandma had asked if I remembered this one in particular.

"What's your favorite part of the story, Ella?" my grandmother asked.

I answered without hesitation. "When Janie changes the colors of her walls. I always wished I could do that. My room gets a little dull, too."

Grandma nodded. "You could really feel it, couldn't you, when she added all that color to those boring cave walls? And a meadow."

"And a pond, and a sky with billowy clouds, and a garden full of flowers, and tiny critters," I said. "And fairies."

When she used to tell me the story, Grandma never failed to asked what color Janie should make the walls this time. Then she'd invite me to help Janie imagine a landscape. Lying bundled up in my bed, imagining a perfect world, I could feel it in my chest when Janie, Grandma, and I finally sang the magic syllables and set our wills to the task of creating it.

"I know exactly how involved you were in the story," she said to me, "because once, when we were singing Princess Janie's rhyme, the wall over your bed turned pink."

"What? Uh-uh," I said. "No way, Grandma."

"I never lie to my favorite granddaughter. It went from blush to bubblegum and was well on its way to fuchsia before I could change the subject and distract you."

"But ... but ... I was just a little kid back then."

My grandmother, to her credit, didn't state the obvious. Instead she said, "Ella, I saw it happen."

"Um, wow," I said. "It can't be that easy, can it?"

"You're right. It's not easy. In fact, it's completely impossible," she said. "Unless you come from a magical lineage and have the imagination in you to pull it off. Then it's entirely possible. In fact, it's completely natural."

Grandma mention lineage. Lineage meant family and family meant genetics. We learned a little about genes and heredity in science class with Mrs. Kendricks. How fruit flies got the color of their eyes and the shape of their wings from their parents and even their grandparents. Was being a witch merely a matter of the chromosomes built into you?

My grandmother said, "For a born witch, learning magic is mostly unlearning not using it."

"Does that even make sense?" I asked. "It sounds like something Holly would say."

"It does make sense," she replied. "And it's especially true for you, dear one, because I've been sowing the seeds in you all along. Most girls don't have that advantage. They start learning magic—"

"They start unlearning not-magic—" I said.

"From scratch, usually as teenagers."

"Like the story you told me about my ... about Buttercup?"

"By the time someone grows up enough to perform magic artfully and wisely, they already have a great deal to un-know. Some never accomplish it. You, on the other hand, have accepted the use of magic all your life. You need only to relax and discover what you already feel in your bones."

"It sounds confusing, Grandma."

"A witch's magic is like a reflex," she said. "Like a twitch or a blink. It's over before you think about it or even realize you've done it. More often than not, you have to convince your body not to use magic. You train your heart and mind to control it.

"At the same time, you absolutely must understand and accept the responsibility you're taking on and the rules that come with it. That's where witches like us differ from the others."

"Hmmm," I said.

"Hmmm," my grandmother echoed. "You'll also find that the control of magic requires a great deal of preparation. Taking proper care of simple things. Which is another way of saying that it involves a lot of tedious drudgery."

"Oh, great. Magic is the same as school?"

"Yes, now that you mention it. Magic is quite like that." She winked. "So let's give it a go, shall we? There's no time like the present."

"Wait. What? Now?"

"I have to gather a few things from the pantry," she said. "Then I'll meet you upstairs by the tub."

She picked up the brooms, balancing them gently in her arms like she would a small child, and marched off toward the kitchen.

I wondered if flabbergasted was really a word or simply nonsense syllables like the fairy-tale rhyme that Grandma taught me to sing.

FYI, flabbergasted is a real word. I looked it up. It means astonished, usually in a bad way. People use it to describe how utterly confused they are. Flabbergasted has the word aghast hidden inside it … sort of … which is the same idea, so its definition kind of made sense. If it did make sense, it was the only thing in the last ten minutes of my life that even came close.

5

Grandma entered the bathroom, carrying the two brooms and an armload of cleaning supplies.

"Start the tub, please, dear," she said. "Not too hot and not too cold. Fill it about a third full."

A rubber stopper dangled from a beaded chain. The chain looped over an arching brass faucet that fed Grandma's old-fashioned claw-foot tub. I squeezed the stopper into the tub's drain and gave it a twist to tighten the seal. The tub looked like a rowboat had grounded itself on top of four squat, stubby legs. The legs ended in sculpted bear feet ... not bare feet ... which made the claw-foot tub a paw-foot tub, according to Grandma.

This particular paw-foot tub had probably squatted there on my grandmother's black-and-white tiled bathroom floor since the day her house was built two million years ago. Small orange patches of rust marred the tub's surface where bone-colored enamel had chipped away over the years.

The quirky fittings on the tub's spigot weren't half as rusted as the tub, or half as well behaved. They dribbled water out stingily until I shoved them full-opened and got Niagara Falls. I had to crank the creaking levers back and forth a bunch of times until the water temperature felt about right. By then the tub had filled up more than I wanted.

Grandma peered in at the result. She dipped a finger in the water.

"That's fine, sweetie," she said, and dumped a capful of something that smelled like lavender into the water.

"Let's start with your broom," she said.

My broom? I liked the sound of that! I liked it even better when Grandma pointed to the unburnt one.

She handed me a pair of pink rubber gloves that matched her yellow ones. We put them on and cinched up the fingers. The pink ones came up to my elbows. Grandma wrapped a rubber band around the upper part of each glove and folded a little of the extra material back to seal me in.

"Rest the broom's handle in one hand," she said, and laid the broom — my broom — on the surface of the water. "I've got the other end. You don't want it to sink. Pretend you're giving a baby a bath and you have to keep his head above the water."

As an only child, I had never given a baby a bath, so that particular instruction was kind of lost on me. Anyway, I long ago made up my mind to never have a baby. Who needs that responsibility? And diapers? Yuck! The decision held doubly—no, triply—for a baby boy. I mean, who needs boys, anyway, baby or otherwise? All in all, I counted baby-bathing as a life skill I'd no intention of ever acquiring.

Broom-bathing, on the other hand ….

"Like this, Grandma?" I asked.

She lifted my hand almost out of the water, until the handle of the broom barely touched the surface.

"We have to be extra careful," she said. "Water destroys certain kinds of magic."

"Like the Wicked Witch of the West in The Wizard of Oz?" I asked.

"Sometimes it's almost that drastic," she agreed, tweaking the position of my hands. "We want nothing of the kind happening to these brooms."

She dropped two clean washcloths into the water and let them sink.

"We're trying to wash the dark magic out of the brooms without harming their essentially magical nature. It's not simply a matter of dousing them in water. That would destroy all the magic and leave us with something not even good for sweeping the floor. It would be like drowning a puppy to get the mud out of his fur."

I frowned at the disturbing image.

She said, "We're going to cleanse the broom of the evil that Matilda's witches pumped into it over the years, while leaving most of the pure magic in. Like this."

She rescued one of the sunken washcloths from the bottom of the tub. Starting at the tip of the broom handle where it rested in my hand, she stroked the washcloth ever so softly down the shaft and toward the sweep, almost as if she meant to tickle the broom. She did the same thing to the bristles.

"Now, watch closely," she said as she wrapped the washcloth around her hand.

Grandma began to squeeze the straw, starting at the top near the shaft and moving down toward the cut end of the bristles ... suspiciously like milking a cow or a goat.

For the record, I had about as much intention of ever milking a cow or a goat as I did of having a baby. In Witch Haven, we lived a stone's throw from the country ... from real people with real farms with real animals that really needed milking ... but I was no country girl.

Grandma didn't seem so squeamish. As soon as her hand reached the cut ends of the bristles, funny things started happening. And I don't mean ha-ha funny.

She gave a little extra squeeze as her fist slid off the bristles. The broom shivered ever so slightly in my supporting hand. At the same time, the water at Grandma's end of the broom bubbled and fizzed and turned dark brown, like someone had dropped a cup of coffee into it. A familiar foul odor assaulted my sinuses. The witch's decaying shoe all over again. I retched a couple times.

After a few seconds, both the black ink and the disgusting smell disappeared. The broom gave one final tiny shudder and the water turned clear again.

I let out my breath.

"There," my grandmother said. "That's what we have to do to get the bad juju out."

"Are we done already?"

Being a witch seemed pretty carefree and easy at that moment.

"No," said Grandma. "Barely begun."

"Oh."

"Since this is to be your broom, Ella, you will need to do your share of the work from here on out."

"Okay, fine," I said. "I'll do almost anything for a flying broom."

"First, I want you to tickle the broomstick with the washcloth, like this."

She caressed the stick end once more. "That helps to attract its interest."

I nodded.

"Next, fit the washcloth around your hand. I want you to take your hand and squeeze along the broomstick. Imagine you are pushing thick, black energy down toward the bristles. That's exactly what you are doing, by the way, so take it seriously. The evil in the broom will want to stick to whatever touches it. Be careful. I'll handle my end."

I did my best to follow Grandma's instructions. I didn't have to imagine the energy moving down the broom. It pulled at me rather than the other way around. As I stroked my heavily protected hand along the broomstick, I could feel the magic inside the wood. It felt sticky, like tar. Like it wanted to stay attached to me forever.

My grandmother's open hands waited at the other end of the broom's handle, and I kind of pushed the icky energy into them. When she forced it out of the broom, the water around the bristles boiled and sputtered like the idling outboard motor at the bow—or was it the stern?—of Uncle's Ron's powerboat. Everything in the tub turned inky black, not chocolate brown this time, and the all-too-familiar overpowering odor bubbled up stronger than ever. I held my breath.

"Good, Ella," Grandma said. "Excellent. I don't even have to ask you if you felt the magic moving."

"Let's do it again," I said with the last of my saved breath.

My grandmother said, "We have to, dear. There's no turning back now."

The power tugging at my hand grew less with each pass and the churning of the water tapered off with each stroke. It disturbed me that I could hardly feel the energy anymore. Had I already lost my touch?

Right on cue, Grandma said, "You probably won't feel the magic as strongly as you did a minute ago. That means the process is working. You feel it less because there's less to feel. Try closing your eyes."

With my eyes closed, I could tune out some of my surroundings and concentrate on the magic in the broom. I felt the energy again. The same stuff, but thinner somehow.

"With a little bit of practice, you'll be able to zero in on different kinds of magic right away," she said. "I think, though, that you're starting from a good place."

We continued the cleansing for another five minutes or so, until I only pretended to feel movement and no more black ink squirted out from the bristles.

It surprised me when Grandma said, "Good enough. Any questions?"

I'd been so concentrated on the broom, I forgot the world for a while.

"How about a million of them?" I asked. "Like, where does the evil go when we empty the tub?"

"Oh, it's already gone, dear. The water absorbed and neutralized it, like a catalyst. Do you know what a catalyst is?"

Thanks to Mrs. Kendricks' chemistry demonstrations, I did. A catalyst is a chemical the helps change other chemicals without changing itself.

Grandma said, "Once the water turns clear, the bad magic is no longer active. You could drink the water."

"No, ma'am. I definitely could not."

She laughed and said, "Trust me, if the magic was still left in that broom or in the water, you would know it without my having to explain."

"Should we do the other broom too?" I asked.

"Oh my word, yes," she said. "I don't want that kind of magic hanging around the house for a second longer than it needs to. Are you up for another round?"

"Bring it on," I said.

I refilled the tub with no more luck controlling the temperature than the first time. I added the lavender oil and we put our gloves back on. Grandma lifted the fire-scorched broom and, as she had before, carefully laid it on the surface of the water.

The broom jumped as if the water had scalded it, and then settled down.

I used my washcloth to tickle the broom like Grandma had showed me; then I wrapped the washcloth around my hand. About halfway along on the first stroke, I got stuck. The magic wouldn't move any farther and neither would my hand. Grandma found a little chink in the wood right at the spot where I felt the energy bog down. She helped me push the magic past that place a couple of times. The broom bucked in our hands.

When she returned to her end and began to squeeze out the bad magic, the broom coughed and belched like it had when my mother rode it up to the roof of the barn. Grandma struggled to keep the broom under control. The bristles writhed like a hundred worms, each one with a purpose of its own. They reached out to grab at my grandmother's hands. The water in the tub blackened and thickened. The air around us stank like rotten eggs and worse.

It took much longer for the ink to dissipate than it had with my broom.

My broom!

At one point, the blackness in the water began to crawl up my grandmother's forearms, inching along the rubber of her gloves like a living slime. She had to stop her work on the bristles to squeegee the determined sludge off with a finger. Once, after she scooped the goo away and swished it back into the tub, the oozing, inky mass started swimming my way slowly, like a demon jellyfish.

"Grandma," I said, "I think the goo's coming to get me."

"Tell me if it gets too close," she said. "I'll move it away. Don't do it yourself. In the meantime, hold still and don't let the broom slip under the water unless I tell you to."

The broom lurched especially hard in my hands.

"But," she added, with the first hint of strain in her voice, "if I do give the word, don't hesitate for an instant. Push it down to the bottom immediately." She panted. "And no matter what else happens, hold it under the water as if your life depends on it."

As if. Right.

The broom fought us to the end. It thrashed and shook and spun in our grip for most of an hour. The gooey sludge that poured out of the broom during the disgusting ordeal seemed darker than dark, as if it ate light. I guess they don't call black magic "black" for no reason.

When we eventually calmed the broom enough to satisfy Grandma, she pulled the stopper in the tub. As the water gurgled down the drain, she peeled off her gloves inside out, like a doctor does, so nothing on the outside of the gloves touched the bare skin of her arms. She showed me how to do it.

I screamed when I saw what the evil magic had done to my hands. They were deathly pale and wrinkled, as if they had aged a hundred years.

Grandma laughed. "That always happens when your hands sweat inside rubber gloves and the moisture can't get out," she said. "It would've been no different if you'd been helping your mother do the dishes." She thought about that. "Which obviously you've never done before, but probably should have."

I said, "Dad usually does the dishes. And cooks. And dusts and vacuums. In fact, I don't know if Mom actually does anything around the house. I guess not doing dishes is a trait I inherited from her.

"Along with a lot of other stuff we definitely need to talk about," I added under my breath.

Ignoring the comment, Grandma tossed me a fluffy towel. "Dry your hands," she said. "They'll be fine in a couple of minutes. Then dry the brooms."

The last of the water slurped down the drain as I patted the second broom dry.

Grandma said, "A very evil witch owned that broom for a long, long time. I never would have risked this if I'd known. Are you sure it wasn't Matilda's broom?"

"No," I said. "I mean yes. I mean … I would definitely recognize Matilda's broom and this one isn't it."

Grandma stared off into space for a second then said, "Let's check each other for black slime. It gets everywhere if you're not careful, and it's worse than fleas to get rid of."

6

We each had a quick rinse in the shower down the hall, and then met on the patio in Grandma's backyard. With the evil purged from the two brooms, I assumed we were done for the day.

But, Grandma said, "Okay. At last, we can get on with the fun part."

When I looked confused, she added, "Anything worth doing is better done outside under the trees and the stars, don't you think?"

"And the rain?" I asked.

Thunderclouds had piled up behind the hills to the west of Witch Haven, as they always did this time of year. Lightning flared inside the towering clouds like flashlights winking on and off under a sheet. Dull rumbles followed a quarter of a minute later, building up from silence to a growl then fading away to nothing. Quite a performance.

One that would be happening directly over our heads in an hour or so.

"Magic comes in many different shades and flavors," Grandma said. "Our craft is based on the earth and the sky and the best of what makes us human. The other kind of magic, the dark kind, is based only on the selfish whims and the worst humanity can imagine. We ultimately draw on the same power, the same source, but through very different means and with entirely different intent."

Despite the chilly autumn air, a warm flush of pride rose in my chest. She had said "Our craft."

I'd wriggled into a snuggly sweatshirt and pulled the hood up over my head before stepping out of the house. The shirt had the same Navy logo as my father's old, beat-up sweatshirt in the garage—or wherever it was now—but looked twenty sizes smaller and twenty years newer.

Grandma wore a long-sleeved, full-length dress woven out of some coarse black fabric. Her formal attire for special occasions, she explained. A stiff round collar encircled her neck. It reminded me of the clerical collars pastors wear instead of ties. A necklace ran around the high collar and halfway down her chest. An odd charm dangled at the end of the necklace, in the shape of a symbol like … what do they call it in The Hobbit? … like a rune.

Truth be told, my grandmother looked suspiciously like a witch.

Rather than point out the obvious, I asked, "What should I do with these, Grandma?"

I held up the two brooms wrapped together in a plush towel.

"Exactly what you're already doing, Ella," she said.

So I hugged the brooms in my arms while she spread a white tablecloth over a round, glass-topped table. The table sat in the middle of an elaborate patio in which an intricate arrangement of hand-set stones spiraled like a maze to a pentagonal section at its center. Each of the table's five feet rested on a corner of the pentagon.

Odd. I'd never noticed the unusual shapes built into Grandma's backyard or the extra leg on her table.

She said, "Over the years, humanity has made a big deal out of a cup of tea."

"Ummm, I guess we have," I said, although I couldn't figure out how sipping tea related to magic and brooms.

Often, when the Saturday morning weather cooperated, she and I would sit at this table—or something that looked a lot like this table, but with fewer legs—and made an elaborate ceremony out of our breakfast toast and tea. The details of our invented ritual were as complicated as the patio's stone pattern. Performing the ceremony we had created out of hot water, ground tea leaves, and our imaginations provided tons of fun. I loved our tea ceremony and, I'm certain, so did my grandmother. She said they had similar traditions in other places like China and Japan and even England.

As I grew up, I noticed that the process left me with the same sense of awe and wonder you get under a starlit sky. Or when you enter a big space like a cathedral or even an old government building, one with carved stone columns, two-story-tall windows, and way-high domed ceilings. Grandma used the word solemn to describe it, but I don't know. Solemn sort of means sad to me. I only felt amazed and happy, like the best thing in the world that could ever happen had happened.

That feeling, whatever you chose to call it, became no less a part of the ceremony than the words we said or the actions we performed. In fact, for me—and I think for Grandma too—it became the whole point of making tea on the patio.

Grandma said, "We're doing something a little different here tonight."

She handed me a lighter. "Help me get these lit, if you don't mind." She held up a rack of candles in one hand. "And these," she added, holding a fistful of incense in the other.

A new touch, incense. The long sticks looked like Fourth of July sparklers, but smelled like sandalwood or maybe patchouli. Either way, they smelled good.

Grandma cupped her hands around each of the candles to protect them from random gusts of air pushed our way by the incoming storm. When all the candles were flickering in the breeze and the sticks of incense puffing like miniature smokestacks, she began to sing a sort-of song in her rich alto voice. Grandma sometimes used little chants, almost like nursery rhymes, in her stories, but tonight's song contained no words I recognized.

I felt myself drop into a quiet place, like settling into a comfortable chair. I realized that Grandma had taught me to locate this feeling of serenity without even knowing how I did it, the same way she had taught me about magic and witches.

"Grandma," I asked, "how did you—"

"Shush, child," she whispered, "We're trying to create a space here."

7

As Grandma waved the burning sticks of incense over the table and me and the entire patio, a definite mood settled on us. Peaceful and solemn. But happy solemn, not sad solemn. A sense of expectation hovered in the air, as potent as the smell of the incense. It seemed to me that my grandmother had invited the star-filled night itself to a seat at our table.

It took me a moment to recognize the familiar feeling. The lights, the chilly air, the anticipation, the joy. It felt like the night before Christmas, my favorite few hours of the year, times a thousand.

Grandma spoke quietly, voice deep in her throat, so that the sound seemed to come from inside me.

"Pull off that hood, Ella. You want to be as open to the universe as you can be."

I shook the hood off. As my unruly hair spilled out, I felt the night cold and crisp on my scalp.

"Now, lay the brooms out on the table with their handles pointing north."

I unraveled the towel on the table, and … "Which way is north, Grandma?"

She raised her eyebrows in the way she always did when she wanted me to think something through for myself.

"Do you remember how Harold and Kay found their way off the frozen lake?"

Of course I did.

One of Grandma's stories described the McDougals, a New Jersey family on a cross-country skiing vacation, who were waylaid on a frozen lake by a roving band of Norwegian cannibal dwarves. The dwarves kidnapped their daughter, proclaiming her both the guest of honor and the main course at their upcoming midwinter feast. Living mostly underground, the dwarves had little interest in the night sky. So the McDougals won their daughter's release with help from some simple celestial navigation and a hungry bear with a personal grudge toward dwarves.

I spun around on my grandmother's patio, scanning the heavens for something familiar. On my second turn, I spotted the Big Dipper, the most recognizable constellation in the Northern Hemisphere.

Two stars formed the ladle, the outer part of the spoon—where the water would pour from if the Big Dipper really was a big dipper. I tracked along the dome of the sky about five ladle lengths and located the next bright object. Polaris, the North Star. Impossible to miss, once you knew what to look for.

I aimed a finger at the star and whispered, "There it is."

I whispered because sometime after we lit the incense and my grandmother began to sing, all the sounds had gone out of the world. Even the distant thunder, it seemed, held itself at bay outside of the circle formed by Grandma's patio. It would have been rude to speak any louder than I just had.

Grandma nodded and turned her eyes toward the table. I did my best to arrange the brooms so they would point in the right direction.

"Do you remember the verse?" she asked me in a low voice.

I nodded, not wanting to interrupt the stillness any more than necessary.

"When you're ready," she said, "you can sing it to your broom."

Okay, stop right there. Even—or especially—in the midst of the magic my grandmother had conjured up for us, singing a lame nursery rhyme to a scraggly old broom seemed pretty ridiculous. When I opened my mouth to inform her of the fact, she cocked her head a little to the side and put an end to my objection.

"And when you do," she added, "I want you to put all of this feeling into it."

She opened her arms to the sky and did a slow circle to show me the feeling she spoke of. It sounds kind of silly when I describe it, but had you been there, you would know exactly what she meant. I could sense the peace and wonder and infinity. So real, it felt like a tingling mist on my skin.

I did as she asked, of course. I sang the little nonsense syllables to the sad old broom lying on a scrap of white linen atop some cheap patio furniture. The process turned out not to be as stupid and embarrassing as I'd thought. Especially when the broom started to hum along!

I cast a startled look at my grandmother.

"Pick it up in your two hands, dear," she said. "Very gently, like you held it in the tub a while ago."

I followed her instruction without question and, taking my time, raised the broom off the white cloth. I felt the shaft vibrate in my hand as it continued to sing.

"Remember when you squeezed the bad magic out of the brooms?"

I nodded. It wasn't that long ago.

"Now you are going to rub new magic back in. No need for gloves. Your bare hands will be fine."

"New magic?" I asked.

"This," she said, opening her arms up to the sky once more in an attempt to indicate … everything, I suppose.

"Close your eyes," she said, "and pretend you are drawing it down through you, out of your hands, and into the broom."

I shut my eyes and imagined stars rushing down from their perches in the sky so I could give them to the broom. Before very long, though, I don't think that I imagined it anymore. I felt a force moving through me as real as my breathing.

When I was little, our family had a black-and-white dog of no particular breed. "Half this, half that, and half something else," my father used to say. Jake was already old when I was born. I loved Jake and he loved me.

On sunny summer days, Jake and I would plop down next to each other on the grass in back of our house. I threw a leg across his boney ribs, and he put a paw on my chest. We would lie there content, until something else to do occurred to one or the other of us. The relationship required no language. Good thing, too, because no matter how much I tried to teach him to talk, Jake never spoke. Not a peep. Not a word.

If you take that friendship with an illiterate old dog, add to it the feeling Grandma had created around us with her chanting, candles, and incense, then toss in the moon, the stars, and, while you're at it, the whole infinite universe, you would have some idea of what went on there on my grandmother's patio.

I swam in an ocean of joy. The mood felt realer than real, like I'd been dreaming before and just now awoke. Have trouble getting your mind around that? Me too, because I don't think that my mind had much to do with that flood of awareness at all.

Standing there on my grandmother's patio with nothing separating me from the galaxy, I latched onto a memory of old Jake lying in the grass, looking straight at me with doggy love in his eyes. In my imagination, I reached toward him.

"Jake," I said.

But Jake was gone. The memory of my parents' backyard collapsed around me as if someone had abruptly stopped a movie in the middle of a scene and turned on the lights. The broom jumped clear out of my hands. It hovered three feet above the patio stones, halfway between my grandmother and me. Grandma stepped forward and grabbed it, probably out of an instinct to protect me. She stood there clutching the broom in both fists like she was going to sweep the deck with it. I'd never seen that look on her face.

I screamed, "Jake. Come back!"

The broom shook violently in my grandmother's grasp, wrenched itself free, and leapt across the space between us with such force it knocked me backwards. I wrapped my arms around the thin oak handle and held it to my chest like the skinniest of dolls.

Grandma's eyes went up. "The broom has a name?" she asked in a hoarse whisper.

A broom with a name seemed to surprise her more than a broom that flew on its own and came when I called.

"Yes," I said. "He's Jake."

She thought about that. Then, in a calmer voice, she asked, "Can you tell me what happened, Ella?"

I told her about the feeling of the stars, and about my old dog, and how the memory of him lying in the grass came to mind when I sang to the broom.

"I remember Jake," she said when I'd finished. "You two were so funny together. Your mother and I used to laugh ourselves blind watching you play out back."

She tapped her chin with a finger. "I don't think anyone has ever had a name for their broom before," she said. "Not right from the start, at any rate. I choose to take that as a positive sign. And I've never known a broom to show … loyalty … any more than a bicycle or a hat would. That could be a very positive sign."

I shrugged. Positive sign or not, I had a broom. I hugged Jake closer.

Grandma said, "You asked me about bindings before. Remember?"

I nodded.

"Well, that was a binding, sweetheart," she told me. "An especially powerful one, if I'm any judge."

With a nod in the direction of the broom, she added, "The two of you have formed a bond. You've convinced it to cooperate with you. Our kind of magic uses respect to do that. And love when it's appropriate. Matilda's kind of magic, by contrast, uses intimidation and demand to get its way. That's one important difference between us and her."

"How could someone force themselves on anything in light of all this?" I asked, gesturing toward the heavens exactly as my grandmother had a minute before.

"Matilda and her magic had nothing to do with light," she said.

"Could I do it again with another broom?" I asked. "Maybe we could make a whole flock of them."

"Would you want to?" she asked. "Now that you have your own … uh … Jake?"

I realized that I wouldn't.

"Anyhow," she said and gestured at Jake, "there was already magic in this broom. Matilda's witches took care of that part for us. Small favor."

She laid a gentle hand on my shoulder. "What we—what you did was create a binding with a magical object. One with magic already in it. That's not the same thing as creating a magical object from scratch. And before you ask, yes, that part is quite difficult. It will be years before you even get to try."

"Doesn't matter," I said. "I have Jake."

"Yes, you do," she said. "You do. And because of that, you now have certain obligations and responsibilities."

"Like what?"

"For starters, you will have to reenergize the bond regularly. That means, among other things, that you have to spend time doing what that broom was originally created to do ... what the two of you were meant to do together."

"Fly?" My voice sounded hopeful.

"Fly," said my grandmother.

I whooped with glee.

9
Which Witch?

My grandmother said I could fly!

One exclamation point wasn't nearly enough, so I added another dozen in my mind. That made ... oops, thirteen. So I took one back.

Still, Grandma said that Jake and I had to fly. Together! She said if we didn't, the magic in him would waste away and he'd be nothing more than a fragile old broom. Without Jake, I'd be a sad, lonely girl. So we had to fly!

"Well," said Grandma, "what are you waiting for?"

"I'm not waiting for anything," I said, "but Jake and I would be happy to stay here forever, if it's alright with you."

We stood together on her patio, immersed in a magical bubble she had chanted into creation. A space of indefinable joy. I held Jake in my arms.

"Forever is too long, Ella. Ten minutes is too long. First I'm going to make sure the other broom survives, and then I'm going to undo the wards and bring the circle down. Technically, it's a modified sphere, not a circle, but we can leave that explanation for another day. After that, I think you and Jake better go for a—"

"Flying will have to wait," said a voice behind me.

I jumped in surprise. But before the adrenaline made its way fully through my veins, I recognized my mother's voice.

"Mom!" I spun, ready to tell her everything that had just happened, about slurping bad magic out of the brooms, about the glorious feeling Grandma had conjured down from the sky, and, most especially, about my new broom, Jake. Who also might be my old dog, Jake. The excitement sputtered out of me like the air from an untied balloon. Even her silhouette, backlit by the kitchen lights glowing through Grandma's back door, looked grim.

"We have to talk," she said to my grandmother.

"It can't wait until we complete the binding with the other broom?"

The disappointment in Grandma's voice told me she already knew the answer.

"Okay then, dear," she said. "But I still have to release the elements before we can break the circle."

To me, she added, "Sit tight for a few more minutes, Ella. I have to undo the magic around us and set the feeling free. It must be released or it isn't—"

"Free," I said. "I understand, Grandma."

She handed me the other broom. The one that wasn't Jake. "Please be careful with that," she said. "It's in a delicate state right now."

She tossed me the fluffy bathroom towel the brooms had lain on. I wrapped a corner around each of the brooms and cradled them together. My grandmother stared into the heavens, waving her smoky incense as high as her arms could reach. I felt the vibration of her rich alto voice chanting syllables too faint to make out.

The quiet that had surrounded us during the ceremony dissolved as Grandma unraveled it, taking down a magical house of cards, one by one, without toppling the others. It felt like the whole world sighed as my grandmother removed the last support, undoing whatever she had done to create the circle—or modified sphere, whatever that meant. My mother, my grandmother, and I sighed, too. All at once. The ritual had ended.

The wonder that had descended over Grandma's deck, the same power that created Jake, wasn't gone. I still felt it. But not so deeply. No longer inside me, but out there, as distant as the stars. I held my breath, as if by pressure alone I could keep the spark of that serenity in my heart.

Then I remembered Jake, and the sense of loss vanished. I hugged the towelful of brooms.

2

"Okay, Stella," Grandma said, "what has you so troubled?"

My mother said, "I've just spoken with the mayor, and there's another witch in town." She almost groaned it. "A very bad one, I think."

Grandma shrugged. "We've lived with bad witches before."

My mother shook her head from side to side, like Grandma had missed the point.

"This one knows everything about Ella."

They glanced at me, then quickly away.

"What do you mean, everything?" I asked, not certain even I knew everything about Ella.

Instead of answering, my mother said to my grandmother, "Can we take this conversation inside?"

Grandma said, "Whatever you say, dear," and put her arm around my shoulder.

We had taken a step or two toward the house together when Grandma stopped.

"Can't leave all this stuff out here," she said. "Follow your mother inside, Ella, and take the brooms with you, if you don't mind."

She gathered up the incense and some of the candles she had used in the broom ceremony.

I found my mother sitting crossed-legged on the couch when I crab-stepped sideways through the living room doorway, protecting the brooms. I opened the towel on the table, arranged the fabric as kind of a mini-futon, and laid the charred broom on it.

Certain I'd made the damaged broom as comfortable as possible, I plopped onto the other end of the couch, with my own broom resting on the smooth leather between us, its handle end resting on my thigh. "Meet Jake," I said to her, unable to keep the pride out of my voice.

It took Mom a beat to respond. "Jake?" she asked. "How did your broom end up with the same name as our dog?"

I gave her the short version.

"Does that one have a name too?" She indicated the broom on the table.

"Sadly, no," I said. "You interrupted us before Grandma could make it hers."

She nodded without a word.

"But," I added, "she said she'd make it hers for only a while. To protect the broom, I think. She wants you to have it eventually."

"Did your grandmother purge the brooms first?" she asked.

I didn't know what that meant, exactly, so I told her about washing the brooms and about feeling the foul energy and about the black goo that had tried to walk up Grandma's arms.

"Was Grandma satisfied that you cleaned them out thoroughly?" she asked.

I nodded. "But we had to fill them back up with good energy. That's why we were out on the patio."

She processed the information.

"Okay. Good. I need you to be quiet and still for a few minutes, Ella," she said. "Can you do that?"

Of course I could. I was a witch, after all. A witch with a broom named Jake.

"Why, Mom?" I asked.

"I'm going to find out what I can about the broom on the table."

I noticed that, with its broken bristles combed out and most of the char stroked away, the burned broom had cleaned up pretty well.

"I need to ask it some questions."

"What can I do to help?" I asked her. "I have my own broom now. I've already done this once. How do you ask a broom questions?"

That brought a smile to her face. "The best you can do to help me right now is to sit calmly, with your broom and—"

"His name is Jake, Mom," I said. "Anyway, I'm a witch now, like you. I can help."

My mother's smile faded. Her little girl had changed a lot since she'd dropped me off at school that morning.

With a reluctant smile that looked like it hurt, she tapped the sofa next to her and said, "Please sit here calmly with your br—with Jake—on your lap. Better yet, you can lay him down on the table."

But I didn't want to lose contact with Jake. Apprehension fluttered in my chest like a flock of butterflies, at that prospect. What do you call a bunch of butterflies all in one place anyway, I wondered? A herd? A school? A gaggle? Certainly not a murder! That's what you'd call a flock of crows.

Naturally, I looked it up. A zillion butterflies, all flitting about together, is called a kaleidoscope, which makes a lot of sense if you think about it.

My mother said, "I need you to help me, sweetie. To do that, you'll have to concentrate and not be distracted by your broom. If Jake sits close to the other broom, maybe he can help too."

Did brooms make friends with other brooms? Did it really work that way? But my mom had made her point. How could I help her if all I thought about was my new broom?

I laid Jake down on the table, noting the direction of the patio and the orientation of the room. I slid one end of the table over a few degrees and then reset the brooms so they pointed toward the kitchen.

My mother looked confused.

"I'm pointing them to the north," I said. "That's what Grandma had me do out back."

"Oh," she said. "Sure. That would be best."

She knelt on the floor on the same side of the table as the blackened broom and smoothed out the towel.

"The best thing you can do, Ella, is stay there quietly while I find out what I can about this one."

I didn't want to sit alone on the overstuffed sofa. I was a witch, like my mother. I could help, somehow. Anything would be better than sitting on my butt, doing nothing.

"A good bit of your training from now on will amount to being still," she explained. "And you'll find that by simply sitting there and paying attention, you add power to the process. We … we witches tend to do things together and that's one reason why."

She sat back on her heels and put a hand on my knee. "You being … who you are … is probably harder for me than it is for you, sweetie," she said. "I always … I only … wanted to protect you. Now, for better or worse, you're in this for the rest of your life. And we both need to get used to it."

True! It would be harder for her than me. I'd never been happier.

She said, "You can sit here next to me, Ella. Or better still, sit on the floor, across the table. Next to your broom."

"Next to Jake," I said.

She smiled. "I need you to stay absolutely silent and still," she said. "Don't even think. Let me do the work. Your attention is all I need. And if I ask you for help, please do what I say for once, without making me explain why. Understand?"

I agreed.

My mother started in as soon as I settled down on my side of the table. She whispered a few words that I didn't catch and slid her fingers under the charred broom. A few more mumbled syllables and she lifted the broom in her palms.

Grandma put a lot more ceremony into her magic, I thought. I had way more fun with her.

"Pssst," hissed my mother, "I need your attention here, Ella." Busted!

I realized, in a way I hadn't with my grandmother, that my new status as a witch carried certain responsibilities. It would never be all fun and flying.

"Right, Mom," I said. "Sorry."

Once again, without any additional pomp, she said her words. Maybe, I thought, she had mumbled those same words a second ago. I tried to recall the sounds. But—whoops—my mind had wandered already. So I forgot about the words and watched my mother do whatever magical thing she did with the broom.

She breathed in and out several times. I paid attention. She moved her hands in flowing patterns over the old broom like she wanted to hypnotize it. I paid some more attention. In one smooth motion my mother bent her forehead down until it touched the broom near the end of its shaft. She made some odd faces and then relaxed a little.

That was all. The end. Not half as cool as my grandmother's show on the patio. Mom laid the broom back on its towel.

"Well," she said to me after a moment, "it looks like you and your grandmother did a good job with these brooms. There's only a hint of the old darkness left. Nothing I can't deal with later."

Good news. Though I didn't know how I would deal with any leftover darkness—whatever that meant.

"When you drove the blackness out, you robbed this broom of the only energy it had," she added. "It's very weak and wouldn't have lasted the night, so I pumped in a little juice to tide it over. Like a sip from one of those energy concoctions Charlotte likes to drink. But we'll have to rebind the poor thing to one of us soon, or there won't be any point."

My mother picked up the broom and turned it twice, while moving over to my side of the coffee table.

"Still," she said, "it should take only a couple of minutes to make the transition. We might be able to—"

A single solid rap on the front door interrupted her. We stole a glance at one another. Who would be outside my grandmother's house this late at night? Grandma never told me she had a friend coming over.

I realized who it had to be.

Dad.

I stood, intending to answer the door, but my mother grabbed my wrist. She put a finger to her lips.

I was about to protest—I had so much to tell my father—but Mom shook her head slowly from side to side. Her normally tanned and healthy face had turned white, like she hadn't seen the sun for a year.

She drew me back.

"Hello," came a raspy voice from the porch. "Is it possible that little Ella is hiding in there somewhere?"

I must have turned pale too, because I could feel all the blood leave my limbs and congeal as an icky glob in the pit of my stomach.

"I have a wee bone to pick with her, I do," the voice wheezed. "Oh, I most certainly do."

3

Knock. Knock-knock.

"You only get one chance to answer, you know," said the voice. "Then I'll huff, and I'll puff, and ..."

The voice outside laughed. I guess. It sounded more like a rhinoceros sneezing.

Knock-knock.

"I promise to take but a moment of your time."

Knock-knock.

"Of course, you'll only have a moment once I get my hands around your scrawny neck."

Knock-knock-knock-knock-knock.

"I know you're in there, little pest."

"Mom?" I half whispered and half whined.

"Shhh."

The night sounds outside had all gone dead quiet. The voice from the porch stabbed into that stillness like a snake's forked tongue.

"Aha! Question answered. Thank you, little one."

My mother flopped against the couch. She didn't look at all like Captain Mom, the levelheaded helicopter pilot I'd known all my life. Jake—the dog, not the broom—used to panic whenever it thundered outside, at least until he grew too old and deaf to notice anymore. My mother's eyes looked like Jake's had during a storm. She put her hands to her forehead and slumped over until her head bumped the table.

The voice said, "I count two hearts beating. Beating fast. Beating like frightened rabbits."

When the voice said rabbits, the front door bowed in, exactly like my parents' basement door had a couple of nights ago. But Grandma's door did not explode. Instead, a shriek from the porch rattled every window in the house.

"Abigail," the voice bellowed, "you will pay double for this."

We held our breath as silence sifted back in behind the echoing scream until, without warning, a horrible sound, not a voice, but a screeching, scraping, fingernail squeal came through the door. It started at the top and worked its way down, past the doorknob, all the way to the threshold at the floor, like a dragon draggin' (homophone!) its talons along the blackboard in Mrs. Kendricks' classroom.

The terrible noise ceased as abruptly as it began. A couple of light taps at each of the door's corners followed.

Then, nothing. When the silence had endured so long that I could no longer hold my breath, the voice outside croaked again.

"It's a pretty good bit of protection you put on this door, Abby. I'll give you that. The wards go deep. So deep, I can't scratch through them. Wasn't expecting that, I must say. Not much reason to defend against marauding witches these days, I'd think. But, you ..."

A few more taps on the door.

"You added some expensive precautions nonetheless. Oh, yes. Your spell even knocked a few chips out of my broom when it struck the door. And look. One of the splinters pricked my arm."

Was that Matilda's voice on the other side of the door? It had the same telltale rasp, like maybe she'd swallowed a handful of gravel before she started talking. But where Matilda had sounded like an adventure-movie pirate, the voice outside had a singsong lilt like some British actress in one of the BBC television shows that my parents feel the need to watch.

If that was Matilda outside, I thought, and if she turned out to be immortal like sometimes people did in myths and legends, then … then … then what? Then it wouldn't be fair, that's what. And, if Matilda had somehow survived the blast of sunshine, I'd bet she'd be even crazier than before. Crazy enough to carry on a conversation with an imaginary friend.

But I'd seen Matilda explode into a thousand … a million? … a billion? … pieces in the first light of morning two days ago. And there's no way even a witch could survive that, right?

Right?

Matilda, powerful witch that she was, had made her fear of my grandmother quite clear in the basement of my parents' house. I imagined my grandmother, even now, creeping around the corner of the house to shout "Boo!" and end the whole episode. I wanted to tell the witch on the other side of the door that she should have stayed dead. I wanted to put the fear of Grandma in her.

Instead, the voice spoke to my mother through the door.

"So, here we all are, eh, Stella? Those few of us who remain," it said. "A shame Matilda couldn't make it, eh, reckless and unruly as she was."

My mother's brow furrowed.

"We all had a nice little chat this afternoon, didn't we, lovie? You, your husband, and I. After which you ran right over here like a frightened bunny."

"Wait, Mom," I said in her ear, "who—"

She held up a finger to silence me.

When Mom and I drove past our street earlier this evening, I saw two people standing on our porch, talking with my father. One, clearly a uniformed policeman—or maybe a police-ogre, judging by his size—dwarfed the other, a petite woman in a flowered skirt.

"Oooo," said the voice, "we will get to who soon enough, sweet child. Oh my, yes. And then we'll get to *you*."

My mother stiffened. She shook her head like a ninja in a movie would shake off a punch.

"No," she said. "No, you won't."

The ice in her voice marked the return of Captain Mom. She squeezed my shoulder once, like she sometimes did before an important soccer match, and spoke to the voice behind the door.

"You'll have to deal with me and me alone. But first, I want to know how you tracked me here. I was very careful."

"Oh, you were, my dear. You were," said the voice. "No one could have followed you on foot, or even in an automobile."

My mother smacked her head with a palm.

"But I had no trouble at all on—"

"Your broom," said my mother.

"Just so."

Mom muttered that word under her breath. The one I was supposed to pretend I'd never heard before, even though it's the third most common word my parents used around our house.

"Okay. So you followed me here. Why bother?" she asked.

"I think we know the answer to that," the voice crooned. "There is the matter of a little girl to consider."

"There's nothing to discuss concerning my daughter." Mom's clipped voice sounded as harsh as the voice outside the door.

"Oh, there most definitely is," the voice replied. "My sister and her coven are smoke in the breeze two days old, you see. There are consequences. Payment is required. Revenge. Why don't you invite me in and we can discuss it amicably?"

"Why don't you wait outside for the sun to come up?"

I counted five rapid heartbeats before the voice responded.

"At the risk of seeming undiplomatic, someone else's time will run out long before that."

I had a quick premonition and felt a chill blossom along my spine.

"I'm so sorry, dear," came a different voice from the porch. "I was out on the patio, straightening up after our picnic, when she completely surprised me."

4

"Grandma!" I shouted at the same time as my mother yelled "Mom!"

That brought a cackle from the porch.

"By my sister's pointy hat," said the gravelly voice, "I'll wager that was no picnic out behind the house. Magical residue is spattered over everything. Oozing from the ground and dripping from the trees. In truth, Stella, my lovely, I could have traced the magic alone without troubling to follow a single turn of your convoluted route."

I could almost feel the witch shrug through the door.

"Grandma," I shouted, "use your magic and run away. We'll be fine."

"Oh, I wouldn't expect too much from your dear grandmum, little one," said the voice. "Abigail is … tied up right now. She's well enough. Well enough for the time being. Though we do have a bit of catching up to do, she and I."

I heard a sound like a person trying to scream through a pillow.

"Who are you and what do you want from us?" my mother asked the voice beyond the door.

Her words came out flat and toneless, as if she already knew the answers to the questions.

"Why don't you invite us in for a chat," said the voice. "For a little face-to-face-to-face-to-face? Call it a family get-together. We could decipher all this in no time."

My mother bit her lower lip and closed her eyes, thinking things through. Concentrating.

"Of course," came the voice, "I could force the matter."

My grandmother grunted in response to an action I could only imagine. I'd already jumped to my feet with the intention, I suppose, of rescuing her. My mother grabbed the waist of my jeans and tugged me back.

The voice began again. "As Abigail, here …"—something bumped into the door and my grandmother went "Oof"—"was the one who initially worked the spells that protect her home and castle from the likes of me, she could certainly remove them if she wished to do so."

Another crash jarred the door.

"As enjoyable as it would be for me to coerce her cooperation, I would prefer to move things along more efficiently."

Making an effort at stealth, my mother picked up my broom from the soft towel on the coffee table and laid it in my lap.

"So few of us remain, you see." The parched voice became a hiss. "Thanks to the scrawny white witch who has so recently diminished our sisterhood."

My mother looked around the room for something, but seemed unable to find it. Instead she pushed the towel aside and squiggled her index finger along the coffee table's surface.

"Mom," I whispered, and silently shrugged a "What are you doing that for?"

Instead of answering, she made a V out of two fingers and touched them to my cheeks, one below each eye. Then she patted the same fingers on her chest. "Eyes on me," her fingers said. Anyone who has ever watched a spy movie knew that. Roughly translated, she'd told me to shut up and pay attention.

I did. There's a first time for everything.

My mother rubbed her finger on the table again. It took a few seconds before I muttered my "Oh" of recognition. She had already etched out a dozen or so invisible letters before I caught on.

I grabbed her wrist and swished my free hand over the spot where she had pretended to write, erasing her nonexistent script. She started over.

"G ... O ... O ... U ... T ... B ... A ... C ... K," she scribbled.

I nodded that I had read and understood her invisible instructions. My hair must have rustled against my shirt or something, because Mom made a silent shushing signal, touching a finger to her lips, three times. I guess quiet wasn't good enough. Only very, very quiet would do.

"What's this?" came the disembodied voice on the front porch. "Cooking up some secret little plans together, are we?"

My mother spoke again to the door: "Tell me you who you really are, witch. I don't think I know you."

"Perhaps Abigail, here, should tell it," the voice said. "I trust you will believe what she says, hmmm?"

My mother sketched out letters. "T ... H ... E ... N ... F ..."

We heard another "Oof" from outside. My mother's hand stopped, hovering in place above the table.

Grandma said, "Stella, you remember Brunhilda, don't you?"

I'd never heard of anyone named Brunhilda. From the look on my mother's face, she definitely had.

"You're one of Matilda's sisters, aren't you," my mother said.

"Oh, aye," came the voice. Brunhilda's voice. "As you are already well aware."

My mother, her hand still holding station above the coffee table, said, "I don't understand." Though something in her demeanor told me she did.

The voice outside said, "Can you clear it up a bit, Stella? For you and your uncomprehending daughter?"

As my mother asked, "What's going on out there, Mom?" she wrote, "T … H … E … N … F … L …Y …" an inch above the tabletop.

We both winced when something bumped hard against the door. My grandmother gasped.

The witch outside said, "Explain the mystery for us, Abigail, my sweet. Yes, do. For all of us to understand."

The words came painfully from a place low in Grandma's throat. "Brunhilda is … was … more than Matilda's sister in magic, Stella. They're truly sisters, from the same mother, long ago."

"Helga," my mother said, groaning the name.

That seemed to brighten Brunhilda's mood.

"Why, yes, my dear," she said. "It appears that at least some of the old legends live on, even in these disrespectful times. Even in your vermin of a daughter."

Confused, I glanced at my mother. Discounting my own family, of course, I'd met my first witch only two days before. Now a whole flock of flying evil had invaded the town. As far as I knew, none of them were actual family members.

I whispered, "Okay, wait, Mom, —."

She held up a hand to silence me. And somehow it worked again. She put her V-shaped fingers to my eyes. With her other hand, she continued her invisible writing on the table.

"F … L … Y … H … O … M … E," she wrote.

"F … A … S … T …"

Adding a quick exclamation point (!) for emphasis, she tapped Jake and indicated the back of the house with a flick of her eyes at the corridor leading to the kitchen.

"N ... O ... W."

I shook involuntarily, more frightened than I had been, even when facing Matilda alone, two miles high in the sky. My mother stood, drawing me up with her.

"Okay," she said to the door as we rose. "You win, witch. I agree we have some things to discuss. Let my mother go, and we can talk."

My mother nudged me down the hall, toward the kitchen.

She moved toward the front of the house, timing her footfalls to match and to mask my steps. The first part of her plan, I realized, was to invite the witch indoors. The next step was to keep her there while I, the naïve girl who brought nothing but trouble to her family and friends, went outdoors and ran—flew—for my life. Despite all the evidence to the contrary, my mom was no ordinary PTA mom. She was a hero who could think and act under pressure. She'd already have a third step to her plan.

As I passed down the hall and into the kitchen, only a few strides from the back door of the house, my mother spoke to the voice outside once again, this time more loudly than before.

"Okay. Here I come," she said, one notch below a shout.

Would even her loudest voice distract a witch who could hear our hearts beating from the other side of a wall?

"I'm going to open up on three."

Two doors separated Grandma's kitchen from the back porch, an inner wooden one, thick with cracked white paint and six panes of glass, and an outer screen door that held the bugs at bay when Grandma opened the inner door to let in the sweet-smelling air on summer evenings.

"I'd like to keep this between us, Brunhilda," my mother shouted. "Can we agree to leave my daughter and my mother out of it?"

The witch said something I couldn't make out.

I wrapped my hand as quietly as I could around the smooth brass handle of the interior door.

"Good," yelled my mom. "Then I'm opening the door now. One. Two. Three."

A commotion at the front door. Brunhilda—what a stupid name— had stepped inside. At the other end of the house, I eased open the kitchen door with a twist of its ancient knob. The hinges squeaked so softly that I wouldn't have noticed if my life hadn't depended on it.

I felt that tickle in the spine that you get late at night as you tiptoe—okay, sprint—up the stairs to bed with all of the lights in the house turned off behind you. I imagined Brunhilda scurrying into the kitchen like a spider from her lair, reaching out with taloned fingers to grab me. I couldn't help but peek back through the kitchen, toward the corridor beyond.

Of course, no one could have made it all the way from the foyer to the kitchen in the short span of time since my mother had opened the front door. Witches are magicians, not track stars.

I tightened my grip on Jake and wiggled the handle of the outer screen door. My movements were jerky with panic. Although it squealed like a stuck pig, the handle swung down easily enough.

I heard a croak from the front of the house.

"What's that?"

So much for the secret part of Mom's secret plan.

"Why, you sneaky little girl," Brunhilda roared.

But the witch was too late. Broom in hand, I leapt toward the patio, toward the great outdoors, toward the limitless sky, toward freedom … and slammed with a noisy crash into the unopened and remarkably sturdy screen door which a deadbolt three-quarters of the way up still held shut.

5

I may have—may have—said that word. The one I'm not supposed to know yet. I may have screamed it, actually.

"Oh, really, Ella?" shouted my mother from the living room. "You and I are going to have a little talk about that one, young lady."

Great, I thought. I was in trouble with a crazed witch and with my mother.

Step, drag, clomp. Step, drag, clomp. Brunhilda scurried down the hall. She had a worse limp than Matilda. The poor broken broom probably doubled as a cane.

Like every screen door in the world, the latch on Grandma's had a little metal barrel that slid into a catch mounted on the doorframe. Standing on my tiptoes, I fumbled with the slide. Its rusted old latch always creaked, and scraped, and resisted any but the most dedicated effort to free it. I stuffed Jake between my knees, using both hands and all of my weight to haul on the latch.

Brunhilda had taken one stumbling step into the kitchen by the time I released the catch. My mother trailed behind her, one hand clenching the witch's curly-toed black boot for dear life—for my dear life. In Mom's other hand, the charred old broom that had been Jake's companion on the coffee table left charcoal streaks as Brunhilda dragged them both across the floor.

A jagged, eight-inch-long shaft of wood stuck like a dagger through Brunhilda's forearm, the splinter that had "pricked" Brunhilda when she slammed her broom against the door. Blood dripped onto Grandma's tile floor in a steady rhythm.

If ugly was money, this witch would have been a millionaire. Stooped over, with a hunched shoulder, she stood shorter than her sister—former sister—Matilda. Remember Igor, Frankenstein's little helper in those old silent films? He and Brunhilda would have made a perfect couple. Their humps would have balanced out.

"Go!" shouted my mother.

Fumbling at the handle with shaking fingers, I only managed to crack the door open before Brunhilda crooned, "Noooo. Sssstay."

Something in the sound of the witch's silky hiss froze me inside. An odd overtone in it, almost a second voice, commanded my attention. The voice brooked no disobedience. I realized how much easier it would be simply to remain where I stood. Much easier than running away. I would never get very far anyway. Old and wise, Brunhilda would find me wherever I hid. My hands relaxed on the partially opened screen door.

"Yessssss," she said. "Sssstay right there, brat, because you are mine."

By now, my mother had dropped the wounded broom and wrapped both her arms around Brunhilda's waist in an attempt to tackle the witch. It should have worked since Brunhilda couldn't weigh any more than I did. Instead, Brunhilda seemed rooted to the old linoleum like a granite boulder.

Brunhilda took another awkward step toward me, my mom in tow.

"Ella," screamed my mother, "run! Now. Run!"

I both did and didn't want to. My mind screamed for me to jump on my broom and fly away before the monster could take her final laborious steps and grab me. But my body had its own agenda. One bent to Brunhilda's will.

My mother's face contorted with the effort of holding the witch back. In contrast, the witch's face looked calm and serene as a summer's day. She took another step. … And another. … I knew I didn't have many witch-steps left to live. The hideous mudslide of her face occupied my entire world. It loomed like a billboard above me.

I recognized something in the witch's face. Something familiar behind all the ugly. Something I'd seen on … on a … on a billboard!

"Mayor Bloom," I asked, "is that you?"

6

The witch stopped in her tracks. Dead still. Not even breathing. I don't think any of us in the room did, either. The space around her shimmered, wavering like the heated air above a campfire. Brunhilda inched arthritic hands up the shaft of her broken broom. She grew taller and straighter. The round hump of her shoulder smoothed out in creaking, popping stages. And there, as if by magic … in fact, precisely by magic … stood Witch Haven's plain-looking, hard-working, and very popular mayor. Plain-looking was a big improvement, in this case. Her winning personality shone like a ray of sunshine in the eye of a hurricane. My mother still dangled from her side.

"Why, yes, dear," she said, "it is me. I thank you for noticing."

The harsh rattle in her voice had disappeared. She no longer sounded like an English nanny. She spoke plain, vanilla American, like they did on the TV news.

I blurted out the first thing that came to mind. "You sent the witches after my friend, didn't you?"

She tapped a finger on the tip of her broomstick as she thought through her answer. "How we all came to this point is a longish story," she said. "Perhaps you would like to hear it one day? The four of us could meet for lunch downtown to discuss it."

"But how … how could you …" I stammered. "Why?"

"Of course, your grandmother, Abigail, figures prominently in the history. You wouldn't believe it, but she once—"

At that moment, to everyone's astonishment including her own, my straining mother finally managed to hoist the suddenly lightweight Miss Bloom a couple inches off the ground.

The mayor's face darkened. Reality rippled. With a high-pitched scream like a scolding crow, the humpbacked witch crashed to the floor, shaking the entire house. Knocked to her back by the impact, my mother lay sprawled by the sink, the charred old broom nearby.

"Drat, drat, drat!" exclaimed Brunhilda. "I had not expected you to see through me like that, little witch. No, I hadn't. It proves you have some promise, though. Quite a bit of promise. Oh, yes."

Brunhilda turned to my mother. "A shame she won't live to make good on it."

My mother stared wide-eyed, her chest heaving.

The witch spoke to me in that special voice. The same voice Matilda, dangling from a bare oak over the edge of a cornfield two days ago, used to force me to retrieve her hat. "You were about to hand me that broom you're straddling."

Right, I thought. Yes. I planned on doing exactly that. The broom belonged to her. I'd stolen it, after all. The gnarly old broom was a mindless pile of sticks and straw strung together with a thread of twine. What could I possibly want with it?

She held out her hand.

"No, Ella," my grandmother's voice boomed from the other side of the kitchen.

She stood in the doorway to the corridor, leaning on the jamb for support. A stream of blood seeped from the silver of her hairline onto the tatters of her elegant robe. My mother, the battlefield medic, had taught me that scalp wounds look worse than they are because the skin on a person's head has a lot of tiny blood vessels. Even so, Grandma seemed in pretty bad shape.

Brunhilda, her body still facing mine, craned her head like an owl's until it had rotated halfway around to stare straight over her spine at my grandmother.

Creepy!

She raised an arm, the one with a bloody wooden spike sticking out of it. Like a policeman stopping traffic, she pointed her open palm at Grandma.

"Stay right there, Abigail," said the witch. "We shall have our own chat soon enough."

My grandmother snapped to attention, standing straight, frozen in place like a statue. Brunhilda cocked her wrong-way-around head to one side, admiring her work.

That moment of self-congratulation turned out to be Brunhilda's first mistake. As her focus left me, so did her hold on me. I woke up inside. The fog evaporated from my thoughts as if someone had turned on a window defroster inside my head.

Brunhilda's second mistake? Freezing my grandmother in place without first shutting her up.

"Ella," said my grandmother as she teetered from side to side like a reluctant bowling pin deciding whether or not to fall, "hold on tight."

I guess some cobwebs remained in my brain because that made no sense at all.

Brunhilda aimed her skewered arm at Grandma for a second time, and bellowed, "Silence!"

But before she got the two syllables out, Grandma had somehow managed to grunt, "Jake. Fly!"

With a jolt that wracked my spine, the broom lifted me from the floor. Not half an hour before, my mother had told me flying would have to wait.

Now I had to fly—or die.

10
Have a Great Fall!

Jake shot through the opening like one of those crazy-fast jets my dad used to fly. We leapt across the threshold, bounced off the half-opened screen door, and rocketed across the wooden porch in a blur. I recoiled at a burst of pain when my foot struck the edge of the wooden railing at the far end.

Jake rose above the stone patio where we had held Grandma's broom ceremony not an hour ago. No speck of that peace remained. I fumbled for a grip on the smooth broomstick handle while Jake soared up over the shed and out past the line of trees separating Grandma's yard from her neighbors'.

The last time I rode on a broom, I'd had to plan every move like a kid learning to ride a bike or to ice skate. I'd been so awkward a flier that Matilda's coven of witches nearly caught me with my feet still stuck to the ground.

With Jake, I realized, I didn't have to try to fly. I didn't have to think right, or left, or up, or down, any more than you would deliberately give those directions to your feet as they walked you down the street or your hand as it lifted a glass of water to your lips. Flying with Jake was just flying. He managed all the details himself.

He had obviously understood Grandma's order to fly and I'm pretty sure he'd been listening in on my mother's instructions, too.

Go home, she'd said.

Go fast.

Go!

2

Jake whisked me into the sky at a speed I couldn't have imagined. Despite the thrill, I worried that I'd left my family behind to deal with a powerful and insane witch. I felt terrible, running away … okay, flying away—although, I admitted in some corner of my mind, the flying part wasn't so terrible. And, I thought, the danger to my family disappeared once I fled the scene. Brunhilda wanted me. Not my mom or my grandmother. Me.

In the dim distance I heard my mother cry out. The screen door slammed and she screamed again. I realized how wrong I'd been to leave them behind.

Jake must have, too. At the sound of my mother's scream, he whipped around in the air to face the direction from which we had come. Momentum carried us back along our original path as we slowed to a halt.

From my perch in the sky I saw Brunhilda struggle through the kitchen door, using her broom handle as a crutch, like a mountain climber hauling herself up the final peak. Even from a distance the broom's shaft looked crooked.

My mother trailed the witch through the door, crawling over the sill on her hands and knees. She must have seen me floating in the sky a block away.

"Ella," she called out, "what are you waiting for? Fly!"

But I couldn't stand by … hover by … while Brunhilda hurt the people I loved. Instead of flying away or even staying at a safe distance, Jake and I drifted slowly back toward my grandmother's porch.

"She's after you, Ella, not me. Go. Now. Get away."

As if to prove my mother's statement, Brunhilda pointed at me with a finger as crooked as her broken broom, and shouted, "I'll get you, my pretty. And your little dog, too."

No. She didn't really say that. That line came from a different story about a girl, her dog, and a crazy witch who had lost her sister.

Instead, Brunhilda yanked the broken broom around, holding it in front of her like a pole vaulter starting her run. I doubt the poor thing was worth the price of the wood and straw it was made from, who knows how many years ago.

Despite all the pictures you see in kids' books of witches holding scraggly sticks, no broom I'd seen in my encounters with real witches looked anything but smooth and perfectly straight—except for Brunhilda's. Matilda's ancient broom had some nicks when I saw it, and it had a knob on the end. But it must have been sleek once and was still straight as an arrow even after years ... decades, centuries? ... in the possession of its evil owner.

Maybe Brunhilda, in her fury, didn't notice the state of her broom. Maybe she was so angry that she didn't care. The witch crouched on the porch, holding her broom's bent shaft in both hands, and took two asymmetric running strides—step, limp, step, limp. She tucked the broom beneath her as she leapt into the air.

No. She didn't do that, either.

Well, she did the broken run, the tuck, and the leap. But her fractured broom couldn't help with the flying part. Instead of up, up, and away as she had intended, Brunhilda slammed face first into the solid wooden railing at the edge of the porch, the same railing I'd bumped my foot on a minute before.

With a noise like a tree breaking in half, a dozen of the railing's spindles—the vertical pieces of wood that prevent little kids from falling off the porch—blew out in a cloud of splinters. The witch's grunt sounded more like a crow's caw. Her broom shattered like glass, exploding into uncountable pieces.

I watched in amazement as the determined witch hauled herself to her feet, shook like a wet dog to free herself of debris, and without another second's delay, scoured the deck at her feet looking for a broom that no longer existed. She stooped to pick something up. With a disgusted "Ack," she threw it back down and stomped on it once or twice or a dozen times. By stomped, I really mean hopped. On one foot. With her broom in shards, she had nothing to use as a crutch and seemed barely able to stand.

Brunhilda turned abruptly and hopped back into the house, leaping high, maybe five feet into the air over my mother, who knelt near the kitchen doorway. Unless she could hop up into the stratosphere, though, Brunhilda wouldn't be chasing me tonight. I'd be home. Without me to pursue, she'd have a long hop back to wherever she'd come from.

I followed the witch's progress through the kitchen window as she rummaged about inside. Pots and pans crashed. Brunhilda gargled out incomprehensible epithets. She had stopped to crane her neck around in that creepy owl way, when I lost sight of her.

Lost sight?

I had to crane my neck to see better through … the leaves. How did I end up in a tree?

3

Grandma's favorite tree in the entire world, a hundred-year-old sugar maple, grew in the corner of her backyard where the picket fences met and formed an angle. She'd named the tree Ginger because of its vivid orange color. Ginger looked like a giant's red-haired wig. Even this late in autumn, a thousand five-pointed leaves hung on for dear life to a thousand tiny twigs. Each leaf flickered like a candle in the porch light.

Ginger's foliage blocked my view of the house. Although I could see Grandma's kitchen through the branches, I doubted that anyone looking the other way would notice me in the darkness.

Good thing, too, because a second later Grandma's screen door sprang from its hinges and spun away across the deck. Brunhilda burst from the kitchen, grasping something in her hand. My heart sank as I recognized the broom that my grandmother and I had cleansed earlier in the evening. Brunhilda came through the door, yelling like a banshee. Her shrill screech sounded like my dad's ancient table saw ripping through iron.

"Thought you could hide this from me, eh, Stella?"

My mother covered her ears and cowered on the deck. Then, like someone had flipped a switch, Brunhilda's rage ebbed.

"Well, you failed miserably, didn't you, girl?" she asked in a matter-of-fact tone.

She held out the broom. "I have need of this, if you don't mind too very much. There is someone out there I have to find. Oh, I do."

She tapped her chin with the tip of the broom handle. "But what happens once I find her? Eh, Stella?" She put a hand on her hip like a petulant child.

My mother said something, muted by distance, and grabbed at the broom. Brunhilda slapped her hand away with the bristles, like she would flick a pile of dirt into a dustpan.

"Well," she said, "it's true I have need of a new apprentice."

Wait! I sucked my breath in. Apprentice? Who? Me?

"But I owe her for my sister, you see," Brunhilda said. "Oh, I do. And I'd be remiss if I failed to make good on that obligation. Killing her outright is so much simpler. I wouldn't feel right otherwise. I'm sure you agree. No? Of course, there's nothing you can do about it. I've decided. Thank you for the broom."

With a one-two jump, she bounded into the air, shooting away from the deck in the same direction Jake and I had headed when we took off. She flashed past us in a wink and disappeared from sight.

4

Jake drifted clockwise around the tree, keeping Ginger between us and Brunhilda. She'd shot off like an arrow from a crossbow. How long before the witch realized we hadn't gone that way?

My father would no doubt have interrupted at this point to say that crossbows don't exactly shoot arrows.

"They do," he'd add, "but back in the Middle Ages, crossbow arrows were shorter and fatter and they were called quarrels."

I have no idea why people called them that. Though, with a range of a mile or more and the ability to pierce a knight's steel armor, they probably did end quite a few quarrels.

And before you ask, the answer is no. Quarrel and quarrel are not homophones. Actually, they are, I guess, because you pronounce them the same. But they're spelled identically, making them homoglyphs as well. That means they're homonyms—different definitions of the same word—basically the same entry in a dictionary.

My mother's quarrel with Brunhilda had left her a sobbing heap on the porch. Grandma stepped out from the kitchen, moving like a zombie—stiff and slow, her arms stretched out in front. I suppose it took a while for Brunhilda's paralysis magic to wear off. A terrible possibility wormed into my thoughts. Had the witch turned my grandmother into a zombie? Zombies gave me the creeps. Zombie grandmothers, in particular.

Grandma fell to her knees beside my mom. She rested those weird wooden arms on Mom's shoulders. Despite the awkwardness of the gesture, Grandma didn't look like a zombie. No sunken, bloodshot eyes. No skin flaking off. No slobber. When my mother returned her embrace, I felt relief down to my toes.

"Mom," I said as Jake drifted toward the porch. I sorely needed some advice about my next move.

Two faces snapped around, looking for the source of the sound.

"Ella," my mother hissed, half shouting, half whispering, like the actors sometimes do in plays at the town theater. "I told you to go right home to your father. Why are you still—"

She never finished her question—at least, I never heard her answer—because without warning, Jake shut down his magical motor and the bottom fell out of my world. We dropped ten feet in no time, like moths do on nature shows when a hungry bat swoops in for the kill. Something whooshed over my head so close it blew wisps of hair across my face. I fought for a grip on the broom shaft as Jake restarted his engine—or whatever it is that gives a household cleaning accessory the ability to fly.

Before I had time to yell or panic or even breathe, Jake had us back in the air and away. I heard Brunhilda's horrific scream close behind.

"How?" she yelled. "How did you know? I should have ended you right there, you sly little girl."

Sly little girl? I thought. No. Sly little broom. Jake had jerked us out of harm's way before the danger even registered in my mind. Was that normal behavior for a broom? Grandma's stories never mentioned it.

Up, up, and up we flew. It felt a lot like the last time I'd escaped a murderous witch on a flying broom, but a million times faster. Tonight, though, I had an even worse witch way too close behind me, one with a far saltier vocabulary. I could make out Brunhilda's deeply personal and quite specific curses over the whoosh of air pounding at my ears. Jake seemed to sense the seriousness of the situation and clawed for altitude.

My father once complimented my quick thinking after I talked my way out of a fight with two bullies at the playground. "Baby doll," he said, "when the going gets tough, your brain gets going." He was right. My dad's almost always right. I probably inherited the cool-headed gene from my mom. The worse things became, the harder I thought. Somehow, even with a crazed witch cackling in my ear, I still found room in my head for a couple of relevant facts. Maybe three. Maybe four. Whatever.

First, I remembered how quickly the temperature dropped the higher I got. Two nights ago, frigid air nearly killed me before the coven of witches even got their chance to try. Once the sun went down, the mild autumn days we had enjoyed during the last week inevitably turned into crisp fall nights. The hooded sweatshirt I'd left on even after Mom showed up earlier had barely kept me warm during the broom ceremony in my grandmother's backyard. It wouldn't be enough higher up.

Second, it dawned on me that as long as I flew around in the wide-open sky, I'd be visible to anyone for miles around. "Anyone" included a certain evil presence I could feel not nearly far enough behind me. Even if Jake outdistanced Brunhilda, she would still be able to spot us against the stars. The sky was no place to hide.

On the other hand, that evening's thunderstorm loomed ponderous and inevitable to the west, lumbering toward town like a slow-motion avalanche. If I managed to reach it, if I got that far, if I managed to shake the raging witch off my tail for a moment, if a thousand things went exactly right, I could hide in the cloudbank until morning.

But even as Jake, somehow sensing my thought, adjusted course toward the storm, a croaked "I think not, little one," from behind me scratched that hope from my list. Brunhilda wouldn't be fooled by such a desperate and obvious ploy. And what about the rain? Clouds mean rain. A drenched sweatshirt offered even less warmth and protection than a dry one. I'd freeze solid before the sun broke the horizon.

In my memory, I flipped through all witches who had died in my grandmother's stories. There weren't that many. Witches, it turns out, are pretty durable. The thirteen I'd accounted for—twelve all at once—could well be a one-time record. In all the tales I recalled, I couldn't find a single trick or delaying tactic that would end in Brunhilda flying into the sunshine as Matilda's coven had done. Too much night remained.

Finally, I understood how lucky I'd been the last time I'd tussled with witches in the sky. Things wouldn't have ended nearly as well had I not thought ahead and—of all the unlikely possibilities—tossed

on a parachute that happened to be sitting around on a shelf in our
garage.

I added it up and realized, despite the apparent freedom offered
by the sky above me, up was a dead end. With an emphasis on dead.

My only advantage was Jake.

5

As if he'd been waiting on that conclusion, Jake took over like a
stunt pilot. He turned us upside down in a half-roll. I caught sight of
the thin line of a distant horizon, the earth on top and the star-filled
sky below, and I held on for dear life. Jake shut off his rockets and we
plunged nose-first toward the ground. As we fell, our path traced the
curving semicircle of a roller coaster loop that I hoped, hoped, hoped
would flatten out before we ran headfirst into a sidewalk. I felt a
force pushing me outward, against the broom, squeezing me like
gravity into my seat, and I understood why Jake had gone all topsy-
turvy before beginning his dive.

Centrifugal force is what slingshots you off the merry-go-round
on your school playground when the boys spin it really fast. Mrs.
Kendricks says it's not really a force, it only feels like one. I'd put off
trying to understand the difference until at least ninth grade. Force or
not, I mentally thanked Jake for keeping me on the inside of his loop
where something-that-was-maybe-not-a-force pushed me tighter
against him rather than flinging me away. I doubted I would have
had the strength to hold on for long.

Jake's trick maneuver took Brunhilda completely unaware. Far
above, I heard her "Ack" of surprise. Brunhilda's agility in the air did
not come close to Jake's. In a series of glances over my shoulder, I
saw her slow to a full stop before jerking the front of her broom at a
sharp angle and then follow us toward the ground.

I narrowed my watering eyes to slits against the windy rush of
our descent. The thick fabric of my hoodie whipped and cracked in
the buffeting air. I'm pretty sure the high-pitched sound I heard was
me screaming.

Another mysterious force—the force of air molecules piling up
against my chest—tried to push my body backwards off the broom. I

hunched forward, flat against the wooden handle, which improved our aerodynamics and, as it turned out, kept me a little warmer. As we picked up even more speed, Brunhilda shrank to a black speck among the stars.

Jake plunged toward … um … I hadn't the faintest idea where we were headed. Did he have someplace in mind? Did Jake even have a mind?

My mother, of course, had instructed me in no uncertain terms to go home, where my father would be sitting on the porch in his favorite rocker, twiddling his thumbs, awaiting my arrival so he could fix me some cookies and milk before Brunhilda stopped by and ended us both. That no longer seemed like the best plan. She'd already stopped by our house in her guise as Mayor Bloom. She would certainly figure out that home was the most likely place for me to go.

And what could my boring father do to thwart such a major-league hag? Him, alone, against a very old and very evil Brunhilda, wouldn't turn out so well. He'd need a squadron of pilots to fend off this rampaging witch, and Dad got out of the jet fighter business years ago.

Home, I knew for sure, was one place I couldn't go. I needed to throw Brunhilda off the scent, confuse her, and lead her in a different direction. Not too difficult, I thought, given Jake's talent for sneaky flying.

Anyway, how could she possibly predict my escape plan when I no longer had one?

6

We plummeted toward the ground like a meteor. There's no way to judge speed on a broom in the sky, but it felt like a thousand miles an hour. Jake leveled us off above Witch Haven's Main Street. In my mind, I thanked him for not flying us into the ground. We rocketed past cars like they were standing still. It took a second to realize the cars were standing still. The light at Third and Main had turned red. Half a dozen late diners bound for home were stacked up behind it. So maybe not a thousand miles an hour, I thought, but we'd definitely slowed down after our all-out descent. My sweatshirt no longer seemed about to blow off.

I twisted around to look behind and scan the starry night above me. No evil witch in sight. Except for the cars at the stoplight, the town below appeared as deserted as the sky. Where to go from here? With home no longer an option, I thought about the best place to hide. Charlotte's house? Ariel's? Nope and nope. Completely off-limits. I couldn't risk bringing this kind of trouble down on my best friends. Involving Holly's bewitched family would be doubly, triply, and quadruply a bad idea.

Returning to Grandma's didn't strike me as a workable option either, although I longed for the protection of the only two people in the whole wide world who understood my dilemma. But Brunhilda had breached those defenses once already and she might guess I'd head there.

So I couldn't go back. That left only forward.

Ahead of me, a block away to the south, our somber town hall squatted, drab and gray like a tired mountain. It's the building where the local politicians worked and everyone went to get their driver's licenses and building permits. Would anyone be there this late? I knew for a fact that the mayor wouldn't, despite her reputation as a late-night worker. She'd turned into a witch and was currently somewhere in the sky trying to murder me.

Jake slowed our pace and came to a stop beneath the overhanging umbrella of a lone elm. The tree lived in a hole cut through the sidewalk outside a block of small shops. Just as he had hidden us from sight behind Grandma's sugar maple, Ginger, Jake now hid us from the sky. Smart broom.

I caught snatches of Brunhilda screeching at the top of her lungs somewhere overhead.

"Skinny skunk … incompetent infant … waste of a witch …"

Did alliteration somehow carry farther than regular words in the cool night air? I held my breath as the echoes of her tirade passed directly above us and then faded away.

Two-story buildings formed the brick-and-mortar walls of a man-made canyon. I recognized my dad's favorite hardware store and, across the street, Mom's favorite bakery that, even in the middle of the night, smelled like sugary cookies.

Behind me, a narrow alley stretched between buildings like a railroad tunnel. I spotted the town's police station at its far end. The police station seemed the natural place for a person in trouble to go. Witch Haven's safe haven. But even if I convinced the officers inside about my impossible story—and why would they believe me—what could a couple of men in blue do against a witch who had overpowered my mother and my grandmother, without breaking a sweat?

I wondered what I could say or do to make them understand my plight. I could call my parents or my grandmother, and let them explain the situation in grown-up language. Not as far-fetched a strategy as it sounds. Witch Haven had a history. Everyone knew the stories. If that didn't work, I could turn on the tears. Crying always helped win arguments with grown-ups and, honestly, it wouldn't be so hard to do right now.

Or, I realized with a jolt, I could simply fly into the station on Jake. End of discussion.

I had a plan.

Which I never got a chance to put it into practice because, an instant later, a voice too close and clear, hissed, "Peekaboo, brat."

7

Brunhilda hovered above the road's center strip fifty feet away. Before my jaw had time to drop in surprise, she leaned forward on her broom and came at me.

I realized too late what combat pilots must have figured out long before my fighter pilot dad had ever been born. All the advantages in the air belong to the higher flyer. Jake had easily outmaneuvered Brunhilda and her clunker of a broom like a jet fighter would an old-fashioned biplane. But it hadn't mattered. The witch simply kept us in view below her and drifted back to earth in our wake.

Jake wheeled around before I recovered my wits, and we peeled away, ducking and dodging electrical wires, traffic lights, and even a flagpole, like characters in a video game. I used my feet to push us off the wall of the town's only Starbucks as we made a whipping left-hand turn onto a cross street.

Brunhilda followed, crazed and cackling. She skidded to a clumsy stop at the intersection behind us and yanked the head of her broom around, trying to point it down the street in our direction. She obviously had a different relationship with her borrowed broom than I had with Jake.

I saw the police station a few blocks distant. Behind me, at the far end of the street, Brunhilda completed her awkward turn and barreled after us. I froze like an ice sculpture as she grew closer and closer, larger and larger. To my great surprise, and hers, the broom gave a little hiccup not quite halfway along the block. I could see the startled look on the witch's misshapen face as she lost altitude.

When Brunhilda had broken her own broom on Grandma's door, she'd "borrowed" the same charred broom that had sputtered and nearly dumped my mother as she floated near the roof of a rickety old barn, the same broom Grandma and I had fought against living blobs of evil to clean, the same recycled broom we'd been about to recharge when Mom had disrupted our ceremony on the patio. Brunhilda's broom had an empty gas tank.

I, on the other hand, had Jake, who spun and took off as fast as he could fly toward the police station.

A uniformed policeman stood alone on the curb in front of the station's frosted-glass double doors looking wan in the dinghy, yellow cone of light that dribbled from the street's single lamp pole. The trunk of his patrol car gaped open. The cop, twice, maybe three times the size of anyone I'd ever met, towered over the roof of the car.

As Brunhilda rounded the corner a block away, her broom coughed. A puff of black and oily smoke belched from its bristles. The witch dropped once more, this time almost to street level. Her scream of rage—one that included exactly the same word my potty-mouthed mother had used when the broom nearly gave up on her—rattled storefront windows along the empty avenue.

Brunhilda's shout may have frightened her faltering broom. I know it did me. As if startled out of a reverie, the broom leap away from the ground and accelerated along the street. Not two seconds later, though, it coughed again and slipped so low that Brunhilda had to bounce along the ground to stay aloft. Lifting her long robe with one hand to keep it from dragging on the pavement, she half flew, half paddled down the street using her good leg for propulsion like some two hundred-year-old grandmother on a skateboard. Despite the encumbrances, she came at us racing-car fast.

A memory, a recent one, tugged at my attention as Jake slowed to a crawl near what I hoped would be the safety of our local police station. My brain ran a brief video clip of a Witch Haven patrol car with lights ablaze, half-in and half-out of our driveway, while Mayor Bloom, a.k.a., Brunhilda, the vengeful witch, strolled toward our front porch accompanied by a hulking patrolman ... or maybe an actual Hulk patrolman ... to discuss the day's events with my father

I felt Jake rev his rockets. He'd come to the same conclusion about the station, and the enormous policeman outside it, as I had. The streets of Witch Haven, this one in particular, were no sanctuary for a girl on the run—on the fly—from a rampaging witch. We would fly toward the coast as fast as we could. We'd fly until dawn, if necessary. It might be uncomfortable, but Brunhilda would never catch us on her borrowed broom. I wondered how long Jake could keep it up and how I could refill his tank if the mysterious, magical juice that powered him ran dry.

But that plan changed an instant later when Brunhilda's charging mount officially gave up the ghost, slamming to a sudden stop in midair like it had jerked to a halt at the end of a chain. The charging witch flew off the front of the broomstick.

Maybe flew isn't the best word. With no broom under her, she "flew" forward only a short distance before smacking down onto the rough pavement in a tumble of rags and elbows.

I heard the sharp sound of asphalt cracking and the muffled sound of bones breaking. I heard the slap and splat of soft skin smacking the road's hard surface. I cringed at a disgusting series of squishes and gurgles as the witch's body dissolved into a kind of rolling puddle that oozed to a stop in front of the police station. A line of dents in the road marked the path of her crash ... maybe crush is a better word. Brunhilda's exhausted broom fainted and fell to the pavement with a hollow wooden clank.

Jake and I stopped dead—okay, stopped alive and glad of it. We floated in place, immobile with horror, mesmerized by the violence of Brunhilda's disastrous demise. Brunhilda lay in—no, Brunhilda was—a heap of sticky glop in the center of the road. I told myself the thick slime seeping from the pile had to be blood that only appeared black under the eerie, incandescent glow of the streetlamp, but I somehow knew it was really the same evil, black goo Grandma and I'd washed out of the two brooms.

For quite some time, nothing on the street moved or made the slightest sound. Not me, not Jake, obviously not Brunhilda, not even the gigantic policeman who remained at attention next to his car.

When I realized I'd been holding my breath for too long, afraid to break the stillness, I tried drawing in some air, sort of as an experiment, but managed only a series of gasps. My racing heartbeat felt more like a low tone than a pulse. I sensed that Jake wanted me to go back and retrieve the broom on the other side of the tar patch that was once Brunhilda. But I wanted nothing to do with the sickly mound of glop lying across the road's center stripe. With dawn still hours away, I wondered what affect daylight would have on it.

"Later, Jake," I said, refusing to let my teeth chatter. "We'll come back with my mom in a little bit. This whole witch thing is finally over."

8

The puddle in the middle of the road went blurp.

Remember that famous scene from The Wizard of Oz? The one where Dorothy accidentally splashes the Wicked Witch of the West with a pail of water and the witch dissolves into smoking oblivion? That's exactly what happened next, only in reverse.

Before my astonished eyes, the muck in the road began to bubble and boil and steam. A lump grew from its center, expanding like one of those time-lapse videos of a mushroom blossoming. A dome formed at the top of the lump and took on a skull's eerie silhouette. The skull levitated on a pillar of gore that rose up from the road in uneven fits and starts with a disgusting chorus of liquid slurps forming the soundtrack.

In a matter of fifteen seconds, or twenty, or maybe thirty, the gooey glob of slime had morphed into a fully formed, humpbacked witch, complete with robes and warts. In a horror film, she would have emerged slowly, dripping with slime, then pushed herself up onto hands and knees with grunts and groans and a straightening of creaking joints. But that's not what happened. In real life, she simply grew head first into her black gown, straight up from the ground, as if a little elevator underneath the street had lifted her from below.

It was by far the creepiest thing I'd ever experienced. And that included a lot of creepy stuff in the last few days including a baker's dozen of exploding witches, truly vile-smelling footwear, and a flock of pulsing black globs trying to escape Grandma's bathtub by crawling up her arms. For the record, it also included Justin Grieves, the boy who sat behind me in Mrs. Kendricks' class.

The reconstituted Brunhilda stood erect in the beam of an overhead light, her back to me. She hitched her shoulders a bit to straighten out the robe. Long, loose sleeves slid down over her talon-like hands. A tremor went through her like a wave along a jump rope. It started at street level and worked its way up her misshapen torso. When the pulse hit the crown of her head, both her arms flew high into the space above. She brought them down slowly once, twice, and again, like a vulture drying its wings.

Brunhilda spoke to me without turning. The gravel in her voice had its own power. "That hurt," she groaned in a rumbling baritone. "That hurt quite a bit." She shivered again and repeated the entire vulture dance.

Paralyzed by what I'd witnessed, I would have collapsed to the ground if collapsing to the ground didn't mean a thirty-foot drop from a hovering broom.

Brunhilda's voice contained … I guess you'd call it weight. I felt its echo bounce around inside my chest and drop into the pit of my stomach. My arms felt heavy. Even Jake seemed mesmerized.

"I'll most definitely tally this little episode to your account, young witch," she said, "along with the evil you did my sister and her minions."

I blurted out, "Hey! None of that was especially my fault. Matilda tried to kill me first."

Brunhilda hunkered, silent and motionless, for a long moment.

"Not hard enough, it seems," came her considered reply.

"No," I objected. "She did try. She tried really hard. I just killed her back." The panic in my voice made it sound all wobbly. "It wasn't even me, really. It was the daylight. She was stuck in a tree and I was helping get her down. The sun came up and that was that."

Brunhilda turned to face me. A coal-red glow burned in the depths of her eyes.

Okay. Everyone has seen the red-eye effect in photographs when the camera's flash bounces off someone's retinas just as the shutter opens. That's spooky enough. The glow from Brunhilda's eyes had nothing to do with that. This coal-red radiance came entirely from within her, casting a faint crimson aura around her sunken eye sockets.

"Uh-oh," I said to Jake.

Brunhilda pointed her open palms at me and muttered an odd-sounding syllable. Something hit me square in the chest. It knocked Jake and me back ten feet in the air.

At least we were heading away from the witch, I thought.

"More's the pity," Brunhilda called into the stillness. "You've shown extraordinary promise for one so young. Extraordinary."

She limped toward us.

Fly, Jake. I concentrated as loudly as I could. She's coming.

But Jake seemed stuck in place.

Brunhilda stopped next to the policeman. She stood half his height like a little girl beside a larger-than-life statue. A statue he might have been. The officer hadn't budged a whisker during the entire episode.

"Incompetent innocent that you are," the witch said to me, "you've still destroyed every practitioner of value in this part of the world. You are far too dangerous to let live."

I could feel Jake returning to his senses … whatever that means when you're talking about a broom. He inched ever so slowly backwards along the street, putting distance between us and Brunhilda. But Jake didn't fool the witch.

"Oh, I think not," she said.

Her hands went up again and she shot another solid blast of energy like the one that had knocked us back a moment before. As if he expected the attack, Jake did that moth thing, and we dropped four or five feet without warning. I felt a puff pass over my shoulder, like the wind itself had formed into a fist and tried to punch me.

Brunhilda cocked her head to one side, eyebrows raised in interest. She tossed another spell at us, more as an experiment, I think, than as an honest attempt to do harm. Jake dodged to the side.

Brunhilda grunted a "Hmmm," and held out an open hand to the immobile policeman. "Give it to me," she said.

Like a zombie—I hate zombies—the officer lifted a witch's broom from the trunk of his patrol car and dropped it with a soft splat into the palm of Brunhilda's arthritic hand.

Flash back a million years to this afternoon. As we were pulling away from the barn with two brooms and a stinky shoe in the back of Mom's van, I'd seen a pair of figures in the shadows at the far end of the cornfield. I knew, now, who they had been and what they had found.

I recognized the broom in Brunhilda's hand. I'd seen its notched shaft and distinctive knob. Matilda's broom, the first broom I ever rode, had apparently survived the fall to earth in better shape than its owner.

The sight of it shocked some adrenaline into my limbs. My ability to move returned along with my will to survive. I whirled Jake's nose around and we headed away fast.

Brunhilda shouted, "Halt!"

Jake stopped dead with a jerk that almost threw me off. He hovered in midair, pulsing and shuddering like a spaceship at full thrust trying to launch but still tethered to the earth. I could almost hear him snarl.

The witch stood in the street, leaning on Matilda's broom like a crutch. A wisp of wind, a suggestion of the oncoming thunderstorm, kicked up street debris and rustled Brunhilda's tattered robe in the swirling breeze.

She made a little twirling motion with the pointing finger of her free hand, like someone stirring tea, and we rotated around to face her.

"You see, little twit, your youth, your promise, and even your pet broom mean nothing to me."

The malevolence in her voice hit me like a slap.

"No. No. Nothing at all."

She wiggled her pointing finger back and forth several times. "No."

Jake and I yawed back and forth, her finger shaking our whole bodies.

"I will have you gone from this world," she said. "Oh, yes I will."

This time she waggled her finger up and down, like a nodding head. We rocked "Yes" in the air.

"And soon, too."

With a flick of the same finger, she beckoned us closer.

"Followed by your pesky grandmother and her heroic daughter."

I could feel Jake's resistance. He shook and trembled but, in the end, Jake proved as powerless as I against an old witch's magic.

"Because of you …" —she spat something gloppy and vile onto the ground—"my sister fell from the sky to her death."

"Technically not true," I objected. "She—"

Brunhilda roared, "Silence!"

A violent physical force drove into me, pushing the air out of my lungs. No question of finishing my sentence or, it seemed, of ever speaking again. I gasped for air, but it all seemed to be somewhere else.

"There are so many ways we could do this," she said. "Yes, there are. But …." She raised her finger in the air like she had just come up with a good idea.

Echoing the gesture, Jake's nose pointed skyward. I slipped backwards along the shaft and only barely managed to hang on by wrapping my legs around the sweep at the end of the broom.

The witch said, "I thought maybe we could have a little fun with it."

Brunhilda straddled Matilda's broom and floated serenely up to our level.

"Have you wondered how it feels to be the one alone in the sky with nothing between you and the hard ground but your terror."

She swept her hand up toward the night sky, and Jake took off. He would have made my jet fighter father proud.

9

Up, up, up, and up we flew. I squeezed my legs even tighter to keep from falling off backwards. The brittle edges of the bristles pressed into the back of my thighs like a hundred needles. I grasped Jake with both hands and held him to me, pushing the wooden broom handle against my chest until I felt my heart next to his. I could sense his helplessness and despair. In my mind, I pleaded with him not to drop me.

Brunhilda accelerated heavenward beside us. She stood on the sweep of Matilda's broom, with her palms draped casually over the knob, chin resting on the back of her hands. The fast-moving air plastered the steel-gray hair flat against her scalp. Her robe fluttered and crackled.

The air grew cold. Really cold. A shudder wracked my body as I cried. My tears blurred the world.

"High enough for you, precious?" the witch shouted over the roaring wind of our passage. "Just say the word."

Too cold and too scared to talk, I said nothing.

"No?" she asked. "A little higher, then."

And on we flew.

Frightened and frozen, I knew that, when we stopped flying, I would start dying. Brunhilda would do something magical and cruel that I couldn't counter. Compared to her, I was no witch at all.

"Ah," said Brunhilda a minute later. "I believe we have arrived."

We came to a stop high above the town. I found my balance atop Jake as he leveled out.

"Follow me," she said, and we flew sedately west … toward the outskirts of the town and the developing storm. "There is a place I want you to see."

It took no more than a minute to reach our destination. Black storm clouds piled up not far away, stretching from the earth to the stars. Random thunder thumped against my chest and rumbled in my head. My teeth chattered, whether with cold or fear I could no longer say.

Brunhilda asked, "Do you know what that is directly beneath us, brat?"

I didn't look down.

She leaned out into space and searched the ground below as if seeking some landmark.

"Oh, my," she exclaimed with mock enthusiasm. "That's your family's mansion down there, isn't it?"

My family lived in a typical suburban house which, for some reason, my parents called a cottage. Ours was one among hundreds of others on the outskirts of Witch Haven. It had three bedrooms, including the one over the garage where my parents slept. And slept.

And slept. Once, I heard a real estate agent tell my dad that the house had two and a half baths. Did that mean you could only shower one side of you at a time? I couldn't imagine a house being any less like a mansion.

Brunhilda leaned out beyond the knobby end of her broom's handle.

"Could this be the very spot where you sprung your trap on my sister?" she asked. "Is this where you lured her and pushed her off her broom?"

She sat back and patted the knob. "Off this broom?"

In a raspy tone of accusation, she added, "Then watched from on high as she fell to her death."

Brunhilda had the details all wrong. It had been neither this place nor that broom. My encounter with Matilda's coven took place farther to the west, over the woods and the fields at the very outskirts of town. We'd drifted pretty far in the breeze that night. I, not Matilda, had been riding Matilda's broom. And, in the end, the fall didn't kill her. The sun did.

Brunhilda bent over again, looking straight down. She seemed to brighten.

"My-oh-my," she said. "Someone is still awake down there. Worrying about you, I should think. The house is lit up like Christmas and, oh …" —she made a great show of surprise— "could that be your father scurrying about the porch?"

I had to look. I picked out my parents' "cottage" easily enough. It was brightly lit against the darkened neighborhood. With the ground so far away—a million miles, at least—I couldn't see anyone on the patio out back, only a yellow glow. I guessed the old witch's eyes saw with magic that mine did not possess.

But as I peered toward the little house centered below my shivering knees, the clear night air seemed to coalesce into a lens. Whether it was a natural phenomenon or some magical influence, I'll never know. In the magnified image I did notice someone down there dashing to and fro like a lost ant.

Brunhilda's voice grew thick with malice. "Won't he be surprised when his daughter drops in?"

In absolute silence, she approached me on her broom. The witch circled me once … twice. I could feel her behind me, a tangible presence blacker than the night, like a black hole that sucked all light

and joy from the earth. On her third pass, Brunhilda stopped in front
of me—so close that even in the darkness I could see uncountable
moles splattered across her ashen skin. Her yellow, red-rimmed eyes
were marbled by blood vessels. Coals still seethed and flickered in
the depths of her eyes. Half dozen straggling black hairs protruded
from her crooked nose. I recoiled from the rot of her breath. Behind
the witch, a menacing black wall of thunderclouds boiled toward us
from the west. Their peaks towered out of sight.

Brunhilda dragged a scaly knuckle down my check in the
perversion of a caress. "So pretty," she muttered. "What a shame."

Her eyes snapped back to mine. They bore into me. I felt them in
the pit of my stomach as she rummaged about in my soul.

A thick drop of cold rain splattered on her check. Then another.
She didn't even blink.

The dark witch leaned in so close that one bony shoulder nudging
against mine. Her frigid lips brushed against the lobe of my ear.

"Now," she whispered, "die."

At those words, Jake bucked violently, tossing me into the air. I
crashed back down on him a second later, off center, arms flailing for
a handhold. When he flipped over on his back, I found myself
dangling in empty space, clutching Jake with hands so cold I could
barely feel them. My numb fingers slipped on the slick broom
handle, unraveling as I watched. I glanced at the ground and
wondered where I would land, not wanting my father to have to live
with the image of his daughter's terrible death.

I saw our house framed between my feet. I saw the brightly lit
deck. I saw my father running like a rat in a maze. A strange blue
glow emanated from the center of the deck, identical to the hypnotic
azure of the ocean when my family had vacationed in the Bahamas,
somehow bluer than the sky it had reflected. Brighter than any lamp
should appear from this height.

One hand tore free from the broom.

Jake screamed. I could feel it in my heart.

Brunhilda leaned out from her broom, leering at me with a
strange intensity. "How does it feel," she croaked. "How does it feel
to fall?" Her wheezing laughter sounded like a cat's hiss. "How does
it feel to die?"

Something bright like lightning shot past us.

"What?" she screamed.

The storm must already be here, I thought. Sooner than I'd expected.

It happened again. The lightning. But something was wrong with its color. And where was the thunder?

"No!" screamed the witch.

With perfect clarity, I saw the light in the center of my parents' patio roil and bubble. A beam of iridescent blue stabbed up from its center like a laser. It caught the knob at the end of Brunhilda's broom, evaporating twelve inches of the handle. As the severed end of the stick smoked and sputtered, Brunhilda lost control and peeled away with an "Ack!" Falling fast, she disappeared from view.

A third beam of light flashed off in the direction the witch had fallen. She screamed something. Maybe that word again. I no longer cared because, at that moment, the roiling storm clouds engulfed me, obscuring all vision, and my hand lost its tenuous grip on Jake.

I dropped like a bag of stones.

ant to know two good reasons why people shouldn't skydive in the rain? There could be more, I guess ... three or four, maybe, or W... nope. There's pretty much just two.

My parents drilled the first one into me over the course of a thousand Saturday morning post-jump breakfasts. Visibility, they'd told me, is the most critical requirement for safe skydiving after, obviously, a parachute and a plane. Only a fool would jump out of a perfectly good aircraft wearing what amounts to a bedsheet strapped on her back without first being absolutely, positively, one-hundred-and-ten percent certain where she was going other than simply down.

Keeping a safe landing zone in sight is important for a lot of obvious reasons. I proved this on my first, and probably last, parachute ride when the pointy branches of the leafless oak nearly got me. By luck alone, I'd avoided death from a million pricks and punctures and landed instead in Mr. Hatcher's cornfield.

So, why people don't jump out of perfectly good airplanes in the rain?

Clouds, say my parents. Big, dark, thick, soupy clouds. Clouds come between where you are and where you want to be. They block your view. If you can't see where you're going ... not so much going, like on a walk, but going as in falling, and falling pretty fast ... you might be surprised when you get there, if only for one final instant.

I discovered, all on my own, the second reason people don't skydive in the rain.

It has to do with terminal velocity. Or, to be precise, the difference in terminal velocity between falling rain and falling people.

Terminal velocity?

Despite what we think we know about Isaac Newton and gravity, it's a myth that all objects fall at the same speed. Mrs. Kendricks showed us that Newton was right only for objects falling through a vacuum. Drop a feather and a brick from a second-story window and, of course, the brick will hit the sidewalk first.

Everything falling toward the ground in real life has a top speed, its terminal velocity, at which the force of gravity pulling the thing down is balanced by the friction of air slowing its fall. Terminal velocity is different for different objects. Bricks and feathers fall at different rates. So do bowling balls and butterflies.

According to my dad, terminal velocity is about a hundred and twenty miles per hour for an average grownup. For an average raindrop, it's only fifteen, less for smaller ones. So, when a person falls through a downpour—do the math—there's a hundred-mile-an-hour difference between her speed and the rain's. The skydiver is smacking into thousands of droplets that might as well be standing still. Rain is no longer a stream of cool, squishy, soothing fun, like the water arcing out of a garden hose on a hot summer's day. It's a hail of paintballs shot by an army of stupid boys.

2

I fell out of the clouds into a raging thunderstorm. Raindrops crashed against me, a cold wall of pain. Each little ball of water hitting my unprotected skin felt like a bee sting, as if an entire hive had escaped its box and come buzzing after me in a maniacal, revenge-driven hoard.

Even freezing, the worst part of flying in my limited experience, paled in comparison to the bite of a hundred—no, make that a thousand BBs bouncing off my body in a continuous stream.

As I fell, I naturally assumed the spread-eagle position, legs spread and arms open wide, in an attempt to slow the fall. But the impact of all those raindrops forced me to pull my hands back in and cover my face against the incoming barrage. Goggles might have helped, I thought. I really wished that I had some goggles. But, stupid me, if I'd had one wish, a parachute would have been a better choice. Or never to have had involved myself with witches in the first place.

At one hundred and twenty miles an hour, a fall to the ground from ten thousand feet takes about a minute. My dad told me that once. I had that long to think my predicament through.

Was there something below me to soften the landing—a deep body of water or a swamp or even a haystack? Would it matter if there was?

As I dropped toward the heart of a middle-class suburb with tree-lined streets and manicured lawns, I couldn't recall any swimming pools or lakes or oceans conveniently placed to catch eleven-year-old girls raining down from the sky. As for haystacks, I had a better chance of hitting one of them during my flying adventure out in the country on Halloween night, and that chance had been zero.

Risking a peek between spread fingers, I peered into a charcoal-gray night filled with tiny bullets of hurtling, hurting water. On the ground far below, I saw a splash of electric blue, the same blue the ocean had been when we'd vacationed in the Bahamas, somehow bluer than the sky it reflected ... the same azure hue as the laser that had wrecked Brunhilda's broom. The light between my fingers seemed to brighten as the distance between me and the ground shrank, and shrank fast.

That's when I understood that I was about to die. The time between now and never for me would be measured in seconds. I couldn't think myself out of this dilemma. Nothing I might do or say would change the inevitable. That's what inevitable means, I guess. No wishing, no prayer, no sudden magic, would prevent the abrupt, murderous impact at the end of my fall. I wouldn't wake up in my bed, panting and sweating from a nightmarish dream. Physics was physics. Bodies were bodies. I was really about to die.

About to die! The end of everything.

Shouldn't I feel something? I wondered. Where was the sorrow, the sense of loss, the sinking feeling in the pit of my stomach?

I was falling faster than my stomach could sink, I reasoned. When I got to the punch line of that dark joke, I truly gave up all hope of surviving the fall. For real. No takebacks. Wow.

Only, then ... exactly then ... something inside me floated to the surface. Something that felt more real than real, more me than me. Something so familiar I couldn't believe I'd forgotten it. Something in me that simply watched events, calm and unafraid, full of the same joy I'd felt during the ceremony on Grandma's patio. With nothing left in this world to busy myself about, nothing left to think or worry about, nothing to regret, nothing to do, I became the wide-eyed witness of my own life, if only for the last few moments of it.

I'd read stories about injured people who had flatlined on the operating table and then were revived. Many described a sense of freedom and joy while they were dead. Some resented being drawn back into the world. Now I knew what they were talking about. Dying seemed a pretty high price to pay for a few seconds of that understanding. But dying didn't seem so bad, really. I had lived. Good. Great, in fact. Living had come to an end. That's all. I hoped it wouldn't hurt.

Wrapped in a cocoon of acceptance, I fell through the sky at peace.

3

Less at peace than I might have wished.

The stupid raindrops kept slamming into me and their impacts grew noticeably worse. Staccato collisions that, until seconds ago, formed the pitter patter of my plunge, now combined together into a fast drum roll, then a continuous roar. It really hurt. The individual drops combined into a bombardment, like the plume from a fireman's hose. They thickened, joining together into one single force that pushed against my body.

I pressed down into it. It shoved back up in all its iridescent blue brightness.

Wait.

Wait.

The rain of pain had turned into a stream of Bahama-blue water pushing against me. Slowing me down? Holding me up.? Was it my imagination? Was I falling less? I couldn't tell through the blinding torrent.

Then some sixth sense, or maybe seventh sense, kicked in. Maybe everyone can do it. Maybe only witches. I don't know. Like a dolphin who hears the echoes from the environment all over her body, I perceived everything around me without needing to see it. The water striking me. The movement of air. The clouds. The rain. The ground.

The ground!

Too close and coming up so fast.

I realized in a panic that I was no longer content to die. I flailed inside the stream of water, trying to push harder against it, trying to climb up it or jump clear of it. Trying to survive.

Out of the corner of my eye, in the only direction I could see with all that water ricocheting off my body, something shot past in a blur of wood and straw.

Jake?

Jake.

Jake!

He flew straight into the shimmering deluge. Thrust upward by the surge, Jake slammed against my chest. Soggy whiskers of straw slapped my face. His handle cracked against my shin. Jake added his strength to the stream of blue water, slowing me down.

Twigs and branches smacked against my hands and legs. I fell fast, tumbling through the canopy of an old and leafless tree.

A baseball bat swung up to mash me in my stomach and flip me over.

I heard the crack of ribs breaking.

I felt a thousand whips lash me as I fell backwards.

And a thump.

12
In the Dark

I will never, ever, ever forget the look on my father's face as he resolved into focus. I can't forget it and I can't describe it. Guess you had to be there lying in pieces on the rain-soaked ground. You wouldn't want to be there, of course. It hurt to be there. It hurt a lot. Exactly what hurt, I couldn't say. Easier to think about what didn't. Or not to think at all.

The menacing branches of a gigantic oak loomed over my father's head, reaching heavenward, to touch low, tumbling storm clouds. The color of the clouds cycled in no particular pattern. Red. Blue. Red. Black. White. Blue. Red. Multicolored shadows danced from branch to dripping branch high in the leaf-bare oak. A million tiny twigs winked and glistened, turning the ancient, living monument into a gaudy Christmas tree. Out of the corner of my eye I recognized the yellow ribbon tied around the tree trunk, where my neighbor across the street had vowed it would remain until his son came home from soldiering somewhere on the other side of the ocean.

In the distance, sirens howled at one another like a pack of wolves on the hunt. The wings of a gigantic dragon pulsed the air with a wuh-wuh-wuh, squeezing my head like the pressure of deep water until it overwhelmed all sound and became a kind of silence.

I saw my father's lips form the words, "Ella, can you hear me?" Nope.

I tried to shout "Dad" or "Help" or "Jake," but my own words were inaudible, even to me. Tears dripped from my father's eyes and mingled with the cold rain. I think I'd been crying, too. It sure hurt enough to cry.

I lay flat on the saturated ground, cold dampness against my back. I tried to move at least one finger, without success. A new face materialized from the clouds. I didn't recognize the man, but something about him suggested a uniform. He laid an arm on my father's shoulder and leaned close to his ear. The stranger made his mouth move a little. What's wrong with everybody tonight? I thought. Why don't they speak up, for goodness' sake?

My father's face slid to the side, out of the picture. I couldn't turn my head to follow. My neck muscles weren't listening. Dad! Come back!

Half a million years later, a second person ... or a third, I guess ... replaced my father. A woman wearing the same uniform as the man. The strangers wriggled their arms in between me and the ground. Someone else I never saw clamped their hands around my head. They lifted me and put something hard, like a board, under my sopping back. My vision narrowed to a tunnel. Their faces faded to gray, then black, and I disappeared.

2

Darkness, pain, jumbled thoughts.

People who wake up after they're badly hurt always wonder if they're dead. At least that's how it works in books. When you think about it, though, that whole waking-up-dead thing is an author's trick, a literary device they use to drum up sympathy and concern for their book's fictional hero. If someone is thinking at all, even thinking they might be dead, then obviously they're not.

Exceptions to the rule exist, I suppose. I've heard stories from Grandma about vampires who live their lives undead—whatever that means. She calls them life-challenged. And zombies—I hate zombies—whose life-state can only be described as inconclusive.

I went through the whole waking up process maybe a dozen times before I finally gathered enough energy to moan. Okay, I'll admit, maybe I wondered, dead or alive? the first couple of times, but only in passing and definitely not out loud. When the absurdity of the question finally dawned on me, I laughed. Laughing, even silently, hurt so much I passed out again.

On the first day of school back in September, Mrs. Kendricks taught us about René Descartes, a French philosopher who lived centuries ago. He wrote "Cogito ergo sum," which is Latin. It means, "I think, therefore I am." In other words, "If I'm aware enough to know that I'm aware, then of course I'm alive, stupid." Brilliant philosophy? I don't know. It seemed pretty obvious to me.

In my mind, I replaced Descartes' *think* with a word of my own. "I *hurt*, therefore I am." No one in as much pain as me could possibly be dead. The "ouch" experience requires a living body. Even my hair ached.

Although I spent most of my time unconscious, I recognized the problem with Descartes' philosophy each and every time I awoke. If thinking proves you exist, then what happens when you're asleep and not thinking, or not aware of thinking, if that even makes sense? Are you automatically dead by definition? I'd have to bring that up with Mrs. Kendricks if I ever saw her again.

Bits of conversation floated around me during my waking moments. My memory of the words was vague and confused, but hey, at least I could hear again. Someone writing a book ... you know, a writer making it up rather than telling a true story about something that really happened ... occasionally slips in snippets of stolen dialogue to cue you in on little secrets about the book's characters. The overheard conversation, like the waking-up-dead ploy, is another author's gimmick intended to provide protagonists with information they would have no access to in any normal world.

Protagonist is another Mrs. Kendricks word, by the way. More Latin. It means "the good guy in a story." Protagonist is the opposite of antagonist, which means ... duh ... the bad guy in a story, since "pro" means *for* in Latin and "anti" means *against*. That much makes sense. It's the "agonist" part of protagonist and antagonist that used to confuse me.

Not anymore.

If an "artist" is someone making art and a cyclist is someone on a bicycle, then I was definitely an "agonist," someone in agony. Taking it one step further, since I was very much against pain, I was obviously an antagonist. A new definition for an old word. Lying there alone in my bed, I realized I fit both definitions of antagonist because I also felt like the bad guy in my own story.

Why think that, you ask?

Well, what good guy would trick a dozen people into blowing themselves up on Halloween night? What good guy would yank a little old lady off her broom in the middle of the sky, two miles above anything? What fictional good guy causes this much trouble for the people she loves? Everyone wants to be the hero in their own life, but I couldn't claim that title anymore. I felt an altogether different sort of pain and drifted off.

3

Awake again.

My first thought: the only thing an injured person floating in and out of consciousness remembers is the pain ... the pain and the frustration of trying to let people know that she's still alive in there.

I mean, sure, the overheard conversation is a convenient literary device, like waking up dead, but it doesn't happen that way in real life. I didn't recall a single word of the quiet conversations I half overheard. I only remember that the people who mattered most in my life—the ones whose secrets I shared, the ones who I, the antagonist in my own story, had let down—they all stopped by to visit and to care for me. They sat with me in the hospital room. They stayed for hours. They fidgeted and sometimes snored in the squeaky chair beside my bed.

Did anyone else even know I existed inside my broken body? I thought, therefore I was. Okay, Monsieur Descartes. But what's the point if no one else can tell? I had a thousand similar questions and all the time in the world to answer them.

In the meantime—I had more than my fair share of meantime—I'd figured out that I must have landed in, or near, the old oak tree across the street from my house. And, yes, thank you, I was quite aware how similar my landing was to Matilda's a few days earlier. I knew I hadn't hit the ground at terminal velocity, in any sense of the term. The column of water slowed my fall enough—barely enough— to leave me here in a hospital bed, thinking these thoughts.

Where had the amazingly blue deluge come from? Every witch I knew was busy somewhere else that night.

Where had that amazingly evil witch, Brunhilda, gone? Like her sister before, she had nearly ended my life. Then a blue laser knocked her off her broom.

How, I wondered, could Brunhilda walk around all day in her guise as Mayor Patricia Bloom, when she should be oily smoke and ashes once the sun came up? How did the attractive—well, not entirely unattractive—and charismatic mayor become a repulsive and treacherous witch when night fell?

Or was it the other way around?

I clawed to the surface for the zillionth time and heard my mother and grandmother talking.

"Why did you risk it, Stella?" I heard Grandma ask. "Why send her home? You put Ella and her father in unnecessary danger. She could have flown until the sun came up. Brunhilda would never have caught her."

"I sent her home," my mother snapped, "because my husband can take care of himself and his daughter."

Silence.

I thought I might have drifted off to sleep, until Grandma chuckled and said, "I'm just glad he didn't blow up the neighborhood again. Remember back in Texas when they thought his battalion was under attack?"

"I do, and it was," said my mother. "But not by any weapons they understood. He managed to drive off the ogres, but we had to move off base for the third time in as many years. What were those ogres doing in Texas, anyway?"

A sound must have finally escaped the imaginary realm inside my head. To be honest, I couldn't tell. Every time I awoke, I did so hollering at the top of my lungs, "I'm here! I'm awake!" But no one ever paid any attention.

"Shush, Stella," Grandma whispered. "Ella just said something."

"Impossible," said my mother, "The doctor told us—"

"Shhh."

I heard them tiptoe to my bed, keeping quiet out of habit, I suppose.

Grandma leaned over and said, "Ella?"

I screamed out again, this time without any words. Simply an "Uhhhhhh!"

What came out—I could hear it this time—was the softest of moans.

Two gasps.

"Oh, sweetie," my mother said. She touched my face ever so gently.

"Owwwwwwww!" I screamed.

It came out as a soft "Oooooo."

A third woman's voice—I guessed, a nurse—said, "Ah. She's awake. I noticed the monitors tick up. Sooner than we expected. Much sooner. That's a good sign."

The third voice came closer. "Ella," it was saying, "I think you are awake. How do you feel? Can you tell me?"

"Owwwwwww," I said again even more loudly than the first time.

I guess I made my point because the voice said, "Good, Ella. Excellent. You are a very lucky girl, you know. Stupid as a slug's slimy butt, but much luckier. Thank the goddess for that. What were you doing climbing your neighbor's tree at midnight in the middle of a thunderstorm?"

The "slug's slimy butt" reference made me laugh but, like all the previous times, laughter proved not all that funny.

"Owwwww," I said yet again.

The voice continued. "I know you're hurting, so I'm going to put you back to sleep for a while. It's the fastest way to get you better. Maybe tomorrow you can try out some real words."

Oh, come on, I thought. I'd been using real words for days now. It wasn't my fault they didn't come out.

"But before we do that, is there anything you want to say to your mother and your grandmother?"

Yes! Absolutely!

Tell them I love them and I wanted to be a witch just like them. A good one. Not like Matilda or Brunhilda or, I guess, Holly's mom. I wanted to ask them who had saved me from a hundred-plus-mile-an-hour splat into my back porch. I'd thought about that a lot and figured out who it had to be and who it couldn't possibly be.

I mean, who else would be running around in our backyard at that time of night. The blueness had definitely lanced up from our back porch. But, Dad? Seriously? I definitely wanted to ask them about that before I went to sleep again.

All that came out was "Awah. Awah."

My mother started bawling like a baby.

"Okay," the third voice said, calm and professional. "I put something in your drip. You'll be asleep in a few seconds, Ella, and we'll see you again in the morning. Sweet dreams."

Totally fine with me.

Until I remembered that the blue fire hose hadn't slowed me down nearly enough. The ground had been coming at me too fast. I'd been about to crash hard until—

"Jake!" I screamed inside my head. "Where's Jake?"

But the blackness behind my eyes spun like a whirlpool and I spiraled down into it.

4

Awake again, I heard movement and whispered conversation in the room. I tried opening my eyes sort of as an experiment.

Searing shafts of stabbing light shot through them, straight into my brain. My brain, which still hurt from all the banging it had suffered … how long ago? … instantly shut the experiment down.

I lay there for a bit, deciding what to do next.

Then I remembered.

"Jake," I cried. It came out sounding like "Ack." Not great, but a definite improvement over yesterday.

The room around me went silent for a second, and then my friends spoke up at once. Their voices all together formed an impenetrable cacophony … two Mrs. Kendricks words that, put together, mean a really loud noise. If you have ever walked through an aviary—that's the part of a zoo where they keep two zillion squawking birds in a cage the size of a mansion—then you might have some idea about the tidal wave of sound that engulfed me, overwhelming my aching awareness.

I tried to bring my hands up over my ears, but of course that didn't happen.

"Whoa, whoa, whoa, ladies," said the mystery voice from last night. "No one can hear a word you're saying when you all talk together. Least of all, Ella."

To my surprise, and probably theirs, they shut up. My woozy head thrummed. My tongue felt numb and fuzzy. Was it really my tongue or had someone dropped a squirrel in my mouth?

"Good," said my savior. "I'll go first."

Three clicks that sounded like high heels on a tile floor brought the voice to my bed. I wanted to open my eyes to see this person who seemed to have control over my life.

"Ella," she said in a smooth, professional voice, "I saw your eyes flutter. A second ago, your wrist twitched like you wanted to raise your hand. One of your friends is going to turn out the lights before you try to open your eyes again. I'll close the curtains over the window."

I sensed her make a pointing or a waving motion with her arm and someone shuffled across the room. I heard the swish of cloth. The darkness behind my eyelids grew marginally more so. A soft click, and the blackness grew a couple of shades deeper.

"Got it," I heard Ariel say.

"Now," said the voice, "try the eyes again."

So I gave it everything I had.

When one lid finally came unstuck, it opened to a confusing blur of light. I shut it immediately.

"Great, Ella," said the voice. "Now try again. I am going to help with your left eyelid."

I felt a cool, gentle touch.

"Ready?"

Pop.

Light flooded my battered brain once again and I forced my eyelids shut, squeezing them as tight as I could.

"There was some crud in that one," came the doctor's voice. "You should be able to do it yourself from now on. Ready to try again?"

This time I opened both eyes and willed them to stay open for maybe a second. No more than that. Everything I saw looked all mushed up, like I'd been rubbing my eyes for a long time.

On the next attempt, I caught an orange blur out there somewhere.

"Ariel," I tried to say, and given the poor quality of my vocal performances over the last few days, was rather pleased when it came out "Arrarrar."

My friends laughed, and continued the roll call.

"And Charlotte."

"And Holly."

By now I knew better than to laugh, so I smiled from ear to ear. I could tell because it made my temples hurt.

"Good, Ella. I'm Dr. Ferguson. And you are the luckiest girl I ever met."

I opened my eyes for a full two seconds and focused them in the direction of the voice. Focused might be too strong a word. A yellowish blur that I took to be blond hair floated above a white blur that had to be a lab coat. The doctor seemed young for someone so professional. Maybe the soft focus and my out-of-practice vision smoothed away some wrinkles.

I tried to tell them how much I needed to sleep again. I tried to say "Tired," but all that came out was "Shyuh."

"Of course you are," said Dr. Ferguson. "We can talk some more when you wake up again."

"Ack?" I asked.

"We can talk about Jake then too, if you feel up to it."

"Wuh wih?"

"Yes," she said, "I promise."

"Angoo."

"You're welcome," said the doctor.

"Ah ee."

"Good night to you too, Ella."

Ariel, Holly, and Charlotte chimed in, "Night, Ella," and "Glad you're back," and "Don't fall out of a tree and end up in the hospital next time, stupid."

I felt a cool hand on my forehead. My attention surged into that sensation as if the doctor had drawn the consciousness out from between my eyes. The room, my friends, and my own body fell away behind me.

5

The next time I awoke, or the time after that, or maybe a dozen times later, I felt a warm and comforting presence in the armchair next to my bed and knew before opening my eyes it had to be

Grandma. And something more. A new feeling. In a flash, I recognized it as an old familiar feeling.

Instead of questioning my sanity over such an odd observation, I asked, "How did you get the stars inside you, Grandma? How do you keep them there?"

Not so long ago—maybe days, maybe weeks—she had somehow coaxed the infinite night sky down and put it into a broom. My broom. My Jake. She had been able to manage it because, at some level, she and the sky weren't all that different. A strange situation, I knew. One I could never exactly explain. But I sensed the truth of it, from my still aching head to my blanket-covered toes.

"Ah," she said, "awake at last. I was beginning to wonder if I had time to sneak out and pee before you opened your eyes. Old crones like me count the seconds between trips to the ladies' room."

That made me laugh, which no longer hurt quite so much. Instead of passing out from the pain, I said, "I suppose you've always had them in there. It just took me this long to notice."

"Funny way to put it, my dear. But not entirely wrong. It's a long conversation for someone who can't get out of bed without help. Now that you've noticed, though, I think we'll have to talk about it very soon."

"Where's Jake?"

She sighed and took my cold hand in her soft, warm one. I scrunched around a little on the bed so I could look at her.

"No," I said, and slid my hand out of hers. "Jake first. Then comfort."

"Me first, Ella," said Dr. Ferguson, who had apparently been lurking on the other side of the bed. "Then we'll decide about any additional conversations."

She put two fingers on the inside of my wrist and kept them there for, maybe, ten seconds.

"Pulse is strong," she said. "A bit faster than I'd like."

The doctor leaned over, peered straight into each of my eyes at close range, and withdrew. She raised a hand.

"How many fingers, Ella?"

"Ten," I said. "Counting the seven you're not waving in front of my face right now. Where's Jake?"

"Go ahead, Abigail," Dr. Ferguson said. "She's obviously got her attitude back. It looks like Ella is going to survive after all. We all agreed that she should know."

"Know what, Grandma?"

I hadn't agreed to knowing anything.

I did the backstroke with one elbow as I struggled to sit up. My other arm remained in a sling. Grandma rearranged the pillows behind me for support.

"What's wrong with Jake?"

She reached over again to take my good hand and gave it a squeeze. She asked, "Do you remember falling, Ella?"

"Duh," I said.

"Do you remember landing?"

"Up to a point." I shrugged. "Down to a point."

I described the last few seconds of the fall that ended with me slamming through my neighbor's oak tree and then colliding with his lawn.

Dr. Ferguson, as blond as my first blurred vision of her made her seem, and twice as pretty … maybe three times as pretty, or even four … had already filled in the blanks for me. They included an exciting helicopter ride that I have no recollection of at all. The pilot, a friend of my mom's, had broken some rules getting me to the emergency room a few minutes faster than an ambulance could have, and may have saved my life.

Everyone, at least everyone in the room, knew I'd fallen into the tree, not out of it. Dr. Ferguson explained how the upper branches had slowed my fall enough, and the shrubbery below it had cushioned the impact enough, and the grass of my neighbor's well-tended lawn had grown thick enough, and the rain-drenched soil below the grass had been soft enough, and I was plain dumb lucky enough to end up lying in a hospital bed instead of in the cemetery out past the elementary school.

When I asked her about the geyser of vivid blue water that had come from nowhere to slow me down, Dr. Ferguson suggested the question could wait for a family discussion.

She explained how, despite the mysterious water fountain, many layers of organic cushioning, and my unusual supply of good fortune, I still managed to break a wrist, dislocate a shoulder, crack a couple of ribs, and bump my noggin pretty hard. The concussion, or head trauma, as Dr. Ferguson called it, concerned everyone most. Everyone except me, of course. I pretty much slept through the whole ordeal. The only thing I worried about, once I officially woke up, was Jake.

So I asked again. "What about Jake, Grandma?"

"Well, dear." She shot a glance at Dr. Ferguson. "We think he tried to rescue you. To get between you and the ground. To slow you down. We think—"

"Grandma," I said, to interrupt her, and flicked my eyes at Dr. Ferguson. "Should she really be in on a conversation about magic water and brooms that fly?"

"Oh, you needn't worry yourself about Fiona," Grandma said. "She has been a practitioner for longer than I've been alive ..."

Whoa. Wait.

"And has seen things that would make your head explode, to think about."

The doctor shrugged and said, "For the last couple of weeks, though, I've been doing my best to prevent your head from exploding."

"A practitioner?" I asked.

Grandma responded with a question of her own. "Do you remember our story about your mother and the prom, sweetheart?"

"Of course," I said, though it was a fair question whether I remembered anything after thumping my head so hard against the ground.

"Do you remember the group of women who appeared from nowhere in the parking lot outside the school?"

"I thought they came from Somewhere," I said. "We decided that Nowhere was too far away."

"Right you are, dear. Well, Fiona was one of those women."

I thought about that for a second. "Then, you're a witch?" I asked.

The lady in the lab coat bowed ever so slightly.

"A witch who is also a doctor?"

She sighed.

"That makes you a ..."

Dr. Ferguson held up a finger to stop me. And somehow it did.

"Old joke," she said, "that wasn't funny the first time. Or the next two thousand."

Ah.

Using my good arm as an oar, I wriggled around to stare at my grandmother.

"So?" I asked her.

"Jake put himself between you and the ground, Ella," she said. "There's no doubt that he saved your life."

I waited in silence for the "but ...."

"He seemed to know what he was doing," she said. "Although no one—no one alive and no one in any of the stories I can recall—ever mentions a broom acting like that on their own."

She let that sink in.

"Your broom—"

"Jake," I said.

"Yes, Jake. He certainly helped to slow you down. Enough that you weren't killed outright, at least. But there wasn't enough time to avert the inevitable. We think the crack you heard when you hit the branch wasn't your ribs. They were only hairline fractures, not full breaks, you see. Very painful, but not especially dangerous in themselves. No, the crack was the sound of wood on wood."

I felt my bandaged ribcage. Wood on wood, I thought. Not wood on bone.

"But what about Jake, Grandma?" I asked again. "Where is he now?"

Another look at Dr. Ferguson.

My grandmother bent over on the far side of her chair and came back up holding a tennis racket—a tennis racket cover, actually—sized to hold one of those snowshoe-looking things with the big heads that make it easier for old people to hit the ball. The cover was made of some soft black material that looked like plastic trying to look like leather. She undid the long zipper with a zzzzzzzzz that took forever.

"Jake was still below you, trying to slow you down. He was between you and the branch when you hit it," she said.

Grandma reached into the racket case and drew something out. Two somethings. Two halves of a broom.

"It was a clean break along the grain of the wood," she said.

I gasped. Jake!

"I tried to mend the pieces, Ella. But my best magic had absolutely no effect. I'm sorry."

My eyes burned and I felt a little ball of tightness in my throat.
Two sensations that, taken together, foretold a deep and desperate
cry. A real gusher. With my ribs all broken and bandaged, I knew
crying would hurt. Still, I took in as much of the dry hospital air as I
could manage. About half a lungful before it hurt so badly I had to
let it out.

My grandmother continued. "We need to think about it a little
more before I try again."

"Grandma," I said. "Tell me the stories." I gasped in the smallest
bit of air I could and still call it a gasp. "The ones where they heal the
brooms. Tell me all of them. Right now."

She said nothing.

"Grandma. Please."

Dr. Ferguson waded into the conversation. "Abby, Ella needs to
know, and I need to know, if there is any evidence that brooms can
heal. Are there any references to the topic? Can you tell us what to
expect?"

My grandmother shrugged. "When something magical is broken
…." She shrugged again.

Dr. Ferguson patted me on my good shoulder. Maybe I'd call it
my better shoulder. Or my not-worse shoulder. They both hurt pretty
badly.

She said, "My gut feeling is that this broom might be different. It's
had an extraordinary, if extraordinarily short, career. And I know
something about healing. Why not let me have a go?"

She held out a hand. Without a word, my grandmother turned
Jake's remains over to her.

The doctor, who was also a witch, but most definitely not a witch
doctor, examined the bits. The bristles jutted from her right hand and
the arrow-straight smoothness of the broom's handle poked out from
her left. A foot-long gash of blond wood on the handle marked the
location of the break. A little drop of sap oozed from it.

A big, hard wail bubbled up from the center of my chest at the
sight of Jake's blood. It would hurt, but I couldn't hold it in any
longer. I sucked air in ragged chunks. All the sorrow and fear and
anger from the last … how long had it been? … crawled up my throat
like a swarm of spiders ready to burst out.

Dr. Ferguson put a finger in the air to stop me.

To my astonishment, it worked.

"Not yet, Ella," she said. "Your ribs can't afford it."

Grandma looked as stunned as I felt. Dr. Ferguson shifted the pieces of Jake to one hand and lifted my chin with the other. She looked straight into my eyes. As she did, the panicky swirl of emotions clawing at my gut gradually lost urgency until I didn't notice it anymore. As if she could sense the result, Dr. Ferguson nodded once and let me go.

Satisfied that grief wouldn't consume me from the inside out, she dragged the room's second armchair over to the window and sat like Rapunzel, facing the sill. Instead of Rapunzel's a spinning wheel, she held the sweep half of Jake unceremoniously between her knees. She twirled the knob end over and over in her hands. Sunlight flashed whenever it caught the light color of the severed section.

"Interesting," she said.

She squeezed the parts together, swapped the halves of the broom, and scanned the lower half.

"Be right back," she said.

Tucking both bits under an arm, she marched out of the room.

Wide-eyed, I stared at Grandma and she at me. I'd never seen her at a loss for words.

Dr. Ferguson returned with Jake's parts in one hand and three rolls of gauze tape in the other.

"I feel something in there," she said. "Something that flutters like a life. Something I've never noticed in a magical object before, so I can't decipher exactly what it is. It's small, like an animal's spirit, but without the fear that any animal would feel in a similar situation. I'm thinking that the lack of emotion might prove to be a positive when it comes to healing."

She tapped the pointed toe of one expensive-looking high heel on the tile floor a few times, and then came to a decision.

"Unless someone else in the room has the number of a local broom doctor," —she looked at my grandmother, who shook her head no—"we'll have to do our best and fake the rest."

She held out the three rolls of tape, each dangling from a different finger.

"Ella, I am going to start by taping Jake back together. Let's give him a chance to heal himself. I'm not one hundred percent certain what to do next, but that's the place to start. Pick a color."

A large roll of white tape dangled from her thumb. Smaller rolls—one pale pink, the other deep blue, almost purple—hung from her middle finger and pinky, respectively.

"Go with the blue," I said. "He's a boy."

Dr. Ferguson nodded as if I'd made the right choice and went back to the windowsill.

She rubbed her palm soothingly over the two halves of the shaft, and then used her finger to smear a couple little drips of sap along the wounded wood. She squeezed the pieces together and bound the halves temporarily with short bits from the roll of white tape. The doctor held the assembly up to the window and spun it slowly.

After some thought, she tugged the strips of tape off and started over from the beginning. Only after several such attempts did she seem satisfied. Dr. Ferguson laid the broom down in the full sunlight of the windowsill and said, "I need your help, Abby."

Grandma and Dr. Ferguson spoke a few words in unison, so quietly I couldn't catch the words, then turned away from me and toward the open sky beyond the window. They opened their arms wide and brought them slowly down toward Jake, as if they were scooping sunshine and pushing it into the broom. I realized Grandma and I had done exactly the opposite when we milked the icky magic out of the brooms in her bathtub.

I felt something moving, spinning. It tickled deep down in the pit of my stomach, exactly where I felt all that grief. The whirling sensation tugged like a gentle current at the center of my heart. Although I couldn't climb out of bed easily, and definitely didn't want to disrupt the process of healing Jake, I knew immediately how I could help.

Once—how long ago?—before Brunhilda's invasion of my grandmother's house and the wild broom ride that ended with me here in the hospital, my mother had asked for my silent attention as she examined the poor, wounded broom on Grandma's coffee table. My mind had wandered and she'd noticed immediately. This time, for Jake's sake, I focused, stayed present, and felt the tingling magic fill me up inside.

Without a pause in her motions, Dr. Ferguson said, "Very good, Ella. That's what any competent witch would do in this situation."

They pushed the light into Jake for fifteen minutes. I lay there, doing nothing much, but feeling *so* much. I noticed Grandma's shoulders relax at the same time I felt the tickle in my tummy stop.

Dr. Ferguson turned to the table where she had laid the rolls of gauze tape and retrieved one of them. She wiggled the tape in the air to show me. I nodded.

"Blue it is," she said.

She wrapped more tape around Jake, back and forth, overlapping and extended the wrapping out a little farther each time, until the roll ran out. In the end, the tape nearly covered Jake's exposed handle like a dark blue sock or a super-skinny leg warmer. He looked ridiculous. Better than pink, though.

Dr. Ferguson balanced Jake on the fingertips of both hands and bounced him up and down, gently testing his weight and balance. She held the shaft end to her eye and peered along it. She turned the broom around and ran her hands over the bristles. Then she handed it to me.

"Take very good care of this broom, Ella. If there is enough energy left in it to mend the parts back together, we might—might—be able to return some of its magic later. We'll undo the splint in a week or so. About the same time your cast comes off. You'll be going home before that."

I nodded.

"I think whatever is special about your broom has something to do with it being your broom," she said. "Although I have no idea why that should matter."

She turned to my grandmother. "Abby, I need you to find everything you can about the care and feeding of damaged brooms. In the millennia that magical people have been keeping records, maybe someone has already done what we're attempting to do,. I need to know, and there's no one better at finding things out than you."

"If Mom can bring my laptop to the hospital on her next visit," I said, "I bet I can find something on the Internet."

The two adults stared at me, then at each other.

"She's probably right," my grandmother said. "Ella has a knack for digging up interesting information. She's the family's lead researcher."

Dr. Ferguson shrugged. "I don't see how it could hurt," she said.

I said, "I'll try Wikipedia. It's always a good place to start."

"Do that," said Dr. Ferguson. "But I also want you to try another site. It's called Witchipedia, and you'll need a very special password to access it."

13
Home-ish

I finally made it home. Or near enough.

One cool Monday morning in November, Dr. Ferguson walked me from my room, along a long (homophone!) corridor, down an elevator, through the hospital lobby, and out the double-wide sliding door. The crisp autumn air nibbled, rather than bit, at my exposed cheeks. Despite the chilly temperature, my father met us at the curb wearing shorts and a faded Harvard rugby shirt. He'd hated dressing up in a military uniform every day for three decades and vowed to spend the rest of his life dressing down.

I thanked the doctor for saving my life and, hopefully, Jake's. She laid a comforting hand on my shoulder, and I gave her the best one-armed hug I could manage. She held the car door while I squirmed into the passenger seat and fumbled with my seat belt. Seat belts really take two hands. With Jake sitting comfortably on my lap, Dad and I left the hospital for Grandma's.

Grandma's. Not home. But near enough.

The adults in my life had talked it over, apparently, and decided her house offered more security than my parents'. Matilda had waltzed right in through our basement door the night of the Halloween wakeover while Grandma's front door fought back when Brunhilda tried to break into her foyer. For all I knew, the witch still had an eight-inch-long wooden dagger stuck in her arm courtesy of Grandma's defenses.

Speaking of Brunhilda, she had apparently survived our encounter in the sky in better shape than me. I heard that, in her guise as Mayor Bloom, she had limped into the hospital accompanied

by her police troll the day after our confrontation in the sky above
Witch Haven. She'd demanded to see me but my grandmother and
Dr. Ferguson chased her away.

Surprised? A two-mile drop without the benefit of a parachute
hadn't done in her sister, Matilda, either. Add "falling out of the sky"
to the list of disasters that don't kill evil witches.

In any case, we had to assume that Brunhilda's vendetta against
me remained a work in progress. Being in a coma and all, I'd slept
through the entire episode. I'd slept a lot. And I'd hurt a lot. It would
be good to be home. Or near enough.

2

Two days later, my mother and I meandered in slow circles
around my Grandma's ornate dining room, getting it ready for the
next day's Thanksgiving dinner. She'd planned a big one, part
holiday meal and part welcome home—or near enough—for me. My
friends and their families had all received invitations. Charlotte and
Holly said they'd be there with their parents. Ariel promised to drop
in for dessert. I'd missed my friends.

"Are you okay, honey?" my mother asked. "You've been about to
fold that napkin for the last two minutes."

I held one corner of a limp, monogrammed napkin between the
fingers of my injured arm. The rest of the embroidered cloth dangled
helplessly in space.

"How can she do that?" I asked.

"How can who do what, Ella?"

"How could Brunhilda show up at the hospital in the middle of
the day? I get that she was Mayor Bloom, not Brunhilda, at the time,
but I thought witches turned to toast when the sun came up."

"We aren't really sure what happens to those witches in the
sunshine," my mother said. "Your grandmother thinks it might be
the darkness of their magic that reacts to daylight, not necessarily the
witch herself."

I had to think about that for a minute.

"Maybe Mayor Bloom has a way to keep the sun from touching
her skin," I suggested. "She—the mayor, I mean, not Brunhilda—

wears an awful lot of makeup. And she always has long-sleeved blouses or business jackets when we see her on TV."

"We thought of that too, Ella. But it can't be the whole story. Too risky. Even thick makeup cracks or wears off. And fabric isn't a perfect barrier."

"Come to think of it," I said, "Matilda's witch buddies were completely covered on Halloween night. Robes, hats, the works. Some of them even wore gloves. I don't think their clothing protected them at all when the sunlight hit them."

"Good point," my mother said. "Your grandmother says there are stories about black witches who were functional to one degree or another during the day. But she won't talk about the spells that make that sort of thing possible."

I didn't want to talk about them either, or think about the terrible energies involved. Grandma, a practitioner like my mother and Dr. Ferguson ... and me! ... had used the beauty, wonder, and joyful presence of a starlit night to work her magic on Jake. What horrible emotions did Matilda, Brunhilda, and their ilk call upon to cast their spells? Fear? Hatred? Horror?

Vowing to think about anything else, I helped my mother toss a huge bolt of white linen, the size of a sailboat's spinnaker, across the long Thanksgiving dinner table—actually, two tables we'd set end to end. I smoothed down the soft, white wrinkles with my good hand. It took a couple of tries to get the fabric settled. Although Dr. Ferguson had finally given the okay to remove my sling, the cast protecting my broken wrist still made even simple tasks awkward.

"Speaking of stories," I said, "I found a couple of interesting sites on the Internet that mentioned repairing enchanted brooms."

"Better run them by Grandma," my mother said. "I think she has some ideas herself. And you have to be really careful with so-called information pulled out of cyberspace. You don't want to take any chances with your Jake."

Truer words had never been spoken.

We faced each other across the expanse of Grandma's dining room table.

"Mom," I said, "can we talk about the night I fell off my broom?"

"Which time, sweetie? You do it a lot."

How about that? Mom's developed quite a sense of humor since my coming out. But she'd stopped caressing the tablecloth and stood stock-still.

"Someone on our back porch pulled off some pretty cool magic that night," I said. "I think they got the individual raindrops to cooperate somehow … to squish all together into a stream. So blue, like the ocean water at the bottom of that slide on our vacation to the islands. It slowed me down. It saved my life."

She gave one final tug on a corner of the white linen—it was already smooth as silk—and then plopped down on the chair at her end of the table.

"Keep going, Ella."

"Somebody did some magic," I said, "and it couldn't have been me. I was busy falling."

She nodded.

"And it couldn't have been you. The last time I saw you, you were lying in a heap on Grandma's porch, with her on top of you."

My mother nodded again.

"And Grandma wasn't looking so good, either."

"Your grandmother might have been a little stiff," Mom said. "She recovered pretty quickly, though."

"Mom," I countered, "Grandma was halfway to zombiehood, and I hate zombies. She obviously got better, but not soon enough to drive all the way to our house and conjure up that trick with the rain. And the blue laser that cut Brunhilda's broom in half definitely came from our back porch."

My mother nodded yet again.

"So that leaves …" I said, and waited for her to fill in the blank. She never did.

Instead, she launched into a monologue about the genetics of witchcraft. How, way down deep in the chemistry of life, girls have two X chromosomes, while boys have one X and one Y. And how that Y chromosome can't mask its matching X chromosome. I won't bore you with the details, but the long and short of it is that only females get to be witches. Apparently, it takes a very specific combination of two X's, plus the right environment, to make a witch. It's all in the genetics and boys don't have what it takes—which is so true in so many ways.

"Okay, Mom. That's interesting and all … kind of Mrs. Kendricksy … but you've explained the how and maybe the why, not the what."

She shrugged. "I don't really—"

"What is it about a couple of molecules bumping together before I was even born that makes me able to fly on a broom right now? That makes no sense at all."

She folded her hands together on the table and grew even more serious. "You see, Ella, when a mother and a father love each other, they—"

"No! Stop, Mom! I already sat through that lecture, thank you very much. Geez, Louise! I know how I was born. I don't know how I was born to fly."

"Obviously, you can fly because you're a …"

I wondered if she had the nerve to say it. I could have counted out loud the seconds that passed before Captain Mom—daredevil skydiver, courageous combat pilot, and emergency medical technician who's seen who-knows-what variety of terrible things—came through with the answer.

With a sigh, she said, "Because you're a witch, sweetie. Like every firstborn daughter in our family since anyone can remember."

Wow. She did it.

Of course, I already knew about the firstborn thing from Grandma's stories. What I hadn't known until recently was that her stories were about me.

"Thanks," I said. "I really appreciate that. I do. But it's still not an answer. I want to know what's true about witches, but not about everyone else, that means I get to fly and they don't."

Mom's face brightened. "Oh," she said. "That's easy."

I held out the palm of my good hand in half of an imploring gesture.

She said, "The big difference between witches and other people is that witches can conduct magic."

Oh. Witches can conduct magic. I see.

No. I actually didn't.

"Magic," I said. "What's magic? Is it some force, or energy, or—?"

"I haven't a clue," she said. "And I don't think anyone else does either."

Not exactly the answer I expected from someone who'd been using magic all of her adult life.

"Then how do we conduct it if we don't know what it is?"

"No idea," she said with a shrug.

"But—"

"How do you see, Ella?" she asked. "Or hear. Or smell? How do you move? How do you think?"

She asked me how I'd flown on Matilda's broom that first time.

"I hopped on and did what Grandma said everyone else did when they wanted to fly a broom."

"Not everyone," my mother said. "Only witches. Charlotte and Ariel could do exactly what you did, down to the very thoughts in your head, and never get any higher off the ground than they could jump. Not in a hundred years."

What about Holly, I wondered, but thought better about asking.

"The witch gene isn't uncommon. Lots of women show some of the signs. Some are unusually intuitive, for example. But their talents are never nurtured or developed. There's an environmental component."

I'd definitely have to look into the whole genetics thing on my own. Grandma would have a tough time shoehorning all that information into a fairy tale. I could barely wait to fire up my computer and get started.

I thought about what sites to visit. I thought about what questions to ask. Sometimes the best questions aren't the obvious ones. Sometimes you went down dead-end rabbit holes full of interesting, but not necessarily relevant, information. In an aha moment, I realized the question that began this heart-to-heart with my mother had lead me down one such rabbit hole.

I shrugged and said, "So, I guess Dad saved my life that night. But, I don't know how he could have. He's a man, so he can't be a witch and he can't conduct magic. But it had to be him on the porch. No one else was around. Unless he brought out some top-secret military thing that he definitely shouldn't keep lying around the house, that blue laser was something magical. And the trick with the water …."

My mother leaned back in her chair and examined the chandelier with its hundreds of crystal facets.

"A long time ago," she said, "it was obvious that certain individuals were capable of feats beyond the ordinary. No one could explain how they managed it, not even the people themselves. It was not lost on our ancestors that these extraordinary individuals inevitably turned out to be women."

"The original witches," I said.

My mother nodded in confirmation, saying, "Others ... mostly men ... felt a little cheated."

"That figures," I said. "The boys at school *hate* it when we do anything better than them."

"So they studied those women with unusual powers. They poked. They prodded. They experimented. They sometimes did horrible things."

"But you told me there *is* no secret," I said. "You're either born with it or not, right?"

"True," my mother said. "No secret. But it certainly seemed like a secret. One that all those mysterious women conspired to keep from the men in charge. Genetics hadn't been discovered yet and wouldn't be for thousands of years. Some people could perform magic, while most couldn't. And that was that. There was no consistent explanation."

I said, "Except that a handful of women could."

"When a whole bunch of people want something, Ella, and think about it for long enough, and experiment with it, and keep on trying despite years or even generations of failure, they eventually come up with an answer. When things take so long, though, the question itself often evolves along with the answer. That's what happened in this case."

"They found the answer?"

"Not to their original question."

"Then, to what?"

"Over time, after a tremendous amount of work, tragedy, and lots of mistakes, humanity eventually developed what I suppose you could call the science of magic. The initial question—why can some women do things other folks couldn't—kind of faded away."

I got it. Sort of. "Isn't the science of magic an oxymoron, though?" Oxymoron?

Oxymorons are words that, when you combine them, make a contradiction, like jumbo shrimp, pretty ugly, random order, and — my favorite because it's the street I live on — Park Drive.

"Less of an oxymoron than you would think," Mom said. "Nice word, by the way, oxymoron. Mrs. Kendricks?"

I nodded and said, "So, you're saying that people can use magic without being magical themselves?"

"After a lot of trying, we" — she waved her arms in a circle over her head to indicate, I guess, everyone on the planet, past and present — "finally figured out how to manipulate magic from the outside. It took a while, but we did."

"I thought you said only women can conduct magic."

"That's right," my mother said. She tapped the center of her chest. "You and I can conduct magic, although we have no idea how we do it."

I asked, "How did they use magic if they couldn't conduct it?"

"We can't conduct electricity, can we?"

"Not for very long," I said.

Mom smiled. "Yet we use electricity every day, in obvious ways" — she glanced at the lights in the chandelier — "and in subtle ways." She pointed to the cell phone she'd laid on a side table when we'd entered the room. "The science of electricity is both powerful and subtle. It took a lot of very smart people thinking about it for quite a while to figure things out. They're still working on it. The science of magic is no different. It's been a secret project for a long time now. Real cloak-and-dagger stuff, with an emphasis on the cloaks."

"Okay. Fine. Then, what's the male equivalent of a witch. A warlock?"

Mom said, "If a male witch existed outside of fairy tales, he would be called a warlock, I suppose. Except that a male witch is impossible."

"Because of genetics," I said.

She nodded. "And it's not only men who practice the science of magic. There are plenty of women in The Society. Quite a few are probably genuine witches seeking to supplement their abilities through higher education."

"The Society?" I asked.

My mother put a finger to her lips in an elaborate, shushing pantomime. She made it clear that The Society—whatever it was—meant to keep its existence secret. She made it equally clear what she thought about that foolishness.

She said, "They like to think no one knows very much about them. They like to think they have everything under their thumb, and they get a little edgy when it turns out they don't. No sense of humor at all. Still, you don't want to put yourself on The Society's radar. It's simpler to pretend they're a myth."

"But," I pushed the question one more time, "what about—"

"Your father tends to be pretty tight-lipped when it comes to this stuff. With all that military training, he knows how to keep a secret. But, to his credit, your father is more open than most of The Society's members."

I had to think that through.

"Which means Dad is … what?"

"A wizard, Ella. Quite a talented one, too. It's kind of how we met."

3

Hours later, Grandma and I sat together on the side of my bed.

"Once upon a time …" she began.

But I stopped her. "I don't know if I want to hear any more stories," I said. "Ever."

She squeezed my hand. "That's your choice, of course."

"You've been telling me those stories all my life," I said. "And look where it got me."

She said, "You *have* a life because of the stories I told you, Ella. I thank the stars for each and every minute we spent doing that."

"But—"

"Where would Holly be right now if you hadn't put yourself between her and Matilda's coven a couple of weeks ago?" she asked. "Who would Holly be?"

Who indeed? Or what? I thought about the rumors, the late-night, wakeover horror stories of girls who had gone missing from Witch

Haven. Some of the scariest stories—legends, really—went back hundreds of years.

"You saved your friend from a terrible destiny, Ella—for now, at least—at no small risk to yourself. Have I already mentioned that I couldn't be prouder?"

"Uh, yeah. About a thousand times."

She tousled my hair, but it sprang back to its original shape like a mop.

"You inherited the witch gene from your mother, she got hers from me, and on and on. You'd have learned about your heritage one way or another. Better it comes from someone like me who has your best interests at heart."

"I didn't especially ask to be a witch," I said.

"And you also inherited the gene for bravery from your parents. Both of your parents."

"I didn't really want that either," I said. "Even if there is such a thing as a bravery gene."

She shrugged my comment off.

"Perhaps. But who can say what choices you made before you were even born?"

What?

"On the other hand, you clearly chose your relationship with the mysterious whatever-you-may-eventually-come-to-call-it."

Grandma strode over to the window, swept the curtains aside, and slid the window sash wide open. She always slept with her own window ajar, even in the frozen winter. The chill night air wafted in, crisp and clear and here.

Grandma inhaled a huge draft and held it in her lungs for an extra heartbeat. Exhaling, she marched across creaking floorboards to a far corner of the room where a rickety old rocker had hunkered alone in the darkness since I could remember. A macramé blanket with odd patterns woven into it rested on its high, carved back. Grandma dragged the antique chair over to the open window.

"This rocker belonged to my mother," she said. "And yes, she was there in the parking lot at your mother's high school prom, along with the rest of us. It would have been inconceivable that she'd allow her only granddaughter to face Matilda alone."

She patted the rocker's cushioned seat. "It's yours now, Ella. If you want it. Come on. I suggest you use the blanket as well."

I abandoned the cozy comfort of my favorite bed and tip-toed to the rocker because the floor near the window felt like ice on my bare feet. I sat and tucked both feet under me, freezing toes and all, until my knees splayed out to either side with my thighs rested on the polished wooden arms of the rocker. Jake lay across the arms of the chair, between my legs and my chest. I tossed the cover over both of us.

"I faced Matilda alone," I said.

"And I'll regret that to the end of my days," said Grandma. "Even though I'd done everything I could to prepare you for the eventuality."

She gave the chair a little push and it swung ever so gently back and forth, like a pendulum marking time. None of the ancient slats beneath me creaked, thank goodness. That would've driven me crazy.

"Tell me more about … I guess it would be my great-grandmother."

"Once upon a time …" she said, and gave the chair another gentle shove.

We listened to the sound of the rocker's wooden undercarriage rolling on the floor.

Several pushes later, Grandma spoke again. "You'll have to make some choices soon, Ella. About how to move forward. A return to normal ceased to be an option the instant you left the ground on Matilda's broom."

"A little ominous-sounding tonight, aren't we, Grandma?"

She smiled. "What a boring future normal would be for someone like you. Don't you agree?"

"Actually, I—"

"You're still a child, Ella, but the witch gene is ancient. It awoke in you a little earlier than makes me comfortable. You already know what happened to your mother in high school. One day soon, I'll tell you about my own awakening and transition. Suffice to say, mine wasn't as modern as your mother's, nor was it accomplished as cleverly as yours."

Grandma squatted between me and the window, face close to mine. Her wrinkles seemed soft as the freshly tilled rows of soil on Mr. Hatcher's farm. Up in the sky, Brunhilda's face had looked like a dragon raked his talons across it more than once.

Grandma tucked a finger under my chin and lifted my head until our eyes met and locked. A gust of wind whistled through the trees outside blowing in a puff of air as frigid as the atmosphere ten thousand feet above Witch Haven. I felt the stars in that that breeze, all the way down to my heart. It's like I could smell them. Weird.

My grandma slid her hand away and nodded once, as if satisfied with what she saw. Dr. Ferguson had given me the same once-over a number of times, including an especially long stare the day she signed my release from the hospital. With a little grunt, Grandma pushed off the rocker's arms and stood up. Her shove set the rocker in motion again. Back and forth, back and forth. It felt good … relaxing … so, with a little effort, I kept it up.

"You'll be facing much of what's to come alone, you know. It's your fate now, not mine or your mother's or anyone else's. Even so, you'll have the dual benefits of a strong family and a long tradition to draw on. We can help. We can advise. We can open up a whole new world. But what you absorb, what you discover, what you become is entirely up to you and your choices. Do you understand what I'm telling you?"

It comforted me to rock, so I kept it up. My broken wrist didn't hurt so much, my feet were warm at last, and the heavy blanket felt like a hug. Even Jake, as silent as the stick of wood he came from, seemed content.

"Ella, do you understand?"

Grandma folded her hands across her chest, waiting for an answer I was not ready to give. She bent toward me and did the stare thing again. Against my will, the words poured out of me as if I'd sprung a leak.

"No, Grandma, I absolutely do not understand. Not even close. And right at this instant, I don't really care to. I'd rather rock myself to sleep here under a dusty blanket in this ridiculously old chair."

My response, rude though it was, seemed to please her.

I stopped rocking long enough for Grandma to kiss me on the forehead. She told me that she loved me more than the rest of the universe combined and creaked out of the room. The door swung closed and, for the first time ever, I heard the latch click shut behind her.

www.ingramcontent.com/pod-product-compliance
Lightning Source LLC
Chambersburg PA
CBHW051947220626
47052CB00004B/835